KISSES LIKE
A DEVIL

KISSES LIKE A DEVIL

DIANE WHITESIDE

KENSINGTON PUBLISHING CORP.

http://www.kensingtonbooks.com

BRAVA BOOKS are published by

Kensington Publishing Corp.
850 Third Avenue
New York, NY 10022

All Kensington titles, imprints, and distributed lines are available at special quantity discounts for bulk purchases for sales promotion, premiums, fund-raising, educational, or institutional use.

Special book excerpts or customized printings can also be created to fit specific needs. For details, write or phone the office of the Kensington Special Sales Manager: Kensington Publishing Corp., 850 Third Avenue, New York, NY 10022. Attn.: Special Sales Department. Phone: 1-800-221-2647.

Brava and the B logo Reg. U.S. Pat. & TM Off.

ISBN-13: 978-0-7582-2515-3
ISBN-10: 0-7582-2515-6

First Printing: February 2009
10 9 8 7 6 5 4 3 2 1

Printed in the United States of America

Prologue

The Grand Duchy of Eisengau, somewhere northeast of Switzerland, spring 1896

Meredith Duncan trailed her mother back into the house, her shoulders braced like a guardsman on parade. Scientific curiosity had led her to weigh each double-flounced, steel-braced satin sleeve before it was sewn onto her gown's velvet bodice. She'd discarded the appalling results before she could include the diamond—well, fake diamond—bow, her abominable corset, or the wires in her skirt which made it resemble an umbrella.

At least Mother had been pleased when she saw the results. Meredith almost wished she hadn't passed her exams, just so she could have studied longer and escaped the military band's concert.

They handed their capes to the single housemaid who was still waiting up for them. They'd moved into this large, upscale house a few months ago and only the public rooms were completely furnished in Mother's trademark mix of dark wallpaper, heavy furniture, and the Judge's hunting trophies. They'd economized elsewhere by cutting back on staff.

"My dear?" Judge Baumgart's tall frame almost filled his library's door. "Did you meet any new officers?"

Mother's face, which had brightened, promptly closed. She held out her hands to him. "I'm sorry, my love."

Meredith sighed and turned for the stairs. Maybe, someday, a man would look at her like that. But, until then, some conversations didn't have to be repeated.

"How could she not meet any eligible officers at a military concert? Eisengau is a military country!" The Judge's voice rang through the hallways, underlined by the kitchen door's bang. At least the housemaid had escaped.

He stalked into the foyer, meeting them by the great central staircase.

"Cavalrymen, artillerymen, infantry . . . And this year, tall women are in fashion for once. Surely she could have found somebody to pay attention to her and help the family?"

"I'm afraid not, my love. Even though the band was playing fashionable tunes by someone named Wagner about Nordic heroines with her coloring, nobody did more than say hello to us."

"Well, she does lack your curves. Where are you going, Mary?"

"Meredith!" She took her foot off the bottom stair and spun around to correct him. Nine years in his household and he still wouldn't call her by name.

"Mary." He glared back at her. "Every child, especially a girl child, should have a proper Christian name. If you'd been born here, your father wouldn't have been able to register your birth, let alone have you baptized." As befitted a second-tier judge, her stepfather's ideas were extremely conventional. She still fought him every day on this subject.

Claws scuttled on the hardwood floor upstairs.

"He honored his mentor and fellow college professor." She bit the words off, trying to keep her tone level.

"By giving his daughter the fellow's family name? More likely, he was so drunk he couldn't fill out the paperwork properly," the Judge sneered.

"How dare you say that about my father!" Meredith fumbled for something, anything to throw at the obnoxious wretch she had to live with.

A small black form leaped down the stairs and slammed into Meredith's skirts, badly denting their wire cage. Morro, her rough-coated schnauzer, took up station before her and bared his teeth at her stepfather. Fifty pounds of knee-high fearlessness was growling so deep in his throat it was almost soundless. Dear God in heavens, her young watchdog meant to attack if necessary.

She had to protect him, just as much as he needed to defend her. She slowly sank to her knees beside him, praying all the hours she'd spent training him would pay off.

What would it be like to have a two-legged guardian?

The Judge's usual furious torrent of words halted.

Mother turned pale and her hand crept toward her throat.

"My dear, please! The servants will hear. And, Meredith, you should know better than to challenge your stepfather."

The Judge nodded briefly, which wasn't quite an apology. Meredith did the same, never taking her eyes from him, and slipped her fingers into Morro's collar.

"*Socair ort*," she soothed him in Gaelic. Far simpler to tell him to take it easy than to convince her pulse.

Morro hissed in an octave below speech, still eyeing the Judge. Her stepfather glared back at him, equally hostile.

If Grand Duke Rudolph hadn't sent his best lawyer to Scotland to pick up a new set of memorabilia Ossianic, from that great Scottish epic collected—or written—by Macpherson, she'd still be back at home. Instead of stuck here in Eisengau, an unwelcome appendage to the ambitious lawyer's Scottish wife.

What could they all agree on?

"Morro and I will go upstairs now and say goodnight to Paul and Johann. I'm sure they're wondering where Kavalier's favorite playmate is."

Her stepfather's shoulders loosened.

Meredith had inherited Morro from the Judge's elderly aunt.

But he'd truly earned his place in the household by making friends with Kavalier, the very expensive, silver-gray, Weimaraner hunting dog he'd bought for his two young sons—the apples of his eye and the center of all his hopes.

Upstairs was also where her collection of penny dreadfuls, those lurid examples of low literature, was hidden away. Truth be told, her favorites were their American cousins, the dime novels that were much harder to find here and told stories of strong men along the American frontier. Their heroes were much more interesting than any of the over-dressed popinjays she'd met tonight. After this far nastier than usual brawl with her stepfather, she deserved to curl up in bed with one of them.

Proper young ladies weren't supposed to fantasize about rough men, like the ones featured therein. A tall, dark-haired man with brilliant blue eyes and a blinding smile, who could hold his own against impossible odds. Proper young ladies weren't supposed to masturbate, either. Knowing she combined the two activities would undoubtedly send Mother into high hysterics.

She curbed a smile and waited, donning her best placid-as-milk expression.

"Yes, of course. Good night, daughter; we can talk in the morning." Mother made a shooing motion.

"Not yet." Ice slivered through Meredith's veins at his tone. "We need to decide what to do with M—her."

Meredith froze halfway onto her feet. He'd stopped himself from calling her Mary but she didn't trust him or the subject.

"What do you mean?" Mother spread her hands. "I'd planned to continue taking her out into society."

Meredith finished standing up and guided Morro into his most gentlemanly stance. Appearance, after all, was everything in this house.

"Very expensive—and fruitless. She left Scotland nine years ago but all she has to show for her time in Eisengau is an exam certificate to prove she successfully attended school. She can't even trot out a panoply of well-connected friends."

But breeding wasn't everything!

Even so, she was hardly about to bring home revolutionaries to meet a judge, no matter how good their breeding. And if he heard them talk about how poorly the grand duke treated his workers, her stepfather would undoubtedly throw them out of his house, anyway.

"She doesn't even have a dowry to attract a husband, unless I give her one." His tightly pursed mouth made it clear his wallet wouldn't open for his wife's daughter.

"There's her inheritance from your aunt," Mother suggested hopefully.

"Frau Masaryk was an old woman whose age must have rotted her brain." He began to pace. Meredith drew herself farther up the stairs to avoid coming anywhere near him.

"She left her lands here to you," Mother reminded him.

"Such as they were."

And Meredith was given the pick of her dogs, thank God.

"And her foreign investments for the education of my stepdaughter as her, quote, only living female relative, unquote." He snorted in disgust. "I couldn't even break the will because the monies are abroad."

"But the will does allow us to be paid for feeding and clothing her while she attends school."

Go back to school? Oh yes, please . . .

He swung around to face his wife. "All we'd have to show is her registration at a school. After that, I'm sure I could persuade Heller not to look closely at the receipts, even if I had to pay him a percentage."

"Lovely! After a few months, we could vacation at the spa in Baden-Baden, where we'd meet all the best people." Mother clasped her fingers, her sleeves quivering. "A good boarding school for her might even give her some prospects."

Boarding school? Oh, dear God, no!

And she could hardly tell Mother and the Judge again how determined she was never to marry. What did she know about those schools that they wouldn't like?

"Aren't boarding schools only for a year or so, especially when you're already seventeen?" She ducked her head and tried to smile sheepishly. It was a trick she'd encountered in several dime novels.

Mother frowned, thoughtfully.

"Wouldn't it be better to send me somewhere it would take longer for me to get my degree? Like—"she hardly dared breathe—"The university?"

"Women at a university? How unladylike!" Mother closed her eyes and shuddered, her mouth's corners turned down as if she smelled something noxious.

"Eisengau University is already accepting women now"— for the second year—"And it would take me at least four years to obtain my degree in modern languages. Longer, if I went for an advanced one."

"Frederick, tell her no."

"Four years or more?" The Judge went for the argument's core.

Meredith nodded eagerly. Four years when she could delve into books and spend hours out of this house with her friends. And possibly help the workers' poor children.

Mother read the changing winds just as clearly. "She'd be much more likely to catch a good husband there, than at a boarding school. After all, so many military men pass through the university."

"Yes, every one of Eisengau's officers must take at least one course there. Many of them study under Zorndorf, the grand duke's top cannon designer."

Zorndorf? That pig?

"Or she might meet a staff member from one of the foreign legations," Mother dreamed, wrapping her arms around herself and spinning, as if she were waltzing. "Somebody titled, who Grand Duke Rudolph would thank us for linking to Eisengau. But she must be in the right place to meet such men."

Meredith cast her eyes up to the ceiling. How many foreigners would hang around the university, desperate to marry a local girl? They were more likely to be spies than wife-hunting. She'd personally be happy to study French, or Russian, or pick up another new language.

But it would at least dodge the possibility of a husband.

"The general student body, where all the military officers pass through?" Meredith suggested. She could disappear into that crowd and make friends, or not, as she chose.

"Too *laissez-faire*," Mother sniffed.

"Or Colonel Zorndorf's office. I hear he's looking for a secretary again."

The two women gaped at the Judge.

"Again? But he's always unkind to females," Mother protested.

Thank you, Mother, for thinking of me just once.

"She's not his wife," the Judge retorted. "Every high-ranking officer speaks to Zorndorf regularly because of the summer maneuvers. Where better for M—our daughter to meet them?"

But Zorndorf? He might be a genius but he was famous for being crude and impossible. "Would he even consider a woman?" Meredith asked.

"It's been almost a month since his last secretary left so he's probably desperate. He must have somebody who speaks foreign languages, given all his contacts with the foreign buyers for Eisengau's famous weapons."

The job might not be all bad, if it got her into the university.

Zorndorf oversaw creation of all the new cannons at the grand duke's foundry. If she worked for him, she could help the workers there. The poor cripples, who'd lost a hand or a foot. Her heart lurched whenever she saw them in the street—especially the burned children—but Mother would never stop to give alms.

"For once, Meredith's pitiful drawing skills might even come in useful." Mother's casual, vicious words shredded Meredith's nerves, like a thunderstorm from hell. "She can't create anything but she can copy what she's already seen. Zorndorf might enjoy that, since he's surrounded by draftsmen."

She took a deep breath and pushed the old wound away, reminding herself it didn't matter. The future was what she made of it. Even so—working for Zorndorf? She continued to fight their proposal.

"Surely being his secretary would take too much time from my studies."

"You can only attend the university if you agree to work for Zorndorf," the Judge said firmly, looking down his long nose at her. She could almost hear him hammering his gavel on the wooden bench.

She swallowed, Morro all warm reassurance under her hand. She had to make the best of it. It'd get her out of this house and Mother's husband-hunting expeditions.

"Very well." She'd use this opportunity to attend school and help the workers at the same time.

With any luck, she'd have more pocket money for buying dime novels, too.

Chapter One

Sagamore Hill, Long Island, New York, June 1900

The tiger glared at Brian Donovan, its jaws stretched wide enough to engulf his head. He rubbed it with his boot and swirled his glass of lemonade, grateful for the reassuring chink of ice cubes on such a hot day. Teddy Roosevelt had at least a dozen other hunting trophies here, plus hundreds of books. They could send his conversation off in a thousand unpredictable directions.

Heat and sunlight filtered into the study through the white-draped windows, closely followed by children's laughter. He'd have some kids of his own soon, as soon as he found another good Catholic girl his folks would approve of. But the next one would be reliable, unlike that money-grubbing Mary FitzAllen.

The governor of New York cast a wistful glance over his shoulder then dropped two massive tomes onto his desk. "Heard you're about to leave for Europe, Donovan."

Brian regarded him from under his brows, wondering what this was all about. Like every other Rough Rider, he'd answered his old colonel's summons as soon as it was received. "Yes, sir. I plan to join my parents and younger brothers in Berlin. My brother's trapped in Peking and they've been pushing the European governments to build a unified army."

And paying bribes. They'd transferred all the family's cash reserves to Switzerland, in case it would help.

"So they've been helping merge together that combined force."

"It was the only way to rescue the diplomats besieged in the embassy compounds, which is where we believe Neil is."

Sweet Jesus, may he still be there and alive.

"With those peasants rampaging across all of China—I'd like to see exactly how they earned the name Boxers!—it'd take a sizable command to get those folks out and back home. Your family's to be commended for helping pull it together."

Brian shrugged the compliment off and waited, not offering any details. He'd been stuck long enough in San Francisco, waiting for word from Neil. He didn't need any reminders of how helpless he'd felt while his parents had been working the European capitals. He'd been sitting there for weeks, playing every string of the family's connections across China and the Pacific to no avail, fighting for any news of Neil.

At least he could move into action now, thanks to that asinine European decision to give Russia command of the army's secondary wing. Why the devil couldn't they give it to somebody with fewer Asiatic ambitions—like France or Italy? But no, it had to be Russia, who was always so desperate for gold and land that there was no telling what their troops might do. Charge into battle without orders, just to take a useful port or loot a city? Many of their soldiers were only half-disciplined, too, dammit.

He'd seen it happen once before, on the far side of India's Northwest Frontier. A business trip there had caught him in the middle of the so-called Great Game played mercilessly between Britain and Russia for control of Central Asia. No brother of his would be caught in the backlash of Russia's troops going out of control, if he could help it.

Only Europe still held any traces of the orders given to those Russian troops. When he'd received the cable asking him to come to Paris, he'd immediately handed everything off to his uncles. They could watch for news out of China as well or better than he could.

But nobody else in the family had the experience to sniff out the smallest signs of Russian ambition and follow them to their source. He was damn glad to go hunting overseas to help block any potential threat to Neil.

"You speak German, don't you?"

Why the devil was he bringing that up?

"Fairly well, yes."

"Ever heard of Eisengau?" Roosevelt swung around a straight-backed chair to face him and straddled it.

"I have one of their shotguns," Brian acknowledged, baffled by the change in subject. Eisengau was known for weaponry, not the size of their army.

"What sporting man doesn't?" snorted Roosevelt, making his guest grin.

"It's supposed to be a small place, on the northeastern fringes of the Alps." Brian shrugged off his disinterest.

"Which designs and sells the best cannons in Europe."

Truly? As well as shotguns?

"Why should that make *me* interested?" He was a civilian now.

"Do you think the same lazy fools who gave us those slow-moving rifles in Cuba will find their way there for some good cannons?"

Brian froze, his lemonade halfway to his lips. "Hardly," he admitted.

He shot a hard look at his former commander, who he'd known since earliest childhood. That was something to be said for family connections: he could ask a question and expect a straight answer. "Why do you bring it up? You're not the President. You're only the candidate for Vice-President."

"On the same ticket as the incumbent President."

"That's no guarantee of being elected," Brian reminded him.

Colonel Roosevelt harrumphed and flung himself to his feet, never one to sit still for long. "Somebody has to go there and see what they've got to offer."

"Why the hurry?"

"There's a rumor they've got a gun as big as anything on a battleship." And being an old Navy man, Roosevelt would have heard about it.

"The War Department won't look into it," Brian guessed.

"Not quite." Roosevelt smacked a big fist into his palm. "They simply don't have the money to buy it. Eisengau runs an auction at their army's summer maneuvers where the atmosphere is lax—" *Enough to make Roosevelt, who'd been uncovering political corruption for decades, mention it? Amazing*—"and bidding can run very, very high."

Rich enough to make a former Under-Secretary of the Navy cautious? Ouch.

"Budgets are tight and Congress is out of session—and you, sir, have no authority." Brian sipped his lemonade again. Dammit, he wasn't a soldier any more, charging up a hill with bullets whistling through his shirt. Nobody could make him do anything, especially not when this was somebody else's responsibility. Like the rest of his family, he needed to go help his big brother.

Still, if there were that many countries visiting Eisengau all at once, it might be a very good place to find out what the Russian half of the Peking relief force was actually supposed to do.

Roosevelt's lips compressed. He hated being reminded of limits. "We can arrange for you to be temporarily back in the Army. The War Department has unearthed some loopholes in the regulations."

Brian blinked, caught totally off-guard. Become a major again?

"You have the money to compete, in your own right." Roosevelt lowered his voice.

The younger man eyed him disbelievingly. Go on his own? "But I'm not an artilleryman. I wouldn't know a good cannon from a mediocre one."

"You're a smart man and you know explosives. Buy what looks interesting and bring it back here for the experts to decide."

"Just because I'm rich." Yes, he could undoubtedly indulge in a cannon or two out of his own pocket.

But why should he pull the War Department's bacon out of the fire, after the way they'd left the regiment to rot and die in Cuba without medical supplies, in exchange for making the Spanish surrender?

"Remember San Juan Hill?" Roosevelt shifted to an orator's coaxing croon and he leaned forward. "All those hours when the Spaniards had us pinned down and our men were wounded and dying along the road and in the fields."

Oh shit, and the smells. Brian nodded, a muscle jerking in his jaw.

"Until the artillery came up. Old-fashioned artillery, using black powder, the same as they used forty years ago. Those guns opened a way for us to take that hill."

"Without them, we'd probably be dead." God knows he relived that scene time and again in his nightmares. He rose and leaned against the bookcase, head bowed before the picture of Roosevelt's beloved father.

"Just go to Eisengau, major, and see what they have." Brian's shoulders instinctively straightened at the sound of his wartime rank. "If there's nothing, come home. But if you find something interesting, buy it and Congress will reimburse you."

"Aren't you exceeding your authority or something—sir?" Brian swung around.

"If I'm not elected, then your family connections will certainly look after you." Roosevelt thumped his desk, making the tomes jump and fall over. "And the next bunch of American soldiers who go into battle will have far better cannons than we did."

And they wouldn't have to die, rotting within hours like pigs, the way his friends had. Never again, not if he could help it.

He'd swing through some of the European capitals on the way, just to see what he could hear about the Russian intentions. Then, off to Eisengau to sift every last gossipy tidbit from the all the drunken soldiers there. Somewhere, somehow, somebody had news that would help Neil.

"Are you in, Major?"

"Yes, sir."

Brian snapped to attention and saluted.

Eisengau, July 1900

Meredith quickly took the last steps down into the square from the college, her long black academic robe whipping around her ankles. Her neatly strapped books swung from her hand, ready to be hidden away for the summer, and her headdress's ribbons brushed her forehead. In the grand duchy's modern capital, only female college students wore traditional headgear—and only during the school year. The intricate wreath would be packed away once she reached home, together with her black velvet robes, to spare her mother and stepfather any reminders of their increasingly unpleasant bargain.

After four years, she still hadn't brought home a fiancé. Her opposition to doing so had grown as firm as her parents' determination to force her into an advantageous marriage. Only their income from keeping her in school kept the atmosphere remotely civilized but that had become an ever-narrower bridge across a deep chasm.

Stiff linen nudged her waist, arguing that she quickly complete her sole errand. Oh, she would, she would. She'd finally had the chance to take action and she'd seized it.

She grinned privately and scanned the old market square

for her best friend. She'd won their private race and reached the rendezvous point before he expected her.

Intricate old buildings framed the great expanse, currently filled with a multitude of vendors. They sold anything a house-wife could desire, starting with food, and the aromas made her mouth water. Whether from small carts or large booths, donkey-drawn or set out in front of a store, they were the gaudiest specimens Eisengau could provide and very popular.

There! A sturdy black dog raced in circles around the drink-ing fountain with several other dogs, all of them leaping in the air to catch droplets of water.

Meredith threw her head back and laughed. She wasn't the only one glad to see semester's end. She could hardly wait to tell her friends what she'd done. Now the grand duke would have to listen to them.

Morro's head snapped up and he barked a joyous wel-come. He twisted, changing direction in mid-air, and raced toward her, dodging between obstacles rather than around them.

She grinned and waited for him, her best and oldest friend. She'd buy him a meat roll to celebrate her secret treasure, once she turned it over to be safely hidden.

A whir and a long drum roll brought the great clock, pride of the ruling dynasty for three centuries, whirling into action. Saints and soldiers strutted in circles atop the New Town Hall's bell tower, careless of the humans below them. Church bells began to ring across the city, once after another, announc-ing the noontime hour. Tomorrow St. Martin's Church in Old Town would hold its weekly concert, reminding everyone who'd gained the largest organ in town thanks to the last war.

Flower vendors hastily straightened their wares, while scared cabbies whipped up their horses and raced for safety, desperate to escape the ban on being caught in New Town by foreign-ers. They disappeared under the great barrel-vaulted colonn-ades, originally built to keep businesses above the great spring floods which regularly ripped through the entire valley, and into Old Town's narrower, winding streets. Only the ancient floodwall protected the historic quarter, not broad avenues and squares, or deep underground drains.

The train blew its whistle sharply once, then again on a long, breathy sigh. Steam oozed out of the station and slid down the tracks, veiling Paris Avenue and Eisengau's Old Town's rough walls beyond it.

Meredith gritted her teeth, barely tolerating another view of the daily injustice. She was never sure whether to race through the square at this hour or delay long enough to avoid the train from Berlin and Paris.

Crimson tile rooftops marked houses and shops clinging to the crag below the Citadel. Only a few, privileged newcomers would be permitted to ascend the narrow roads cut into the Iron Mountain and journey to the ducal palace, sprawled like a sated python over the rock. Black smoke slowly spiraled into the sky behind the cathedral's gothic spires, as it had for all the millennia since swords were first beaten out against the peak's unyielding heart.

And that made everything completely normal in Eisengau—or "Iron Mountain" in German.

Morro planted himself in front of her, tongue lolling out from between his teeth, just as the clock sounded its final note. Perfect timing, as ever.

"You marvelous boy," she crooned and bent to scratch his head behind the ears.

"Fräulein Duncan."

Her boss's all-too-familiar Germanic bark sent her stomach diving for her boots. For a moment, her head spun. Remember, he can't see through your robes, she reminded herself fiercely.

The massive, curving bulk of Colonel Heinrich Zorndorf, Eisengau's chief cannon designer, almost blocked the sun. Taller than most men, his waist measurement nearly equaled his height. His nose was as sharp as a vulture's rapacious beak, his mouth was as tight as a python's grip, and his jaw jutted like a tiger's strike. But his eyes were as sharp as a saber's edge.

"Colonel Zorndorf," she acknowledged and rose slowly to her feet. She plastered a smile on her lips, hoping it looked like her usual polite, patient version.

"They will be working tonight at the foundry."

"Again?" The betraying word slipped out before she could stop it. Morro whipped around, planting himself between the two of them.

Travelers streamed past, isolating them in a bubble of concentrated conversation.

"What's three consecutive weeks when perfection is required?" He frowned at her, his bushy eyebrows beetling under his spiked helmet.

When they've been laboring at least fourteen hour shifts and haven't had a single day off?

"I'm sure all will end well." She'd learned long ago what she could, and could not, do. Openly disagreeing with him was profitless. She shifted her books, nudging her elbow against the linen tied around her waist.

Oh please, let him not notice that my robes are much thicker than usual . . .

"You will need to observe and take notes."

"Tonight? After dark?" She gaped at him. The foundry was almost five miles outside town. She went there regularly during daylight—but at night? For a properly bred girl to walk there alone during those hours was unheard of.

"Of course. My name is all the shield you need." He threw back his shoulders, a lascivious sneer curling his lips.

Yes, but that implied she was either his mistress or his fiancée! She could hardly tell him her friends at the foundry would protect her. She should simply say her mother would never agree. She opened her mouth to object.

A soft, rumbling growl rose from Morro.

"I will be attending Grand Duke Rupert's reception for

our foreign visitors," he went on. "Such a pity you can't attend that instead, since the company there will be very *warm*."

Zorndorf leered down at her, his gaze running over her body like a slimy glove. It lingered on her bosom and traveled lower, scrutinizing every fold for clues to the female form hidden underneath. What if he realized she'd abruptly lost her normally trim waist?

Dear God, what if he guessed she was carrying the plans for Eisengau's magnificent new cannon, strapped around her waist? She had to end this.

"Yes, of course, I'll do my duty and go to the foundry tonight." She'd have to visit her friends now, rather than wait until this evening's workers' party central committee meeting. But she should be able to catch Liesel at home and Liesel could hide the plans for her.

"Excellent, I knew you were a good girl." He reached out to chuck her under the chin and she stepped back quickly. Morro deliberately didn't follow immediately, causing Zorndorf to almost trip. By the time her boss recovered, she was standing a few paces away with her very innocent canine companion at her side. Four years of working for the pig had given them far too much practice in that move.

Zorndorf glared at her, puffing out his chest even farther as he drew himself erect. "I'll also need two new drawings of the ceremonial limber, the one which holds the ammunition for the Citadel's antique cannon."

"Two new drawings? Are more countries coming to the summer maneuvers?" She'd thought all the reservations had been received.

"Only one additional—the United States."

An American? What would he look like? Surely nothing like somebody out of her dime novels.

But he might be—fascinating, the way her two lovers hadn't been.

She yanked back her thoughts before they could wander too far. "And who else?"

"The Russians have finally paid enough to attend all of summer maneuvers. So they too will receive the traditional memento, a program with their coat of arms on the ceremonial limber. You will draw the limber from memory and a court artist will add the coat of arms."

Her mouth twisted wryly. A memory challenge but a small one, considering she'd recreated blueprints for entire cannons before. Still, these drawings would be reviewed by the grand duke's fussiest artists and her work had few creative touches to please them.

"Certainly, sir." She blatantly dodged a departing traveler, who was trailed by a cartful of luggage. "Is there anything else?"

Zorndorf frowned, his mouth tightening until his beak of a nose seemed to dive toward his chin. "No, nothing for now, Fräulein Duncan."

She waited, her back rigidly straight, until he vanished into a hansom cab. Then she shook, the priceless plans resting under her ribs.

Morro whined restlessly and nosed her fingertips.

"Yes, dear, I know we must leave." She rubbed his pricked ears, drawing the soft leather through her fingers for reassurance.

He grunted deep in his throat and butted her hand, knocking it away. His gaze was focused, straining toward something far across the square.

"What on earth?" She looked up.

A single man stepped out of the colonnaded station, isolated by a swirl of travelers. He was tall and broad-shouldered, clad entirely in black. His broad-brimmed hat readily identified him as an American, a rarity here in Eisengau despite its famous summer music festival and military maneuvers. His clothes were well-made yet neither dandified nor a uniform. Straight black hair brushed his collar and his skin was tanned golden brown from the sun, something seldom seen amid these stone walls. His blade-sharp nose, high cheekbones, and stubborn jaw could have been carved by a master sculptor.

He paused on the top of the steps to look around, graceful as a hawk scanning a meadow, yet utterly unself-conscious. His brilliant blue eyes flashed over the crowd like light passing through the finest stained glass—and lingered on Meredith.

Her breath caught in her throat. How many newspaper articles about American adventurers had she devoured? How many cheap novels about men like him had she bartered for?

And to finally see one in the flesh . . .

She instinctively rose to her feet.

The young British military observer limped over to him. Broad grins and thumps on the back announced their old friendship. They were gone within a minute, leaving her alone.

As Zorndorf's secretary, she knew everything that went on behind the scenes at Eisengau's summer maneuvers and weapons' auctions. She'd never been allowed to meet any of the guests, nor would she be. But she could dream—after she saw the plans into safekeeping.

Her friends would be completely surprised. They'd never expected her to accomplish the feat so soon.

She grinned again and headed for Liesel's tiny apartment.

"Meredith!" Liesel, a very pretty, plump, little blond, opened the door wider. "Please come in. Will you join us for sausages?"

Meredith stepped inside, twitching her skirts out of the way so Morro could renew his acquaintance with Liesel's beloved mutt. They'd come here so often that the two dogs played together like each other's shadows. The windows were shut at the moment, despite the day's steamy heat.

"I didn't expect to see you this afternoon." Liesel was chattering as usual. She'd talk just as much when she tried to convince Meredith to buy a new dress. "But we're all friends here and there's plenty of food."

There were eight people in the room, crammed into the sofa or perched on chairs. It was more than she'd expected to see.

But they were her friends and the family of her heart. They'd studied together at the gymnasium, before they came to the university. They'd united together here, outraged by the grand duke's treatment of the workers. There'd been good times, too, such as when new records came from America and they could learn the latest dances together. Or when they'd go to the beer houses for fun, not for rallies.

Franz Schnabel, the workers' party's central committee's longest-serving member and Eisengau's archbishop's nephew, lifted his coffee cup to her. Meredith nodded to him, allowing a trace of her private grin to show.

"Gentlemen, slide over and make room for another lady. Shoo, shoo, shoo." Their hostess waved her hands at them. They obediently began to sort themselves into more understandable clumps, always avoiding the worst broken springs in the upholstery, of course.

Where could she sit?

Erich and Rosa were together in the corner, of course, while Franz and Gerhardt had the window seat.

Liesel was fluttering about, unlikely to settle down given her duties as hostess.

"Ernst, please leave some bratwurst for the others!" she ordered and everyone laughed at the familiar plea.

Meredith spotted a spot next to the silent Gerhardt and squeezed onto the ancient, straight-back chair, Morro tucking himself against her feet. There were too many people here.

"Why am I rattling on so much? All these thunderstorms must have shaken my nerves." Her best friend delivered sausages and bread to Meredith, then stood up, dramatically laying the back of her hand against her forehead. "My head aches so."

Meredith paused, her sandwich halfway to her mouth. What was happening?

Liesel tottered backward, heading directly toward the previous silent blond man. His very handsome face promptly shifted into a concerned—calculated?—smile. He reached upward, drawing her down onto the wing chair's arm. She snuggled happily against his shoulder and beamed up at him. "My darling count, how good you are to me."

She trusted the Russian?

"Would you like some aspirin, Liesel?" Meredith asked desperately. "I'm sure I can find you one." She'd do anything to get her friend out of his arms. Heaven only knew what she might have told him.

"Oh no, my dearest Sazonov knows exactly how to make me feel better. Don't you, sweetheart?"

"Always, my darling." He kissed her forehead, his dark eyes sliding over Meredith.

She shivered and bit into her sandwich. Sazonov might be their biggest backer—in fact, their only source of funds beside their own threadbare pockets—which gave him some claim to being their advisor. But it didn't mean he had to know *everything*.

She could wait until later when he was gone before telling the others. They still had time to decide how to use the cannon's plans to help the workers.

"When are you going to steal the cannon's plans, Meredith?" Liesel asked.

She choked. By the time Gerhardt had thumped her hard on the back several times and Rosa had poured water down her throat, her face was red and her brain was fighting for a foothold in reality. At least nobody seemed to have touched her below the shoulder blades.

Liesel's mutt grabbed Meredith's sandwich and it vanished without a trace.

"I'm not stealing anything," she denied, tears streaming down her face and Morro pressed against her heart. It might be a lost cause but she wouldn't admit to anything with the Russian's far-too-interested eyes watching her every move.

"You don't have to be shy in front of Sazonov," Liesel tried to reassure her. "I already told him everything."

Meredith shot her friend a startled glance and took another sip of water. She let it linger on her tongue, trying to buy time until she had to say something.

If she invited Liesel on a shopping expedition—for corsets, maybe? Blech—they could have a more private conversation. Then she could explain the hazards of trusting somebody owing allegiance to a foreign government. Surely his duty to his country would trump his private feelings. (And Meredith would be careful not to mention her own opinions about the genuineness of said feelings.)

"I confirmed it, since he'd already guessed most of the details," Franz added. "Admit it, Meredith: we need his help."

Franz? If she couldn't trust Franz, the longest serving member, who was left to help the workers?

But she'd have to save her tears for later, when she was alone. There was work to be done now. First, she needed to find her own place to hide the plans. She'd have to talk to her friends later in private and try to convince them not to share everything with the Russian.

She shrugged ostentatiously. "Please don't blame me for trying to keep it a secret as long as possible."

An almost audible sigh went up and everyone settled into their seats, clearly ready for a conference.

Meredith's mouth twisted. What could she say and what couldn't she? Oh, to be in a simple predicament with a dime novel hero and his clan beside her.

She set Morro back onto the floor, warning him with a little pat not to relax.

"Are you certain this will work?" Sazonov asked in that deep, guttural voice of his. Liesel batted her eyes at him.

The sound always made Meredith grit her teeth but this time she managed a thin smile. "Grand Duke Rudolph paid one thousand marks for a model stolen by some Italians five years ago."

"A more important set of blueprints—such as the ones for the latest cannon—should make him do anything we want politically." Franz's eyes were shining.

He truly had told the Russian everything. Meredith was glad she'd only had a couple of bites of bratwurst, given how they were jostling each other in her stomach.

"You will need someplace very safe to hide it, while you negotiate with the old bear," Sazonov remarked. "Please allow me to offer the sanctity of my embassy. He'd never be able to seize them there."

"You'd guard them for us, no matter what Grand Duke Rudolph did?"

"It would be an honor. No matter how long it takes." Sazonov managed to bow, despite fondling Liesel. Meredith's skin crawled, even though his actions were the same as Erich and Rosa's.

And the more time in his hands the better for copying them, too.

"We accept, of course!" Franz cried. Liesel kissed Sazonov and the others jumped to their feet, cheering.

I don't.

Meredith stood up and applauded, glad he'd confirmed her estimate of his goals.

But where on earth would she hide the plans now?

The enormous reception hall was full of crystal and gilt, satin and velvet, from the ceilings to the walls to the people. Crystal chandeliers glittered like the women's diamonds below and satin-draped walls formed the backdrop for peacock gowns from Paris. No honest day had ever been so bright, with so few shadows to offer privacy.

Gilded frames marked dead heroes and echoed the sweep of gold lacing over old men's fat paunches. Every European army's most gaudy uniform was flaunted among the living attendees, topped by polite diplomatic ribbons. The men would be living together day and night for the next month, although not in the same glamorous garb.

Brian Donovan was wryly glad to be wearing his Rough Rider uniform. He'd earned every one of his medals on a battlefield, by God. How many of his fellow guests could say the same for theirs?

At least he had one friend here, somebody he could trust socially, even if not in a bidding war for Eisengau's latest weapons.

Captain Gareth Blackwell shifted his cane from his right hand to his left, his brand-new Victoria Cross briefly glinting in the light.

"How's your leg?" Brian asked.

"Does well enough." He accepted another glass of champagne from a waiter, eyeing two Russian ladies with particularly low-cut décolletages. "The ladies love seeing the scars."

Displaying them in a bedroom was probably the biggest benefit he'd gained from helping to save the guns at Colenso, a few months ago. A damn mismanaged battle but very gallant rescue. His invalid status was his ticket to Eisengau's summer maneuvers.

"What about that abscess in your shoulder?" Gareth continued their medical banter. "Bullet started it, not a knife?"

"Spanish bullet at San Juan Hill, and it's finally healed. My father threatened it with the best doctors until it ran away." Brian smiled faintly and finished his cognac. After he'd been carried off that troopship, delirious from that infected wound, his parents had nursed him night and day. Only his father had had the strength and the patience to keep him in his bed until the fever broke, crooning old Irish lullabies to soothe him. Someday Brian would sing the same ones to his own son.

"You're lucky." Gareth slanted an eyebrow at him.

"No, all infections are terrified of alpine climates like this one."

They touched their glasses together, laughing. They'd first met during a battle on India's Northwest Frontier, then sailed back together to Egypt. How many doctors had they heard crisply order their patients off to Europe to escape tropical diseases?

"Those ladies don't seem to be worried about the climate," Gareth commented, nodding at the Russians.

"Very healthy women, those northerners," Brian agreed.

"And nothing like Miss FitzAllen."

"Nobody is, thank God." Brian shrugged and took another snifter of cognac off a servant's salver.

"Sorry, old man, I shouldn't have—"

"Why? It was years ago and she's gone to another. I don't even think about her anymore." Because I'm damn lucky to have escaped her.

Gareth stared at him for a long moment. "You said the same thing back then but I didn't believe you."

Brian shrugged, disinclined to revisit an old folly. "Did you intend to do your bit for God and Country by calling on those ladies?" He made the last word sound overly polite.

"Of course I will." Gareth tossed him a rude salute, screened by his champagne flute. "It's how the Great Game is played, old man. You colonials really should grow up and start learning how to play with the grownups."

"We tossed a four-century-old empire out on its ear from a hemisphere," Brian observed mildly. "Broke the line against well-trained, well-entrenched troops, under withering fire—"

And took far too many casualties.

"Thus earning yourself a seat at the Eisengau dinner table for the first time," Gareth agreed. "The old grand duke is rather a snob. But *we're* glad you're here."

The subtle emphasis made Brian go quite still, his eyes searching his friend's.

"Not that it's likely to change things much." The Welshman smiled wryly. "Now I'm off to tell a few stories to the ladies and see how far they get me."

"Good luck." Brian tossed him a two-finger salute. He sipped his drink, considering his own options.

He smiled politely to the countess of Something-Unpronounceable, wondering if she'd provide the seventh invitation for bed sport he'd received that night.

God knows he enjoyed screwing but even the indomitable Teddy Roosevelt hadn't suggested Brian do it for his country's sake. On the other hand, he hadn't realized all the fringe benefits of his agreement with Teddy, either.

He'd received his first offer in Eisengau from the housemaid who'd laid out his clothes in his bedroom. He'd refused her, a little startled to be propositioned so early in his stay.

Even more surprising, every servant he'd met afterward had been a man. No flirtatious maids here whisking away trays of drinks with a flash of lace-trimmed petticoats—no, not in Eisengau's Citadel! The halls and dining parlors were populated instead by immaculate footmen, either blank-faced and grim or prettier than any Parisian streetwalker. He'd wager a month's income from his Alaska gold mine that any of those footmen, or the maid, could repeat every word uttered by a guest, if requested by the local secret police.

No, not his style at all.

But there was something to be said for an atmosphere which encouraged licentious behavior. After all, he had received five other offers, all from female guests. Gareth, who'd been here once before, had two ladies clinging to him while he played tunes on wineglasses.

Still, the Countess didn't look nearly as interesting as that blond he'd seen crossing the square by the railway station earlier that day. The beautiful young lady with all the ribbons braided into a wreath atop her head and swathed in an academic gown. A college student, by God, and feminine as hell with the soft colors fluttering around her head and a dog at her knee.

There had to be some magnificent fires lurking under all that black velvet. If she'd been in his arms, he'd have made damn sure she was purring—or howling for more.

He grinned and knocked back the rest of his very expensive cognac.

But she wasn't here, damn his luck. So he'd have to make do with the prettiest girl available, or the one who could help America—or Neil—the most.

After all, the next few weeks could change the balance of military power in Europe—and America, if Teddy's sources were correct. Discreet liaisons were always perfectly acceptable in diplomatic circles and they were probably strongly encouraged here.

"That's quite a collection of war heroes hanging on the walls, Countess," he remarked. "Napoleon, of course. But isn't that Wellington?"

"Oh yes!" She immediately turned her back on the man beside her. "And Nelson's over there, with the Duke of Marlborough, a little farther down toward the musicians. Plus, Frederick the Great and Garibaldi, Italy's great liberator. Each portrait says 'thank you' for a successful arms purchase."

Brian turned to follow the line of portraits, bringing the countess almost under his arm. For an instant, the two of them were closer than a breath. She boldly fondled his ass, her long fingers lingering over his thigh before falling away, hidden by the crowd.

Invitation number seven.

He slanted an eyebrow at her, ready to flirt more with such a promising source of information, but a harsh voice cut in.

"Countess, I believe your husband needs you."

Sazonov, the Russian attaché, arrived beside him, medals jangling. "Now."

Her eyes flashed at the unnecessary rudeness before she ostentatiously glanced around, looking and not finding her absent spouse. Brian flickered a significant glance upstairs toward their common bedroom wing and she smiled, cat-with-canary-feathers smug.

He bowed, bidding her an ostentatiously polite *adieu*. His opinion of their interruption was far less printable.

Sazonov was one of the few here under fifty years old. Even rarer, Brian would wager he was one of the two or three guests—beside Brian—who was armed. He was just as gaudily uniformed as any other man there, in a dark blue tunic, a brilliant scarlet sash, and white pants tucked into his high black boots.

"A game of poker is about to start in the library," Sazonov said softly. "Would you care to join us?"

"Us?" Brian queried, equally quietly.

"Simply put—the British, French, German, Dane, Swiss, Serb, myself, and yourself." Representatives of the eight countries most likely to bid high for Eisengau's best weapons this year.

Aunt Rosalind had made sure Brian, like all of his siblings and cousins, knew his way around a poker game from a very young age. He wasn't the best in the family but he was damn sure he could give a good account of himself.

"My pleasure," Brian agreed sincerely. He'd enjoy finding out how the competition like to play their hands.

Firelight washed the room in rich shades of ochre and gold, caressing the century-old tapestried chairs and footstools.

Meredith paced, trying to stay calm and not let her nerves infect the men below. They should have been done an hour ago.

Her notebook lay open on the table, pages of neatly labeled notes describing every step of a complicated process. A cup of tea—genuine, honest-to-goodness lapsang souchong—steamed gently beside it. It had been her father's favorite variety after a visit to the pub. But she never had the heart to refuse it, not after her friends had worked so hard to obtain it.

The only memento of her father she comfortably tolerated was her cairngorm brooch, whose stones had been mined in Scotland. She wore it as often as possible, lest it vanish into Mother's jewel chest the way so much else had.

She could have been anywhere in the world. Edinburgh would have been heaven, a university town offering the soft accents of her birthplace. Her bedroom a few miles away, with its narrow view of Eisengau's university, would have been expected. But not here, not where the heat swarmed over the iron balcony like an army battering at the city gates.

The fire wasn't from a few cozy logs on a hearth. No, it was the great open-hearth forge of Grand Duke Rudolph's personal steelworks. Here Zorndorf's latest handiwork came to life like hell-born beasts. Their sire had assigned her to record this birth like so many others, since females lacked the native wit to understand the weapons' true importance.

She should have been at Franz and Gerhardt's apartment, planning for the rally tomorrow night with everyone else. Sazonov might not have been there, giving her the chance to talk her friends into some discretion.

But she couldn't leave, not when Mayer and Brecht were half-staggering to cast the new gun. Better she roast like a goose in an open stewpot with them than run away, leaving them alone with the secret police observing from the other side.

She'd always done what she could for the children—seen them assigned to carrying messages, rather than heavy steel, and coaxed scholarships for the best in the grand duke's schools. But there was little she could do for the adults except try to talk Zorndorf out of his more appalling calls for long hours—and stand here in solidarity with the workers when that failed.

Sweat trickled down her throat and pooled under her breasts, following every seam in her liberty bodice. A regular corset, such as her mother always wanted her to wear, would have been hell on earth at times like this, with whalebone to force the fiery saltwater into her flesh whenever she sat frozen in place like this. Her linen skirts rubbed against her legs; even the light summer wear an almost intolerable weight now.

Had any torment in a dime novel been worse? Perhaps that American adventurer could tell her about their deserts one day. They might be cooler than this.

She chuckled and finally drank her tea.

Morro muttered deep in his throat from the door, dozing beside the only place where a threat to her truly existed. A few shards of ice floated in his water bowl and a dark, wet ring in the carpet told of its presence here. At any other spot in this room, that mark would have evaporated within seconds.

Eisengau's people had mined limestone in these mountains for millennia. A century ago—when Napoleon had planned to invade Eisengau—the ruling grand duke had hidden his armory's most important forge deep within the maze of tunnels, abandoned quarries, and dammed-up lakes. The entrance was only a few miles from the Citadel yet it was impossible for strangers to find, let alone trace the path to this room.

There were very few people Colonel Zorndorf, the top designer, trusted to accurately record every step of creating one of his great designs. Not even his top two assistants knew all of the steps, let alone his students. She could have done without the honor, even though it brought frequent escapes from home.

At one end of the floor below stood the great hearth, lined with the great bricks for which it was named. It glowed with heat, almost as bright as the noontime sun. Iron tracks ran before it, carrying small, heavy vats. Great cranes on long rods swung across its face, coaxing an immense pot far taller than a man. A single crane brought it forward, red-hot and steaming, a handful of grown men circling around it like acolytes before a pagan god.

If they made a single mistake, they'd be fired and lose everything. No income, no house. No medical care if they were injured unless they paid for it, and the closest doctor was a half mile away. No alternate job, even if the problem had been the armory's fault. They'd become beggars, as they would have been a thousand years ago.

Because the damned grand duke refused to allow any change or any discussion of needing to change.

Brecht shouted and shoved the molds into a slightly different position. His son Anton ran across the floor, carrying a slate bearing orders for the foreman.

Meredith frowned. No children should be working the night shift, only the warier adults.

The boy slipped, skidding across the floor toward a heavy mold, waiting to hold molten metal.

She lunged for the balcony and shouted a warning. The bell behind her was only used for ordering refreshments. Her appeal probably wouldn't be heard from here, not in this racket. But she could try.

Mayer, the foreman—and Anton's uncle—looked around.

Another bucket arced high overhead from one furnace to the next, ready to pour fiery hot steel over anything which brought it to a stop.

A high, thin scream rose to the rafters and vanished, as the boy desperately tried to stop himself.

Mayer dove and yanked Anton away from the mold. He tossed him up, over his shoulder and into the lad's father's arms.

An instant later, the fiery steel spilled into the form with a mighty hiss and whoosh. Steam boiled out and rose, obscuring the forge's open hearth, as if Hades had slammed the door to his domain.

Mayer sat up and grinned at Meredith, his back hiding their understanding from any police spies.

She sat down, shaking. At least she'd accomplished something for one working family today.

And she had stolen and hidden the great cannon's plans. She couldn't forget that. Because Eisengau had to transform and she was going to help it along.

The library wasn't gilded like the reception hall, thank God. Instead it was lined with books and full of big, carved wooden chairs which a hurricane couldn't have lifted, plus an equally solid table. A single, massive chandelier blazed down pitilessly, picking out every detail of the players and their cards. Smaller lamps in the other corners allowed observers to whisper and drink, while not disturbing the players' all-important concentration.

Aunt Rosalind would have greatly approved of it. Brian could have played poker here for hours.

He yawned again and didn't look at his cards, which he hadn't checked since they were dealt. Instead, he'd behaved as if he was eager for his bed—and let the others guess the reason why.

The impassive steward looked around the table again, double-checking that nobody wanted any more cards. Given the monies involved, one of Grand Duke Rudolph's liveried servants was acting as dealer. There were only three players left—Brian, Sazonov, and the Swiss fellow. The others had withdrawn and were standing up now, watching the game.

The Swiss studied his cards, tapping his finger lightly on the table. Brian waited politely, anticipating the decision given the other's tell-tale gesture.

Finally the fellow shrugged and tossed his cards into the center. "Fold," he announced clearly, in a slightly guttural accent.

Brian inclined his head, as did Sazonov, and watched the other go.

"Well?" demanded the Russian. He tossed back another glass of vodka without looking away from Brian. Pity he didn't seem to be getting drunk.

"Call." Brian pushed the rest of his chips into the center. Five thousand pounds, plus another sixty thousand on the table, or three-hundred twenty-five-thousand dollars. A tidy little sum and a fortune to some folks, but not in his family.

"What the hell are you talking about? I've got two pair showing, aces and kings!" Sazonov slapped the table, sloshing vodka onto the gleaming wood.

"You haven't proved you can beat my hand," Brian returned, well aware of the knife lurking in his opponent's sleeve.

An evening spent playing poker with the other man hadn't quelled his anger over the fellow's unnecessary rudeness toward the countess.

The other players began to gather even closer, drinks in hand, decorations gleaming on their chests like ancient oaths.

"You fool." Sazonov shrugged. "Never say I didn't give you a chance." He flipped over his last remaining card. "Full house, aces over kings."

Brian fanned his cards across the table. "Royal flush." *Read 'em and weep, you bastard.* It wasn't much of a lesson but maybe it would teach him a little politeness—and not to judge people too quickly.

Sazonov glared at the unyielding cards before looking up again at Brian. "*Sukin syn,*" he hissed.

The room fell silent, the previous small talk replaced by a deadly hush.

Son of a bitch, indeed. Brian chilled at the deadly insult to his mother. The slim, sharp strip of steel up his sleeve nudged him eagerly. But if he took physical action, here and now, he'd be thrown out of town before he could find out what the U.S. or his brother needed to know.

"When you call me that—*smile!*" he hissed.

Sazonov glanced around, catching watchers studying them like a waiting gun battery. His lips curled but his eyes promised Brian that vengeance for this humiliation was only delayed.

Brian tilted his head slightly, eyes never leaving his enemy's. It was one challenge he'd be glad to accept.

Chapter Two

The beer house's pantry was barely large enough for one person, let alone three and a healthy argument. Wide shelves stacked high with flour and spices muffled their voices, while sausages hung from the ceiling cloaking the light.

"Why did you have to tell Sazonov about the blueprints?" Meredith repeated, holding onto her temper by a shred.

Liesel sniffed. They hadn't spoken a civil word together since she'd realized Meredith wasn't convinced Sazonov adored her.

"We had to give him something in exchange for all his help," Franz answered, finally saying something which sounded like the truth. "None of the socialist parties will give us more than a pretty proclamation, since their governments don't want to lose access to Eisengau's weaponry."

"But the blueprints?"

"Don't you remember how much money he's given us? They're the only guarantee we've got, if the next election fails."

"Of course, Sazonov is so clever,"—Meredith bit her tongue at Liesel's sugar-sweet adoration—"he immediately realized you would be the one to steal the plans."

But did you have to confirm it, thus placing me firmly in the firing line?

"But how can I give them to him? What if he copies them or takes them back to Russia?"

"How can you say that? He'd never betray the revolution like that. He's told me how much he cares about the workers here and in Russia." Liesel sighed. "He can quote poetry, too."

She was sure he could, especially to gullible women. How could she protect her friend?

"Are you committed to the workers, Fräulein *Duncan*?" Franz asked.

Duncan? Why was he calling her that? "What do you mean?"

"Perhaps your weak British blood is leading you a trifle astray."

What? Weak British blood? Astray? Every nerve snapped fully awake, as if fiery needles ripped through her veins.

"You're the only one of us who's hesitating about going forward."

Meredith braced her shoulders, wishing for the first time in her life she was a man. Hitting somebody in the face suddenly made sense. "I feel stronger about the revolution than ever, Franz."

"Excellent. I knew we could trust you." He patted her on the shoulder, his teeth shining in the faint light. "Please forgive me for testing you. I'm sure you know I've been around for a long time and know best. After you've stolen the plans, just bring them to me and I'll take care of them."

She murmured something and stretched her lips across her teeth. She wouldn't have called it a smile but she was still too angry to care. Did he think she was stupid enough to fall in line, just because he'd touched and praised her like a pet animal? Would he give her any reason for obedience other than his orders?

Of course, he was the patriarch of their group, the senior male, and therefore entitled to unquestioning loyalty, according to local law and custom.

Not that she'd grant it.

A knock sounded on the door. "The beer house is filling fast," Gerhardt announced. "We need to start hanging posters."

"Thank you," Franz answered. "Well, we'd best move on so we can speak to the workers. Even if we don't need them as much anymore, thanks to obtaining the blueprints, we still want them to feel involved."

But he didn't have the blueprints. And the revolution was about the workers, not people like Franz and Liesel.

What was changing? Did she want to stay?

On the other hand, she still had the blueprints, not them.

Her smile turned broader and she followed them to the door.

"Entschuldigung, mein Herr?"

Brian glanced up, his fingers closing around shredded telegrams above his sausage and cabbage.

He met narrow gray eyes, a large nose above a bristling mustache, and a receding chin. Thin lips stretched across yellow teeth in a smile's parody, surmounting a stout body cloaked in good tailoring and cheap toilet water.

The beer house around them surged with life, every table crowded with neatly dressed men and women drinking the fine local brews. Their very respectable clothing was clean, the women's feathered hats and men's caps precisely set on their heads. Yet their tailoring was years out of date, held together only by precise darning and repeated repairs. A band thumped out tunes in a corner and a few couples pretended to practice the local favorites on a dance floor which would have fit in his mother's pantry.

Waiters filled their orders with the casual speed of long practice, the glass steins with their overflowing foam glowing like miniature suns in the big room's gloom.

Small pictures of saints and local landscapes were scattered across white plaster walls, framed by heavy wood paneling below and around the doors and windows. Massive tables and benches filled the center, while high-backed booths marched down the only long, uninterrupted edge. A very simple bar stood at the narrow end, where a bartender dispensed beer and rocked back and forth on his feet, eyeing the crowd more than the amber liquid he was pulling.

Comfortable aromas of food wafted through—pork, beef, cabbage, and potatoes mixed with onions, butter, caraway. But they were fainter than he'd have expected at this time, matching the odd fact that this evening's heavy crowds were drinking more than they were eating. And they were an unusually sober lot, even though they'd already filled almost every table and much of the aisles. Even the dogs they seemed compelled to bring everywhere were here, twining around ankles, snuffling at hands, guarding satchels.

Brian had a corner table, granting him privacy in this, the closest beer house to Old Town's telegraph office. It was also the only spot where his London-tailored suit melted into the shadows. He hadn't been about to wear his Rough Rider uniform to read cables from home, even if most of the men at the Citadel were uniformed.

"Can I help you, sir?" He met the interlopers' glare guilelessly, wearing an expression which would have made any of his three brothers wary. He decided to lay it on a little heavier.

"Uh, *wie bitte?*" He hesitated, turning the simple apology into five syllables instead of its normal three. His German was very good, thanks to an extremely brutal Klondike winter which had left him little to do except learn his cabin mate's native tongue.

Crimson washed through the other's face and ebbed slowly, leaving behind ugly splotches. He closed his mouth, his yellow teeth snapping shut like an ore crusher ripping into a ten-ton boulder. He drew himself up, his coat tightening over a fat notebook in his breast pocket and a revolver in his hip pocket.

A Webley? Damn, Grand Duke Rudolph had been bragging how placid Eisengau was so why was this cop carrying a weapon?

Was there any danger to Brian? Probably not, but where were the threats coming from?

Brian's skin tightened, matching nerves and blood and muscles springing to full alertness. He waited, feigning confusion.

The other's gray eyes narrowed and considered Brian with no sign of friendship before reaching a visible conclusion.

"Passport, please." His accent was thick and barely understandable. Two men came up behind him, broader of shoulder and bulkier of pocket—and undoubtedly packing more in the way of guns.

"Of course, sir." Brian smiled a little more broadly, making sure he knew exactly where the other men's weapons were. He slowly eased the all—important document out of his jacket, taking care to look harmless, and handed it over. "I'm the American buyer this year."

One of the thugs bent to say something quiet to the leader. He stiffened but said nothing, simply flipped through Brian's paperwork while listening.

When he looked up, his teeth gleamed in an oily semblance of welcome.

"Welcome to Eisengau, *mein Herr*." He bowed, snapping his heels together. "My apologies, sir, for having disturbed you. I trust you will enjoy your visit."

"Thank you." Brian would have relaxed faster if a rattlesnake had declared undying affection.

A curt nod and the three pivoted. The throng parted before them then closed ranks behind them to avoid contact with the clearly unwelcome officials.

Brian took a drink of his now lukewarm beer and checked to see if anyone was watching him. Nobody, thank God, either his plate or his cables' scraps. Donovan & Sons' cipher was extremely strong but why let anybody else have a chance to read his mail? Especially this batch, which had contained good news for his mission at the expense of bad news for his family.

The Europeans had finally gotten an army moving to rescue the diplomats in Peking. Unfortunately, nobody had yet heard from Neil. So he had full use of all the money—a damned great fortune—they'd gathered to rescue his brother, because nobody knew if Neil was alive or dead.

Worse, he'd learned the Russians planned to attack heavily at any pretext, hoping to seize territory and gold first, then argue about the rightful owner later. The response to his warning lay shredded on the table before him: The Allied army, including its Russian wing, would go into battle long before even the fastest message could reach them.

He slammed his fist into his other hand. He'd rather be a pauper, going into an auction with nothing but his wits to help him.

Big brother had to be alive. He was too stubborn for anything else to have happened. Plus, he had Abraham, Father's Chinese bodyguard, with him and he could speak at least one dialect like a native.

Brian cursed under his breath, struck a match, and lit the cables, removing the last temptation for passersby to steal the shreds and help the competition piece them together. Still, he'd be able to buy weapons faster than anybody else because he could do so on his signature alone, rather than begging for permission from his masters back home.

Paper blackened and curled.

He poked it, suppressing the urge to add another match. Not here, not now, not when it might draw attention from a policeman. He found himself clenching his fists and gritted his teeth.

Be patient, dammit. The first telegram was gone, at least.

Perhaps he could pick up the ashes and crush them under his boot heel? But in a beer house?

He snorted at his own stupidity. The band crashed into a long chord and stopped.

Brian looked up, automatically seeking the next song's start. It was too soon for the set to be over so why were they filing off now?

The band disappeared through a small door, neatly concealed in the woodwork. Their dancers were gone, replaced by men tacking up banners under a young woman's direction. The signs were big with strong, bold lettering—"Vote Now," "One Man One Vote," and more of the same ilk.

But the woman? Praise the saints, she was the girl he'd seen yesterday in the town square, crowned with golden hair. She now wore a surprisingly well-tailored blue suit and white shirt, a higher quality version than the usual Eisengau's working woman's wardrobe. Her high collar was pinned with a chased gold brooch, highlighted by a darker golden stone.

Her movements were direct and confident, her commands staccato. Her forces worked eagerly and quickly under her direction, accomplishing their tasks remarkably fast.

Her features were etched in strength, rather than a passing moment's prettiness. Her eyes were gray, flashing with passion as she considered the best position for each sign.

Ah, to be the lucky man who was the focus of her lambent gaze in the bedroom.

Brian instinctively crammed his paperwork onto the embers, answering the fire sheeting over his skin and down to his feet, marking a path to her.

"Ladies and gentlemen," a man shouted.

Brian shot an irritated glance toward the bar and discovered a young fellow, hidden behind a voluminous mustache and beard. The naïve fool probably thought it made him look more impressive.

The crowd promptly fell completely silent. Was he whom everyone had been waiting for or was there somebody else?

Like half the people there, Brian pulled out his chair and stood on it to see better.

"Ladies and gentlemen," the fellow began again, "we have come to discuss this fall's elections when the duchy's entire council is up for re-election. We urge all of you to vote!" His voice surged to a room-filling roar on the final word.

Nobody spoke. A quick glance showed dozens of intent faces, except for the policeman and his friends. They'd scattered to stand by every door. More of their kind joined them, marked by the better clothing and eyes which paid no attention to the speaker.

"If you do, we can elect enough candidates to change the rules here," the orator went on. "No more one hundred workers' votes for every shopkeeper or one *thousand* workers' votes for every noble, crushing us into the ground!"

The crowd cheered heartily, while the policemen signaled to each other. The room grew silent, waiting for the orator's next words.

"And then we can have . . ." He hesitated, looking out at them. He tried again. "We will all know the benefits of . . ."

Somebody shifted unhappily.

The girl whispered to the orator behind her hand.

"Then we can have a six-day work week!"

The crowd cheered again and the orator looked relieved. He glanced down at the girl and she leaned sideways toward him.

"A medical clinic at the foundry to quickly tend any injuries!" He pumped his fist in the air.

"Hear, hear!" someone shouted. An old woman muttered what sounded like a prayer, her careworn face lighting up with hope.

"A new start for Eisengau," somebody muttered.

The blond girl folded her hands, her brilliant gaze considering the audience. Jesus, Mary, and Joseph, it didn't take a degree from Harvard to figure out who was the brains behind this rally.

The cops started moving forward, sliding through the crowd like snakes. Dammit, the armed one was heading for the girl.

"But *all* of us must vote," the man crooned, his eyes shining bright enough to light a path to heaven. "Every one of us or this won't work."

"Vote!" somebody shouted in the back. Somebody else promptly echoed him, "Vote now!" Others took up the shout, lifting their caps into the air.

One of the cops blew a whistle and pointed at the two speakers.

Shit. There were too many innocent women here for this to be just a good fight.

BOOM! The front door burst inward and uniformed cops poured into the beer house. A woman screamed, long and shrill. A man cursed, deep and guttural, and swung a ham-sized fist at the cop next to him.

The air-headed orator ran for the kitchen door with its likely escape to the alley.

The armed cop lunged for the girl who'd been coaching the speaker. She jerked away, barely evading his foul grip.

Brian growled and jumped for the next table, dodging a pair of fighters.

A woman screeched in terror. She was shoved aside and onto the floor by truncheon-wielding cops.

They were attacking the onlookers, too? Mother of God, hell's fires were too good for them.

Crockery sailed past to break by the dozen, fast and loud as any gun. Overhead, the big lamps were swinging wildly, shards of glass falling like hail which had been brought down by the various missiles flying through the air. Feathers floated past, symbols of hats torn off innocent ladies' heads.

The bastard grabbed the girl by one elbow but she hit him in the stomach with a beer stein. He doubled over but didn't release her.

Good try, milady.

Brian took the next table in a single bound.

The men who'd been hanging banners started to disappear

through side doors, just ahead of the police. Women were sobbing and fighting to reach the nearest exit.

One man threw a huge roundhouse punch at him but Brian simply stepped inside the arc and hit him in the face, using the heel of his palm, then waltzed past to wait for any counterstrikes. Both he and Neil had been trained in Chinese street fighting, although Neil was far better.

The fellow yelped, falling back, and Brian leaped again.

He ran down the next table's center, dodging obstacles both living and not, moving and still.

Hold on just a little longer, lady; I'm coming.

A flying wedge of other policemen, too many to be deterred by the fighting, headed for them from less than half a dozen steps away.

Brian grabbed a half-empty beer stein and hurled it at her captor. It caught him on the head just above his ear, stunning him—and freeing her.

For an instant, their eyes met, the riot now only a frame for their world. Hers were enormous and silver-bright, spilling light like a river between them.

Brian's breath hung in his throat.

"Get that man!" the policeman roared, pointing at him.

She shook herself and ran for the door, skidding only briefly on the slippery floor. But the cops were close on her heels.

Brian snarled and gathered himself to follow. They would *not* have his girl.

Two hands grabbed his ankles and pulled, yanking him off the table and onto the floor.

Brian whirled, taking his attacker down with a slashing kick to his knees.

A hard blow from behind caught him unawares and he staggered. He looked up to reorient himself—and found himself staring straight into a lamp's blinding glare, just as it began another wild swing. Brian blinked, momentarily blinded. An instant later, three men piled onto his chest and he was handcuffed.

"Damn you, find her!" the lead policeman howled.

At least his girl had escaped.

Brian smiled proudly and lashed out with his feet, doing his best to distract her would-be pursuers.

A half hour later, a loud shout and whip crack sent the paddy wagon skidding around yet another corner on its way uphill. All of its occupants were thrown against each other and onto a single bench, sliding along the rough wood like toy dolls. It bumped, bounced, jolted, every cobblestone ringing through the iron wheels and metal walls like a fusillade.

The other police wagon could barely be heard behind them, driven by a much less reckless driver. After all, it carried all the cops who'd torn apart the beer house.

Somebody landed on the floor with a loud yelp.

Brian grimaced sympathetically, bracing himself against similar misfortune. He'd been lucky enough to be loaded last, next to the door and what passed for clean air. Losing his bowler was the least of his problems.

Somebody grunted and cursed. Somebody else prayed to a litany of saints. A third man, far more pragmatic, choked and prayed not to be sick.

The horses thundered forward, harnesses jingling and hooves clattering down the street. The guard was singing something about good beer and pretty women.

Brian braced himself and leaned once again toward the pallid light creeping in through the window high atop the rear door. He had a nicked cheekbone and every breath was an effort, thanks to a policeman's heavy boots thudding into his ribs.

God forbid he should be bailed out by the American consul. That worthy gentleman had already made his opinion of Washington-sent *amateurs* very clear. He might use this opportunity to substitute one of his own flunkeys for Brian at Eisengau's summer maneuvers.

BOW WOW WOW WOW!

A dog's deep bark challenged the paddy wagon from immediately ahead. The horses reared and screamed in alarm, bringing the wagon to a complete halt.

What the devil? Brian started to rise but rapped his head on the roof.

BOW WOW WOW! The dog was barking continuously, triggering all of its fellows in the neighborhood.

The driver cursed and the wagon swayed wildly. The prisoners began to shout and beg to be released.

The first dog was barking at the top of his lungs, apparently running back and forth at the horses. They reared and lashed out. One of them neighed again, a high-pitched plea for help.

The wagon lurched forward and back, then stopped with a screech of iron wheels across the cobblestones.

Brian grabbed for the door.

BOW WOW! The dog proclaimed triumphantly.

The other police wagon sounded its trumpet, ordering all citizens to clear the way.

"Hold the reins, you fool," the driver exclaimed. "I must untangle the horses."

WOOF WOOF WOOF!

Brian pulled himself up to the window. Had the dog arrived by chance? Did he have friends?

His fellow prisoners started to slowly untangle themselves, complaining bitterly of filth and bruises.

They'd stopped in a narrow stretch of street, marked by tightly shuttered shops on both sides. A single, ornate streetlight flickered next to a solidly built wall. The atmosphere was dark and damp, smelling of rain, wet stones, and neglect.

Brian looked down. The earlier rainstorm had broken up, letting the stars peep between the storm clouds.

The girl from the beer house cocked an eyebrow at him, all the while slipping a key into the paddy wagon's lock. Her face was drawn, etched with tearstains in the unforgiving light, under her small, woolen hat.

Dammit, she shouldn't be here! The cops would be here any minute.

"Go away!" he hissed.

"Hush!" She frowned at him and went back to teasing the stiff lock open.

"If they catch you, they'll destroy you."

"You're wasting time and attracting attention."

She wanted him to wait patiently while she risked her neck?

A soft snick, more felt than heard, and the heavy barrier fell into her hand. She slid the bar back and pulled the door open.

Moisture slid down the stone walls and gathered itself on the pavement, ready to turn itself into a mirror for the authorities.

Brian sprang down onto the street. "Come on!"

"Turn around!"

He shot her an incredulous glance but obeyed. Why the hell the driver and the guard hadn't looked around from the panicked horses by now, he didn't know.

Horses' hooves pounded over the cobblestones, their harnesses jingling and iron wheels ringing, echoed and magnified by the narrow streets. The dogs barked and howled, working the paddy wagon's horses into a greater frenzy.

Another key brushed against his palm and she unlocked his handcuffs.

God help him, she smelled of ambergris and cedar, rare and sensual. Heat surged through his skin and into his blood.

She slapped the key into the next prisoner's hand and closed his fingers around it. Without waiting for his thanks, she put two fingers in her mouth and whistled sharply.

The first dog promptly stopped barking, although his compatriots continued the wild chorus.

She picked up her skirts and a piece of shadow reassembled itself at her knee in the shape of her black dog, panting happily. He woofed once.

"*Sàmhach!*" she hissed.

Quiet? She'd ordered the dog to be quiet in *Gaelic*? But her accent wasn't quite Irish. Scots perhaps?

The second police wagon stormed into the narrow street. "Stop them!"

The now silent pair ran for the nearest doorway without sparing Brian so much as a backward glance.

He matched her stride for stride. Logic wasn't part of his reason for doing so.

At least she moved like a young doe, lithe and straight. A modern, S-shaped corset would have left her doubled over in agony after the first few strides.

Hobnailed boots thundered up the pavement after them. Damn, damn, damn. Why couldn't all of them have stayed to help the first paddy wagon?

At the last possible minute, she jogged slightly and slipped between two buildings, diving into a darkness so deep Brian could only hope she'd come this way recently enough to know all the obstacles. She ran it lightly, surely, with the dog leading the way, while the walls snatched at Brian's sleeves.

"Go around, you fools!" somebody shouted from behind them. "You'll catch them in the open."

Maybe he should pick her up. Surely he could run faster than she could.

She burst onto an odd bit of road, neither square nor street, sandwiched between a tiny church with an immense steeple and a handful of buildings. She zigzagged between these and took off, running down a steep, diagonal alley which suddenly opened behind a baker's shop.

Hell, he'd have to let her keep the lead. She couldn't have signaled him in time if she was in his arms.

After all, she was only panting a little.

Brian snarled and kept going.

A police whistle blew behind them, matched by the deep thunder of boots drumming over the stone streets.

Damn.

She still hadn't looked to see if Brian was with her.

They dodged a series of puddles, the dog woofing softly in his throat. She was in fine fettle so far, breathing deeply but not straining for oxygen. Keeping her skirts high and letting her boots take the brunt of any splashes.

Rats scuttled past, their eyes flashing red as they assessed the interlopers.

If she stumbled once, though, he'd snatch her up immediately.

The cops' rough calls were getting closer. "Spread out! Look alive, they can't be far now."

No, they certainly weren't. The American ambassador didn't matter a damn now, compared to getting his girl away safely.

She stopped at a corner and leaned her head back, panting, but still aware of her surroundings. The very narrow alley was lined on one side by garbage, currently being searched by the city's most unwelcome four-legged denizens. Water rushed down the center, gathering the neighborhood's worst smells and souvenirs. The three of them were pressed against the other side, in the highly visible, sole dry spot.

Brian eyed her warily before relaxing, his own lungs rising and falling quickly. Blessed be, she had the constitution of a wild cat, made for running and living—and loving. Not collapsing like a hothouse rose faced with an unpleasant breeze.

Whistles blew again but he refused to openly curse.

She sucked in air, visibly controlling herself, and peered cautiously out from their hiding place. She jerked her head back angrily and muttered something under her breath.

What the devil?

"What is it?" he hissed.

Even in the dim light, he had the impression she blushed.

"We're trapped. We can't go forward until that couple, ah, finishes their business, and we can't go back because of the police."

Does what?

"Let me look." Brian edged past her for a quick survey. She and her dog sidled out of the way, muttering in an oddly identical tone of voice.

He looked out across the park edging the stables behind the Grand Hotel, Eisengau's greatest hostelry. The great linden trees were heavily leafed for high summer, veiling the horses' quarters. Flowerbeds and stone paths meandered through the garden. The distant hotel was brilliantly lit, with a brass band inside belting out enough dance music to deafen anyone within pistol shot. Beyond it stood the long green ribbon of the waterfront parks and promenade, where Eisengau's finest enjoyed watching their great river.

If he and his girl could get that far, who could stop them?

The trees were very close together here between the stables and the Old Town's streets. Dense enough that nobody inside the hotel could see what was happening in the dark. Unfortunately, this was also where the city's less enchanting prostitutes gathered to ply their trade—as demonstrated by the couple only a few feet away.

The man and woman behind the hotel were hardly paying attention to the magnificent vista, though. Given that the fellow's hands were under the slut's skirts and her hand was in his back pocket—plus their grunts and moans—Brian would wager their motives were less than artistic.

He leaned back against the wall beside his girl, striving to keep a safe face. "They probably won't take long," he said soothingly.

Their pursuers' whistles shrilled again, making her flinch.

How much time did they have before the police caught up? Next to none. Crap.

Her dog growled, making Brian glance down. "Be quiet," he ordered sharply in Gaelic.

The dog's bushy eyebrows drew together but he stayed silent.

"What are you—"

Brian wrapped his arm around her waist and whipped her out of their hiding place. A couple of steps—half-dragging, half-carrying her—brought them to a separate linden tree from the amorous couple. He backed her against the solid wood, the sweet fragrance sifting around them.

"They'll see us," she hissed.

BRRRRRR!!! The police whistle sounded from the alley they'd just left. No time now for long explanations.

He kissed her, slanting his mouth over hers to cover any objections. She had a delicate frame to support all the courage she'd shown and her lungs were still heaving from their desperate race, lifting air into his mouth.

She stiffened. Her hands clawed at him, pushing him away. Her knee came up, hard and fast to unman him, and he blocked it quickly. Pity he couldn't allow her any games now. *Steady, milady, steady. Play along with me and they won't take you.*

BRRRRR!

A moment later, her fingers loosened, curved, and curled around the nape of his neck. Her mouth moved to meet his.

Feet ran back and forth, urged on by shouting. He should be concerned about them. But it was hard to worry much, when his girl was warm in his arms at last.

Chapter Three

Meredith flexed her fingers around the crazy American's neck, uncertain where to rest them. This wasn't like either of her affairs, where matters had started in a dance floor's corner after a good deal of beer. It'd seemed like the easiest thing in the world back then to kiss a man, since she was already in his arms.

But now?

He ghosted his lips across hers again, teasing her with the promise of pleasures to come. His breath brushed hers, offering warmth. His arms were strong, protecting cables around her, anchored by steady, impersonal hands, and his torso was a wall against danger. He hadn't grabbed or mauled her.

This was the man who'd run *at* the secret police to help her. He'd risked his neck for her.

Cold washed through her again at the memory and a small sound escaped her. She pulled him closer, sinking her fingertips into his black hair. The strands trailed over her skin like silk, heavy and clean, caressing every inch. She murmured something hungry and shifted, opening her hips to his embrace.

He took immediate advantage, pinning her against the tree as if they'd been lovers for hours.

She gulped. She wanted more. She'd come to help him, as thanks for his aid at the beer house and because she could do nothing for those in jail. She hadn't bargained for hunger lighting up her veins.

"Steady, sweetheart, steady," he crooned in Gaelic and lightly skimmed his fingers over her hair, soothing her.

BRRRRRR!

Dear God, the police. Her heart shot into a staccato beat which would have amazed a bumblebee. Shaking, she slid her hand down his shoulder and pulled him closer.

He rumbled approvingly deep in his throat and his tongue tasted her, delicately at first then more deeply.

She moaned and yielded, fire lancing from his mouth to her breasts and lower, moving rhythmically with the pull of his mouth. Oh, dear Lord.

Heavy footsteps thudded around them.

He cupped her head, supporting her, somehow linking them through the pressure of their bodies and the trees' sweet fragrance. She couldn't breathe anything but him, didn't want to taste anything but him, just wanted to eat his kiss and feel the textures of his hunger coming through his lips and teeth. Even his coat's fine wool reached through her suit's linen to rasp her nipples into aching tips.

"Oh yes." She clung to him, stroking him with her thumbs, her knees.

"Sweetheart," he crooned, nuzzling her throat. She moaned and pulled his head back, desperate for more. Her heartbeat rose to meet them, deepening the fire within her.

His cock was a hot, hard promise against her hips and his pulse thundered under her palm. She kneaded his neck and shoulders like a cat, instinctively sinking her nails into him to beg for more.

He chuckled a little roughly and paused, his cheek against hers.

Had the footsteps faded away? Did she care? She tugged at his hair, blindly seeking more of those drugging kisses.

He gave a hoarse laugh and muttered something in a language she'd never heard before. He kissed her cheek. "We need to stop."

She blinked and instinctively tightened her grip on him.

"Sweetheart, the police are searching the streets. We have to leave."

No more kissing. Of course. She closed her eyes and commanded her body to stop reliving the previous moments. There were more important things to remember, like—"Morro!"

A very soft woof answered her and she looked down. Her oldest friend wagged his tail, almost invisible in the shadows between her skirts and the tree. She gave him a quick pet on the head, rewarding his fidelity.

The American yanked her into motion, heading straight past the amorous couple. Why did she want to linger and copy their every motion with him?

She barely managed to conceal her squeak of alarm when he snatched up the man's bowler hat, which had been tossed on the ground a few feet away.

"Why did you steal his hat? He'll call the police!" she whispered, looking back over her shoulder.

"It's not theft when you leave twice its value behind. Besides, he never noticed."

The woman howled something foul and ecstatic, her eyes screwed shut. Meredith blushed, silently agreeing with the American, but rallied. "It was a hideous risk!"

"We'd be stopped within moments as out of place, if I didn't have a hat. You look every inch the proper young lady—"

"Dusted with mud," she countered. And etched with tear-stains. How could the police have attacked in such numbers when they knew married couples would be present, not just workingmen? How many women had she seen go down under their truncheons before she'd had to flee?

"Not too many flaws for a promenade on a rainy night," he struck back. "But nobody would believe in a gentleman without a hat. Praise the saints, this one fits well enough."

She bit her lip and tried to concentrate on the current

problem. But her restless pulse kept reminding her what he felt like, as if he'd imprinted her like a woodblock through her clothing. She could have announced where his cock would best fit, how his knees cradled her thighs, the grip of her thumbs into his shoulders . . .

Her pulse was beating deep and fast, pushing her toward him in anticipation.

She reminded herself to think about the bowler.

She shuddered and forced her eyes to open far enough to consider the fashionable necessity. The trees filtered light from the hotel's window into a golden haze. "True. It even matches your London suit, if nobody looks too closely."

"But we do need to wash up a bit."

He stepped into a small enclosure just outside the stables. There he found a water faucet, where he rinsed his handkerchief. Good heavens, he had strong hands, with long sensitive fingers. How could a rich man's hands have become scarred? Warmth deepened inside her, reaching out to him. "May I?"

He tilted her chin up and she froze. Tears had swum endlessly onto her face during that long run to intercept his captors. Her lashes were caked in saltwater and brine etched her cheeks, cutting into her mouth. Job's wife had built herself a pillar of salt by looking back at the past. Had that been any more painful than seeing her friends and their guests maimed and injured?

She nodded jerkily and he washed her face, as gently as if he dealt with a week-old baby. How absurdly easy it would be to lean on him.

"Ready?"

"Of course." Looking back helped nobody. It was time to move forward.

He drew her up closer to him, the path narrow and the air laden down by the formal garden's dozens of roses. She automatically tucked her hand through his elbow in the proper style for accepting a gentleman's escort, and matched her pace to his.

He was warm, so warm, even through the layers of cloth. His hips powered his strong thighs forward, every movement transferred smoothly through her skirt and single layer of petticoat. For the first time, she understood her mother's endless lectures about wearing stiff corsets and layers of frilly silks to signify virtue. If nothing else, they'd allow little chance for decadent thoughts to creep in.

Such as admiring the understated elegance of his London tailoring. So many men in Eisengau wore uniforms that students in civilian clothing usually looked clumsy. But his suit was made from the finest cloth, smooth and supple under her hands—or pressed against her skin. His silk cravat had a very subtle pattern woven into it, which gleamed in the streetlights and made her long to slip her fingers inside it and caress the same strong neck it did. Such a foolish thought!

He sauntered in exactly the proper style, too. Not so fast as to attract attention in one of the most fashionable venues in Eisengau and certainly not swiftly enough to satisfy her crackling nerves. She swore she could hear his watch fob rustling against his waist on that solid gold chain, as elegant and restrained as everything else.

"Are you sure we want to go in here?" She tightened her grip on his arm when he started to lead her up the steps to the Grand Hotel's rear entrance.

"They'll never look for us at the most fashionable hotel in town. Once we're in front, we can catch a cab to anywhere we'd like."

Or run into someone she knew, other than the police.

"We must get you to safety before you're captured," the American murmured.

"They'd simply turn me over to my stepfather." *And I'd rather jump off a cliff.* Despite her best efforts, Meredith's voice wobbled. She'd always known she'd prefer the grand duke's medieval prisons to her stepfather's ideas of redemption.

Her companion's head snapped around for a moment, his cobalt gaze all too perceptive. He recovered quickly and touched his hat, honoring a pair of women exiting the doors. "It's nothing you'll have to endure, sweetheart; my word on it."

"Reckless foreigner."

He chuckled—and his warm masculine certainty made her stupid pulse leap. "Brian Donovan, very much at your service, miss."

What kind of adventurer was he, to be so calm? Still, where else could she go but with him? She did her best to match him.

"Meredith Duncan, sir. Thank you for trying to help me, back at the beer house," she added.

She shook her head at him and swept through the great wood and curving brass doors ahead of him. High brass chandeliers and sconces in every corner cast a golden glow over the smooth plaster walls and fine paneling. Great arches adorned the hallway inside, adorned with elegant stencils in brilliant colors. Ethereal brass railings lined the staircases leading to the upper floors, while oriental carpets rippled over the treads.

Only a few expensively dressed patrons moved past them, heading for the hotel's popular street-side café or the private dining rooms upstairs. If they were lucky, most of the nightly traffic would have already dined and left for the promenade, to enjoy the Citadel's fireworks display.

He paused in the central atrium, the space between a massive, square pillar and the railing providing an illusion of privacy. "Where do you want me to take you?"

Or how? She smiled, wondering what her American adventurer's reaction would be to that question.

Morro rapped her knee with his head on the other side, the warning triggering a chill through her body.

"My dear child." The ice-cold voice, dripping with sugar and poison, silenced anything she might have said.

"Mother." Meredith threw her shoulders back a little farther. "Sir." She gave her stepfather the barest possible acknowledgment.

They eyed her coldly, the other hotel patrons giving them a wide berth. It was too late for the theater or a dinner party so they must have just come from a boating party at the hotel's quay. An important one, no doubt, given their clothing.

Mother was dressed in an expensive Irish lace dress, which clung to her abundant curves. She was extremely proud of her figure and took advantage of every opportunity to showcase it in the latest corset. Meredith had only once been angry—and foolish—enough to openly liken the result to a hunchbacked pigeon. The remark had earned her a severe caning, followed by bread and water for a week. Only Colonel Zorndorf's intervention had rescued her from having to live on that starvation diet for a month.

Mother surveyed her slowly, starting with her mudsplattered hem and lingering on her cheeks, which must still be faintly tearstained. She sniffed in disgust and tapped her beribboned cane impatiently, lifting her head until its multitude of ostrich plumes shimmered in echoing outrage.

Oh no. Icy chills raced each other up and down Meredith's skin. She donned her best polite mask and set about satisfying the formalities. At least Donovan would be able to escape, once that was done.

"Mother, may I present Mr. Brian Donovan? Mr. Donovan, allow me to introduce His Honor, Judge Frederick and Mrs. Baumgart."

Donovan squeezed her fingers briefly before releasing them slowly, refusing to show any embarrassment. "Ma'am. Your honor."

Meredith's stepfather, Judge Frederick Baumgart, was tall and narrow, a razor-edged knife beside his wife's curvaceous flower garden—or hand-held rock. His suit was cut on crisply military lines, an impression heightened by his regimental tie and pin. He inclined his head, frowning slightly.

Another group of merrymakers strolled down the stairs, led by a British officer with a cane and accompanied by two young women. They paused to watch Brian and Meredith's party.

Morro edged between Meredith and her mother, the closest member of the new pair. She refused to glance sideways at the hotel's front door, in the vain hope she might be able to reach the house and her bedroom before her mother arrived. Donovan, after all, should be able to look after himself.

"Donovan? Aren't you the American observer for the summer maneuvers this year?" her stepfather asked abruptly.

"I have that honor, sir." Donovan's expression turned unreadable, a radical transformation from her friendly companion.

"What a very great pleasure it is to meet you, young man," exclaimed the Judge, flashing his teeth in a shark's enthusiastic grin. He seized Donovan's hand and enthusiastically pumped it up and down. "My darling, do you see what our dear daughter has brought us?"

Dear daughter?

"The leader of one of the most influential delegations this year."

Influential? They must mean well-greased. Meredith's lip curled at becoming useful to her mother for the first time.

"My dear young man, we are so glad to be introduced to you." Frau Baumgart beamed, instantly taking up her husband's gambit. "Where did you meet my daughter?"

"Mary," added the Judge.

"Meredith," she corrected, bridling at the old insult and automatically protecting her first name.

The Judge's head swung around, his mouth opening to snap out a retort.

"Miss Meredith," Donovan interposed, lingering over the last syllable, "has been teaching me about Eisengau's history, especially its ability to satisfy its commitments in guns. Washington will be very glad to hear these details."

The Judge gave a narrow smile, sharp teeth very much in evidence.

Meredith tried to look as innocent as she had on the few occasions she'd been hauled to debutante balls.

"I say, Donovan, glad to finally run you down." The British officer limped over, his two ladies hovering solicitously at his side.

"Blackwell." Donovan nodded to the newcomer but hardly seemed relaxed. He certainly hadn't eased his grip on her hand. Introductions were quickly made, lighting a predatory blaze in the Judge's eyes. His tongue flickered across his lips and Mother smiled, openly assessing both men from head to toe.

"Please come home with us for drinks, gentlemen," Mother purred. "We can promise you good wine and good conversation with friends of ours."

Meredith flinched at the open attempt to grab both men for social triumph. Donovan stiffened beside her and an unreadable glance passed between the two men.

"Unfortunately, ma'am, I'm afraid Captain Blackwell and I have been planning to meet up with each other. Now that I can hand Miss Duncan into your care, I'm free to join him. But with your permission . . ."

"Yes?" The Judge was breathless, drat it.

"I'd like to see Miss Duncan again after summer maneuvers are over."

Now it was Mother and the Judge's turn to study each other soberly. Meredith held her breath, startled by their reaction to a simple request.

"If we're still in town, you certainly may," the Judge finally pronounced his decision.

"Thank you, sir. Miss Duncan." Donovan kissed her fingers, lingering over them a little long. She had to stiffen her knees.

Morro rumbled contentedly, drat him.

A minute later, a cab was carrying him away from the Grand Hotel toward the Citadel.

Mother and the Judge were silent for a long moment before calling for their carriage.

Chapter Four

Sunlight peered hesitantly into the grand duke's private office through the heavy windows, barely enough to outline the gilded pipes straining to heat the cavernous room. Certificates and photographs honoring the current resident's accomplishments were scattered over the walls—a lion hunt, a repeating rifle's number of rounds fired, and so on—but added nothing to the warmth. The walls were the Citadel's original stone blocks, unsmoothed by plaster. The floors were stone, barely softened by a few jewel-like oriental carpets which had been given as bribes by oriental potentates.

Pyotr calculated their value and bit back another curse. How much more of a gentleman would Grand Duke Rudolph be after a year in Siberia . . . He might even become trustworthy.

The morning gun boomed one last time from its embrasure below them, sending echoes sighing around the valley. Pigeons danced and wheeled in the sky. The lord and master of everything in this tiny, godforsaken country blew on his monocle and polished it with a handkerchief.

Grand Duke Rudolph was wasp-slender and immaculately turned out in his top cavalry regiment's glittering uniform. His mustache was heavily waxed to a hornet's sharp points and his bald head gleamed under the weak, early morning light. Pyotr never willingly turned his back on those pale blue eyes.

Nicholas, his only living son and heir, stood silently beside the windows, his attention focused on the quays below. He wore the dark green uniform of Eisengau's crack Rifle regiment, forming the traditional balance to the older generation's equine interests. He'd surprisingly chosen the workmanlike field uniform for today's departure on summer maneuvers, rather than the fancier service uniform.

Rumor said his beard concealed scars from a cougar, gained during his sole American hunting trip. Pyotr doubted that, given the boy's proven fondness for Oxford University, but couldn't disprove it.

Shouted commands and thuds from below marked the steady progress of luggage being loaded onto the railroad cars. The foreign observers would enjoy every luxury, in hopes of encouraging them to buy Eisengau's finest arms. Even the finest European courtesans would pamper them, arriving tonight when the wives had been left behind in the capitol to rummage through the shops and theaters for the next two weeks.

"Your Excellency . . ." Pyotr began again, trying not to sound like a beggar. Dammit, his family had been noblemen for centuries.

"Yes, Sazonov?" The grand duke yawned and held his monocle up to the light. The dark circles under his eyes were deeper than usual, confirming that last night's debauchery had lasted an extremely long time.

"Surely you can extend credit to Russia, Your Excellency."

"Why?" He screwed his monocle back into place and spun, the silver-rimmed glass glaring at Pyotr like a Cyclops' eye. "You knew the rules when you came. Cash only and Eisengau sells weapons, never the plans. Why should I change them now?"

"Russia is one of the great powers, with an army large enough to overrun Europe."

"Not without cannons, it won't." Grand Duke Rudolph

snorted inelegantly. "How many corpses will laugh at you if you march without the King of Battle on your side?"

"Buying that many guns would be ruinously expensive, even for the British. Let us have credit so we can pay you over time." The words scoured his mouth like ashes. Russia deserved better than begging favors from a minor autocrat, who should be groveling to the tsar instead.

"No. Why should I waste my time on you when there are so many other better prospects? Why, the American can pay with either government or private funds. Even my son would keep him in the auction." He cast a bitter glance at Eisengau royalty's next generation who stared stonily back at him before returning to the activity below.

"I'm not interested in rifles, Your Excellency." Pyotr laced every word with icy precision, refusing to unleash his temper. "Russia already has an excellent one."

"Then buy one of my mountain guns and start thinking about how well you can tear apart Afghanistan, on the road to India." Grand Duke Rudolph picked up a pot and poured himself a cup of coffee.

And fight our way through the Himalayas? We're trying that now and it's not working. No, there has to be a better way to bring Russia the greatness she deserves.

Pyotr hissed in annoyance and started over, trying for a supplicant's sugary tones.

"Russia deserves to buy anything she wants—including the new great gun."

"The one that can outshoot the new French cannon or any of the old British or German guns?" Grand Duke Rudolph didn't bother to look up from the brandy he was pouring into his coffee. "Of course, you can . . ."

Pyotr came alert, hope racing through his veins for the first time.

"You've already paid enough for a model of one." The older man glanced up and laughed softly. Pyotr's lips thinned but he didn't clench his fists. It wasn't the first time he'd considered disobeying his orders and funding an assassination.

"On the other hand, you imperialistic fools, you could have used the same sum to fortify Alaska, instead of selling it for a song forty years ago. Just think—if you'd kept it, you'd control the access to all those Klondike goldfields, not the Americans."

"We'd be rich." Pyotr silently cursed the betraying murmur.

"Maybe, if you didn't ruin your affairs in another way. But you're wasting my time. Anyone who wants to buy our guns, must provide gold."

Pyotr tried one last chance. "What about buying the plans for a weapon?"

"So you can have somebody else build them? Never in our history have we done that." Even his son nodded vehement agreement to that pronouncement.

"Now get out and start packing for the summer military maneuvers." He pinned Pyotr with a long, icy glare. "Unless you want to miss the summer maneuvers entirely."

Dermo, the old bastard was serious. The room narrowed until all Pyotr could see was the desiccated aristocrat, edged in black like the coffin for a victim of his beloved Mosin-Nagat rifle. He forced the vision back, his pulse thudding sullenly in his ears, and did his best to ignore his knife resting eagerly against his arm.

Why the hell wouldn't St. Petersburg allow him to assassinate the old goat? True, it would undoubtedly infuriate the Germans and the other steady clients. But that foolish young cockerel would undoubtedly be easier to deal with than this strutting blackmailer.

Still, he could afford to be polite now, since he had another option.

"It will be an honor to attend the maneuvers in any capacity, Your Excellency." Pyotr smiled, baring his teeth in a smile's caricature.

He'd enjoy showing the old buzzard just who was the greatest power. All he needed to do now was set Meredith Duncan into motion.

Meredith set her satchel down beside the big armchair in the small sitting room, refusing to tug her lapels together in a vain semblance of her academic robe's protection. She'd lost the right to wear it when the school year ended yesterday, together with Frau Masaryk's ribbon wreath. Every female Eisengau university student wore similar traditional headgear, if inherited from another woman in her extended family.

Frau Masaryk, the Judge's aunt, had been Meredith's dearest friend when she'd first arrived in Eisengau. She'd spent most of her time at her estate in the mountains, reading, riding, and working with the farm dogs the old woman doted on. She'd also encouraged Meredith's ambitions of a university degree, training her finest dog to protect Meredith. The Judge still hated to see any reminders of her plebian hobby.

Meredith smiled faintly and went to find Morro, the living emblem of two good friendships.

If she knew him, he was amusing himself while he waited for the precise moment when he expected her to arrive. An instant before then, he'd plop himself down in the perfect spot so he could be ready, looking like a complete angel. Hah!

It wasn't his fault she'd dressed extra fast, saving time by pinning up her hair in loose waves instead of the usual tight braids to support Frau Masaryk's ribbon wreath. Mother and the Judge had been too well-behaved last night. They hadn't asked her any questions about Brian Donovan, for starters. Instead, they'd simply bid her goodnight and informed her they'd talk to her in the morning.

She should be grateful to have escaped a stinging lecture about being seen with a stranger late at night. But she wasn't. Maybe she'd be calmer after she cleaned up Colonel Zorndorf's office for the semester.

As befitted Eisengau's top cannon designer, he was leaving on summer maneuvers to answer any technical questions the buyers might pose. Or that the Eisengau army might ask, although they were usually very well drilled in the weapons by now.

She'd also be able to make sure no partial or draft drawings of the guns survived anywhere. She was almost certain none did—but she couldn't afford to take any chances for the workers' sake.

She dropped her satchel beside her academic robes and followed shouts of laughter in search of Morro.

As she'd suspected, he was running circles around the back garden with Kavalier, her half-brothers' elegant gray hunting dog. The two dogs barked and slammed into each other, for all the world like a pair of good-natured canine jousters.

Paul and Johann, her two half-brothers, waved at her from the terrace. Even with their mouths jammed full of jam-covered bread, they still managed to laugh at the dogs' antics.

Meredith opened the door and joined them, chuckling. She saw them so seldom since they'd been sent away to that Austrian military school. At ages eleven and nine, the Judge's standards for his offspring became higher the faster they grew. "Good morning."

They wiped their mouths and rose, grinning. "Good morning, sister! Did you see—"

They snapped to attention, animation vanishing from their faces. "Good morning, Mother."

Cold ice dove through Meredith and settled in her stomach. Dear heavens, the boys had always been better at reading Mother and the Judge than she was.

She turned and found herself confronting her mother, who was wielding her most arrogant glare. She stiffened her spine, determined to admit to nothing. "Yes, Mother?"

Morro plopped himself firmly down beside her, growling softly.

"Come with me, daughter; the Judge will talk to you now."

She turned and headed back into the house, her long skirts swishing across the carpet like an executioner's march.

Meredith reached for a smile's semblance but the boys saw through it, of course. They'd all had too much practice at counterfeiting contentment.

"Good luck," whispered Paul. "If we're not here when you get out—"

"Send letters to us at school through the French teacher," Johann finished.

"I won't need—" she began, and stopped. The last time Mother had been this succinct, she'd been so furious Meredith hadn't been able to leave her room for better than a month. She nodded jerkily and quickly embraced her brothers.

The Judge spun on his heel to face the two women from inside his office, his desk slicing the room like an altar prepared for burnt offerings. Mother pointed at a narrow wooden chair on the far side and slammed the door, narrowly missing Morro.

The loyal dog objected immediately, his barks barely louder than soft chuffs. Like Meredith, he'd long since learned to watch his tongue in this house.

She quickly silenced him with an outstretched palm and took the highly uncomfortable seat, carefully settling her skirts. There she waited for the real blow to fall, with Morro beside her.

Mother ensconced herself in a brocaded armchair beside her mate and critically studied her daughter.

"We know all about the archbishop's dreadful nephew and his associates, whom you've been meeting for years," the Judge announced without preamble.

Meredith froze. What did they know about the central committee and their hopes for the workers?

Mother shuddered elaborately.

Had they been watching? Did they know about the rallies? Meredith could scarcely breathe.

"We know they've led you astray into strange talk of voting reform and changing the established order."

Oh, no, no, no.

"We've tolerated it all this time in hopes you'd form a good connection"—*marriage?*—"But you've never been able to coax a proposal out of Herr Schnabel."

Of course not, he's studying for the priesthood! She gaped at her mother.

"If we separate you from those foolish hotheads, there will be no trouble for the family." Mother nodded decisively and sat back.

"So we've decided to accept an excellent offer for your hand," the Judge purred.

Meredith's jaw dropped. She'd always been very careful never to make a public speech or have anything in writing for the workers party. Surely her behavior hadn't been bad enough to make them injure themselves.

"What do you mean? If I leave the university, the payments from Frau Masaryk's inheritance are lost." Including the money to them for her room and board.

"Foolish though the old biddy's ideas were, her will can still be satisfied." Mother sniffed haughtily. "Your husband will allow you to continue studying."

Husband? She'd never find one tolerable, even if she believed he'd let her stay at the university.

A positively beaming smile danced across the Judge's face and Meredith's stomach turned cartwheels.

"Your engagement to Colonel Zorndorf will be announced in tomorrow's newspaper," he announced proudly.

Her boss? Ice knotted into Meredith's shoulders and lanced into her stomach, ripping into her knees. She'd have staggered if she'd been standing.

"Zorndorf?" she croaked. "Why me? He's the grand duke's top cannon designer; he could have a far wealthier bride."

"Who cares?" Mother rolled her eyes. "Think of what his connections can do for us."

"He's probably planning to obtain a cheap secretary," the Judge shrugged off any quest for motives. "At least he already knows you, so he can't claim we hid any of your problems from him.

But marriage? Surely nobody with any claim to family tenderness would send their daughter to Zorndorf's household.

"But he beat his wife! She was always heavily veiled, even in the summer. And you commented on her bruised face the one time we saw it clearly, Mother, after the wind blew it aside."

"She undoubtedly deserved to be chastised." Mother yawned.

"Two black eyes was only *discipline*?" She stared from one to another of her parents, unable to comprehend how they could excuse Zorndorf's behavior.

"Exactly," the Judge agreed. "Excellent practice, too, for teaching you manners—starting with how not to be a slut."

"How dare you call me that!" Meredith sprang to her feet. Morro snarled rough and low. She grabbed for his collar, catching him just before he dove under the desk at the Judge.

"I'll name you that and worse any time I choose. I'll give you a dozen good strokes with a cane, too, for defying me."

All the blood left Meredith's face and she fought for breath, using lungs which seemed to have no strength. *Dear God, not again.*

"I thought that might be the one threat which resonates, dear stepdaughter." The Judge tilted his head, his lips curling into a satisfied grin. "Has your back healed from the last time?"

She stared back at him, fists clenched. Mother chuckled and exchanged a smug glance with her husband.

"Zorndorf can't want a woman who's not a virgin." Meredith forced her fingers to unknot and tried to bring her rusty wits back into play.

"We're well aware of how you've debased yourself." Mother shot a look of pure loathing at her. "At least you've never humiliated us by flaunting your behavior in front of our friends."

"Since you've kept your amours infrequent and far from our circle, Colonel Zorndorf is willing to overlook them. In fact, he prefers an experienced woman and forced us not to interfere with your late-night activities."

Meredith ground her teeth. "Surely he can't believe a wedding ring would stop a promiscuous woman."

"I doubt it. In fact, he said he was looking forward to teaching you how to respect your husband and his commands, as he'd taught his first wife. It will be very pleasant to watch." The Judge sipped his coffee, his mustache points almost quivering in anticipation.

A vision of Frau Zorndorf limping into church rose before her eyes. Meredith flinched and bit off another, no doubt futile protest. She'd always thought losing her virginity would guarantee safety from a respectable marriage.

She reached for one last, faint hope.

"Mother, please, how can your maternal instincts accept having a child of yours married to a brute like Zorndorf? His only advantages are his connections to Grand Duke Rudolph."

"What more is needed?" Mother frowned at her. "What have you ever done for me, except be a burden? Do you understand what those long months were like when I was alone, after your father died?"

Long months? Meredith blinked. "You married the Judge less than three months after Papa died in that storm."

Mother drew herself up. "How can you question the depths of my grief? I was alone and you offered me no solace."

"I was eight years old." Meredith gaped at her.

"And you're grown up now, enough to know how to bring credit to your parents. As Zorndorf's wife, you'll raise us up with you into the highest circles of society."

Was that all she cared about? Not even her own daughter's safety?

Oh, Mother, it's been years since I thought you loved me but I never knew you'd auction me off like this. Being abandoned would have been less painful.

"If you don't agree immediately, I'll have the pleasure of disciplining you first," the Judge purred.

Meredith's blood cascaded like an ice fall through her veins. More canings and whippings? More beatings until she'd screamed her throat raw and couldn't sleep on her back for days or weeks?

If she couldn't convince them to change their minds, she did have one advantage: Frau Masaryk's legacy was held in British stocks. If she attended a school outside Eisengau, she'd still have an income and be independent.

But she'd have to cause a scandal large enough to destroy Zorndorf's interest, find somebody to get her out of Eisengau— and help force Grand Duke Rudolph to end proportional voting in Eisengau

She closed her eyes for a moment. The first things to do were to play for time then escape from her parents.

She threaded tears into her voice. "I don't know what else to do, Mother, except obey you." Well, that was true enough— at least for the moment. "When do we meet Colonel Zorndorf?"

"This morning. He wants to introduce you to the grand duke as his betrothed when they tour his labs at the university," Mother answered, fluffing the lace at her wrists.

Now?

"He won't return until summer maneuvers are over." The Judge frowned at her, underlining the meeting's urgency.

Meredith blanked her expression, thinking fast. All of the buyers would be at the university this morning, too. She'd planned to avoid them by lingering in the library, while Zorndorf led his usual, long-winded tour.

However, this just might be her only chance to make a deal with the devil.

Like Sazonov. Tell him where the blueprints were, in exchange for pretending to ruin her.

Her mouth tightened.

"When do you want to leave?" She rose.

Her stepfather frowned at her but stood up. "Certainly— my dear daughter."

Damn, lying, would-be patriarch. If she had to make a bargain with anybody, she'd rather do so with Brian Donovan. At least he'd never lied to her.

Not that he was a viable option.

"Here we are, in the center of Eisengau University," Grand Duke Rudolph proclaimed, his right arm sweeping out to describe his domain. "Here we train our most trusted engineers and design the world's finest arms!"

The covey of arms buyers murmured noncommittally. Many hid their yawns by taking another drink from the mug clutched in their hand, whether it contained coffee, tea, or the hair of the dog.

Brian slid to the side and pretended not to see yet another latecomer sneak into the group. This tour had been touted as the opportunity to understand Eisengau's arms industry's intellectual foundations. It actually seemed to offer a low-key moment for buyers to sleep in, should they need to recover from the previous night's debauchery, before departing on the more intense summer maneuvers.

He did agree Eisengau provided for its technical studies very, very well. The granite edifice was more Renaissance palace than humble study hall. Set into a hillside, it was both light, airy, and a supreme work of engineering in its own right. Window after window overlooked its series of interlocking, inner courtyards or opened onto the outside world from an office or lecture hall.

Fog blurred its outlines, slinking into the alleys that bordered it.

Doors proclaimed themselves boldly or crouched hidden in dark corners. Books were racked neatly on shelves, unnamed potions lurked in glass jars, steel rods and blocks of all sizes and dimensions waited in storerooms.

The visitors had been conveyed quickly by elevator to an observation gallery on the top floor. From here, they could see both the building's outside and the inner courtyards' details.

A few students were industriously tidying up glass cases or writing up long descriptions in marble-backed notebooks. But they were all male and most of them wore uniforms, typical for a Germanic country, especially one dependent on the arms industry. He hadn't found any light, quick steps matched to a faint, Scottish burr.

Brian began to stroll down the hall away from his companions, always keeping a watchful eye into the exterior courtyard. A city carriage would probably arrive there or a pedestrian striding quickly up from the market square. Gareth Blackwell joined him, equally casual.

"If you look down into this courtyard, you can see where we assemble our prototype rifles when the weather is good, like today," Grand Duke Rudolph continued.

Brian looked up to the heavens and prayed for patience yet again. He was allowed to inspect cannons—however informally as a private citizen—but only the official military could select rifles. They were the idiots who'd come up with something chosen to save ammunition but not kill the enemy quickly. The resulting, so-called *military* rifles had done such a purely pitiful job that his friends had been picked off like flies in Cuba, unable to match fire with a few sharpshooting Spaniards. America had won the battle and the war but the War Department didn't seem to have learned much. No, now they were out buying a new type of rifle with damn similar requirements to their last one.

He'd found a simpler answer: he'd bought one of those fine German rifles like the Spaniards had used to damn near defeat him. His Mauser 98 was a pure joy to him, especially since he'd had it shortened a bit to make it easier for carrying on a horse.

He'd be damn happy to be sure nobody had created a cannon which could be a similarly nasty surprise for his countrymen, the way the German rifle had been.

But that wasn't today's hunt. Right now, he was looking for a flash of woolen skirt, swirled by lithe hips. Meredith Duncan was a student somewhere in this university, but probably not in the engineering department. The question was where could he find her?

"I can answer all of your detailed questions," a man's high-pitched voice rasped.

Silence followed, etched in astonishment, during which the assemblage took care not to look at the grand duke. He'd been answering every query himself. God only knew what he'd think of this usurper.

Brian glanced back down the parapet at the speakers. Grand Duke Rudolph was rapidly polishing his monocle, his black uniform and gold insignia melting into the fog like an extinguished torch.

Behind him stood the massive, curving bulk of Colonel Heinrich Zorndorf, Eisengau's chief cannon designer. His offer of a tour could have been heard a block away—or two.

"With His Highness's permission, of course," Zorndorf added, not sounding obsequious in the least.

"Herr Colonel is—indispensable," his highness commented and unclipped a hip flask from his belt. "You could not be in better hands." His lips had narrowed to a thin white line but he waved permission to continue.

"You will start by observing the courtyard there," ordered Zorndorf. "I parade my staff there every morning to review their assignments. For example, my assistants are regularly drilled on range tables, while my secretary can draw blueprints from memory."

"Maybe we won't observe, if we want to keep the grand duke's good graces," commented Gareth quietly and joined Brian at the outside wall. "D'you think the Colonel plans to point out every door and window?"

"Yes, if it means he can tell us exactly what he does at each one." Brian winced and moved farther away, matched by his friend. "We're still missing at least a half dozen buyers, too, so he's got plenty of time."

Gareth groaned. "It might be worth while if he had some female students to brighten up the landscape."

"Do you ever think of anything else?"

"Not when I'm off duty," Gareth retorted. "Besides, they're so much more interesting than the range calculations the old goat is spouting now."

Brian choked with laughter and thanked God his friend was speaking softly.

"Eisengau has some very fine specimens to offer, too," Gareth continued. They strolled after the others, with Gareth leaning on his cane far more than his limp required. "Take that young lady of yours last night, for example."

"What about her?" Brian shot a quick glance at him.

"Nothing, nothing at all. Certainly wouldn't dream of poaching on your territory, old man."

Brian bit his lip, imagining Meredith's reaction to Gareth's typical insouciance about feminine education.

"But I certainly much preferred your Miss Duncan's level-headedness to the former Miss FitzAllen's frequent giggles."

The long-forbidden name made Brian miss a step, nearly stumbling on the limestone pavers. He caught himself, unhappily aware Gareth knew the trigger all too well.

"I rarely think of her now," he answered, choosing to bite the bullet and spit out the truth. Lying wouldn't protect him now against the one man who'd been present when he'd met that Irish chit.

"Truly?" Gareth stared at him. "I'm sure you've had many opportunities elsewhere but—"

"Truly," Brian said firmly. It was the absolute truth. "Once I realized my fury was injured pride—"

"What better cause could you have?" Gareth murmured.

Brian didn't answer that. Some memories were best not relived. "I knew she'd meant nothing to me. I'm sure she'd make any man a good wife and I wish her and Giffard every success."

Gareth hooted. "Two more mercenary people were never joined in holy matrimony."

"Isn't that the truth," Brian agreed heartily. They leaned back against the railing in complete harmony, while their companions hoisted antique rifles to their shoulders and sighted down the barrels.

He glanced sideways at Gareth and read the same thought in his friend's mind: Hadn't the old fools studied any of the weapons in their own armories before coming here? With one accord, they turned away and studied the engineering college's entrance.

"I never quite understood what you saw in Miss FitzAllen anyway," Gareth murmured.

Brian shrugged and gave him part of the answer.

"I was ready to settle down and she seemed exactly the sort of girl my parents would approve of—young, Irish, Catholic, sweet-tempered, obedient . . ."

A carriage stopped in front of the main door below them, performing the maneuver with neatness rather than style. A man sprang out and handed down a woman, whose hat carried so many feathers it could almost take flight.

Brian frowned and leaned a little farther over the edge, his voice dying away. He'd never seen that hat before so why did she look familiar? Her escort was too tall, too thin—too much like a saber poised to strike.

A young woman climbed out unaided, followed by a sturdy black dog. Meredith? What was she doing here? She looked around the narrow street, taking in every person, every movement.

The older woman shook out her skirts to straighten the flounces, before accepting the man's arm.

Good God, they were Meredith's mother and stepfather.

They sailed up the stairs to the portico where the doorman greeted them obsequiously, their voices echoing over the city noise.

Meredith picked up her skirts and opened a door hidden in the college's ornate façade, using the carriage's bulk to screen her movements from her parents. She paused a bare instant, letting Morro enter first, then silently disappeared.

What the hell?

"Daughter dearest?" Meredith's mother turned around. "Where are you?" She stepped back onto the steps to survey the street, bereft of any young women. "Drat the girl, how dare she disobey us again, especially now?"

"Don't worry, my dear. She'll learn not to disappoint us again." The Judge tapped his cane against his boot, his eyes glittering in the darkness under his top hat when he looked around.

Brian cursed under his breath.

Chapter Five

Meredith bent quietly over her desk, unlocking it as fast and as quietly as she could. She'd been able to reach her office fairly easily, thank God. Most of the building was deserted, empty of students now that regular classes were out. As Zorndorf's secretary, she knew where all the demonstrations were scheduled so they'd been easy to avoid. That luck wasn't likely to hold.

All the other copies of the plans were gone, as she'd thought. Zorndorf always had the intermediate drawings destroyed when a gun was ready to be sold, to cut down on the chances for theft.

Now she needed to retrieve the little money she had hidden. After that, she'd have to find Sazonov, which was probably best done through the Russian embassy.

Footsteps resonated through the building, punctuated by the rumbling notes of men's voices. The grand duke and Zorndorf were showing off the engineering college to the arms buyers. If she didn't leave soon, they'd catch her here—and hand her back over to her parents.

Would Brian be equally quick to do so? Americans did have different notions—not that it mattered at the moment.

She had a small, so-called office, barely large enough for her desk, her chair, and the two other chairs set aside for Zorndorf's visitors. Colonel Zorndorf had designed it, like the rest of the office suite, lecture halls, and laboratories. He'd also trained her, his top assistants, and his students in how to use the facilities, although not everyone learned all of the capabilities.

The only window was barred, barely large enough for Morro, and so high only a monkey could have climbed through. The room's real purpose was to guard the doors into Zorndorf's office—and the even more important vault which held Zorndorf's designs.

The drawer eased open silently. Thank God for an engineering school which oiled locks no matter how often they were used or not. She grabbed her pitifully few coins—Mother kept all almost of the funds allocated for living expenses by the trust, claiming they were needed to maintain the family's position in society. But they might be enough to get her to London on a third-class ticket, if she didn't eat anything, with a little left over for Morro.

Her faithful guardian growled.

"Tell that damned dog to shut up," Sazonov hissed.

"What on earth are you doing here?" He never came to the university before noon, although he did know his way to Zorndorf's office, like all the other attachés.

She signaled Morro to let him through and came around the desk to face him. Morro obeyed, rumbling deep in his throat, and stayed close at hand. She cocked an eyebrow at her dear friend's continued intransigence but didn't take the time to make him settle down.

"Do you have the plans yet?" Sazonov hissed.

She blinked, startled by his sudden switch to demanding co-conspirator instead of generous mentor, and lied automatically. "No, of course not. Where would I have put them?"

"I thought you might have hidden them someplace in here." He frowned and spun around to survey the tiny room, before returning to stare accusingly at her.

She propped her hands on her hips and glared back at him. What was he thinking about, when he'd been told time and again she hadn't stolen them yet? "Sazonov, all plans have very large dimensions. They can be as long as my arm or even two arms' length."

"A rifle's length."

"True," she agreed, glad he was showing at least a little sense. If she could distract him by talking about cannons, where could she get help for herself in the meantime? "The plans would be very hard to hide. Plus they're always locked up in trays in the vault." She managed not to glance at the enormous steel door next to her elbow. "You know I didn't have them yesterday afternoon so why would you think I have them now?"

The building was humming a little, thanks to the boots thudding into the floors overhead.

"In that case, steal them now."

"Now? With the tour coming through?" Was he insane?

"What better time? No one will expect it." A wicked gleam danced through his eyes.

"We'd never get them out of the building!" Her pulse started to pound, hard and strong, through her veins.

"Give them to me and I'll claim diplomatic immunity. All will be well."

She gaped at him, a thousand objections springing to mind, starting with what on earth she'd tell the grand duke's secret police, who were undoubtedly trailing their master through the building at this moment.

"My dear Miss Duncan," Sazonov added softly, his lips displaying more teeth than curve.

Was he trying to seduce her, too, not just Liesel?

She shook her head in disbelief, her fingers touching her lips. Her blood was racing through her veins faster than she'd ever felt before, yet her thoughts were assembling themselves into crisp, orderly sets. The workers' party might need St. Petersburg's help but could she take the chance on him absconding with their only leverage?

"Miss Duncan . . ." he warned and lunged for her.

Morro erupted into a storm of barking and Sazonov lashed out with his foot. Only Morro's lightning reflexes saved him from being hurled against the vault. Why, the cowardly brute, to mistreat a small animal that way!

Meredith flung the trashcan at Sazonov's feet, catching him off guard and throwing him off-balance. He stumbled against the filing cabinet and rapped his head against a brass handle, triggering a foul curse.

She ran for Zorndorf's office, the one direction left open. How many times had Zorndorf drilled her in these moves? The man was good for at least something.

"Morro, come!" she called in Gaelic.

Her valiant dog immediately followed her, barking triumphantly deep in his throat. She could only hope it was an omen, since she'd just snubbed the workers' party's most likely ally.

Sazonov started to follow and tripped over the rolling can once again. Thank God, it had bought her a little time.

She slammed the door on him, deliberately not pulling the cord to the very loud steam whistle.

"Miss Duncan, you fool, what are you doing?" Sazonov called and rattled the doorknob. An instant later, he kicked the door, making the wood shiver in its frame.

Morro barked a ferocious—and no doubt unprintable— counterchallenge.

She needed to get out of here before somebody else heard and came to investigate. Sweat trickled down her spine under her corset.

Long training came to her aid. Her breathing stilled and she spotted the books she needed.

She canted the century-old trigonometry text forward, careful to keep it on the shelf. Then the chemistry text three books down, followed by the calculus reference on the shelf below. Her hand was very steady and each title seemed to be outlined in black. Morro's barking was very far and Sazonov's profanity even more distant.

A solid sheet of steel slammed down on the far side of the door, between the wood and Sazonov.

"Dammit, Miss Duncan, you almost cut my foot off!"

She made a rude gesture, which she'd learned in Eisengau's foundries.

An instant later, her desk slid across the floor, blocking the other exit from her office.

"I'll kill you for this!" He kicked the door again, testing the steel.

Time to go.

He wouldn't suffocate, not with the window. Somebody would hear and let him out very soon, given all the people around to help with the grand duke's tour.

Boots thudded through the halls again, echoing like a giant forge beating a death knell to her hopes.

Not while she could find an escape route. After all, the blueprints were still safely hidden, just waiting for the chance to use them to help the workers.

She poked her head out the main door into the corridor—*good, there was nobody around*—and raced for the nearest staircase, Morro close on her heels.

The tour clustered around the college's entrance, where its president was delivering an endless speech from the grand portico about the honor of serving Eisengau. The grand duke was listening appreciatively, while most of his guests looked bored. They probably envied their fellows who'd risen late enough to be waiting in the carriages outside. There was less than an hour to go before they'd board the train for the start of summer maneuvers—and the real party.

Zorndorf at least was nowhere in sight. He'd excused himself and gone outside, supposedly to finish preparing for summer maneuvers.

Brian closed his eyes and slowed his breathing, sliding himself into a world where the droning voice didn't exist. Here tension raced, pounding frantically through the stone floors. Danger was running hard and fast—but where?

He'd been at the crowd's edge; now he slid into the shadows. Gareth watched him go but said nothing, simply moved to block sight of him. An instant later, Brian had disappeared back into the college, where footsteps raced and sound was magnified by stone walls and ceilings.

God help them both, Meredith might still be in here somewhere.

He stopped where a larger corridor intersected a narrow one, probably a servants' passageway and just out of sight from the grand portico. A single electric light swung overhead, offering occasional glimpses of stolid official portraits mounted like trophies on the paneled wall.

He pressed his fingertips against the wall as his mother had taught him, and stilled his heartbeat to listen with more than his ears.

One, two, three . . . One lightweight human, several considerably heavier—and that dog.

It had to be her.

Brian made up his mind and ran down the narrow hall toward those running feet, moving as quietly as possible. He might not be able to stop any followers, given their superior rank, but he should be able to delay them.

Sounds were hard to accurately track in this man-made warren, almost as bad as the mines he'd grown up around. He also didn't have either of his twin brothers' familiarity with schools, having left ten years ago.

She whipped around a corner and slammed into him, nearly bowling him over. Brian wrapped his arms around her and instinct, more knowledgeable than intellect, promptly identified her.

"Let me go!" Meredith shoved him hard.

"No! Let me help you." He held her close. She was gasping for air and sweat was slipping down her face. Jesus, were the police after her again?

"You can't." She looked over her shoulder for her followers. "Please, if Zorndorf or my parents find me here . . ."

Damn arrogant bastards, they had no understanding of a wildflower like her! They'd crush her.

Her black dog circled and came back, tongue hanging out. He watched Brian warily but didn't bark.

Brian made up his mind. "What can I do?"

"Ruin me." She made the outrageous demand with a level stare.

His lungs seized until he could barely grunt. "What?"

"Have an affair with me which even Zorndorf can't overlook."

She wanted to be his mistress? His blood stirred and headed south. Heat spilled into his chest and sparked wherever she touched him. He was close enough to see the curve of her ear under the soft sweep of her hair and the proud line of her neck. How would she respond the first time he kissed her there?

"You're joking." Her followers were only a few feet away, coming on hard and fast. Eisengau's prisons were legendarily vicious, possibly worse than living with her family. "What about your parents? Your mother?"

"Have already sold me to him so he can teach me a lesson." Bone-deep agony etched her face and she tried to twist away. Brian instinctively crooned to her.

"Please, he always beats his wife," she choked out, her gray eyes luminous with unshed tears. "I can't stay with him."

He immediately believed her; nothing in their acquaintance led him to think she'd tolerate such behavior or make up a tall tale.

"Son of a bitch," Brian spat. Any parent—any mother!— who gave their daughter to a man like that deserved a fate far worse than Hades.

She misread his silence and kicked his shin, making him jerk briefly. "If you don't say yes now, then let me go."

Jesus, Mary, and Joseph, what a wildcat—and what a delight she'd be in the bedroom.

Brian made up his mind.

"Very well. You can be my mistress throughout the summer maneuvers. Is that notorious enough?" Should be, with all of Europe's demi-monde present and nary a wife to be seen, especially not beside her own husband. "After that, I'll take you out of Eisengau with me, if you want."

"Yes, thank you!" She kissed her fingertips and laid them against his lips. His cock promptly, predictably surged until even his trousers' zipper was unbearable torment.

Jesus Christ, what had he let himself in for? Had he ever truly considered refusing? He shook the doubts off.

"Come on; we're better off facing him outside." He'd ask later about the police following her, when they had a few more minutes.

He laced his fingers with hers and raced back the way he'd come, slowing just before he reached the door to the outside.

He tucked her hand into the crook of his elbow and smiled down at her. Dammit, he'd been calmer when he'd charged up San Juan Hill into that bullet-ridden hell. "Ready?"

"Yes, of course." Her throat worked for a moment above her white lace blouse with the superb cairngorm broach. She smiled gallantly, her lips only a little tremulous.

Christ, how he wanted to kiss her until she thought only of him.

Instead he wrenched open the door to the street—and met Gareth's all-too controlled eyes. His friend gave an infinitesimal jerk of his head and stepped aside.

Brian flicked a glance. A pair of Eisengau guardsmen flanked the doorway, blocking any hope of a fast getaway. The street was filled with foreign observers, engineering students in their stiff uniforms, and more guardsmen, plus the carriages waiting for the grand duke's guests.

Well, now, wasn't this going to be a hot party, if matters went awry?

He smiled broadly and drew Meredith a little closer. He couldn't have used guns anyway, not with her around. But if his wits didn't see them through, he could always fall back on the fighting style he'd learned from his father's Chinese body-guard. One way or another, he'd look after his girl.

Grand Duke Rudolph strode forward, the crowd falling back before him.

Meredith's grip tightened on Brian's hand but she stayed silent and steady.

"Your Excellency." He acknowledged the grand duke with a small nod but said nothing to the grand duke's heir or any of the tourists.

Zorndorf stepped forward, elbowing past his country's ruler. "Unhand my fiancée immediately," he demanded, drawing himself up to his full height.

The grand duke's eyes narrowed and he fingered his pointed beard.

"Fiancée? I'm not aware of any announcement," Brian countered. "Instead, I'm enjoying dealing with a beautiful young woman whose conversation I *trust*. In fact, I look forward to continuing our acquaintance throughout summer maneuvers."

"You will not! That's scandalous! Your Excellency, I *demand* you make him stop," Zorndorf ordered. "It is an insult to me."

The grand duke stiffened. "What did you say, Zorndorf?"

Guardsmen surrounded him now, the spikes on their polished helmets glinting like spear points. They eyed Zorndorf hostilely, clearly more than ready to seize him.

"Your Excellency." Zorndorf gulped, turning white. "I beg of you, by your mercy, do not permit this man to take her."

"Miss Duncan is old enough to speak for herself," Brian commented softly, hoping that held as true in Eisengau as it did in California. "In fact, she's already persuaded me to stay the full two weeks, instead of only one. I'll wire the extra money immediately to your chancellor."

Grand Duke Rudolph's cold gaze traveled over him.

Brian raised an eyebrow, daring the old autocrat to ask for more. He'd just promised to pay ten thousand dollars to have her at his side, a sum which put her company equal to the highest rank of courtesan who'd be visiting the summer maneuvers. However, all of it would stay in Eisengau.

Morro crouched at the edge of her skirts' folds, for all the world like a guardian lion in perfect position to attack anyone who threatened her.

"What's going on here?" Judge Baumgart shouldered his way through the crowd, which reluctantly parted for him. He was closely followed by his wife.

She shrieked when she saw her daughter. "Meredith, step away from that man at once. What will people think of my household if you behave like that?"

Meredith snorted softly and moved even closer to Brian. "I'm here to interpret the summer maneuvers for my protector."

She kissed her fingertips and lightly stroked them across his lips. It was a lover's gesture but not too daring for public display.

"Meredith!"

Brian met the grand duke's reptilian gaze and deliberately smiled rather lasciviously. She hadn't exactly lied but she had used a term more commonly applied to men who kept expensive mistresses.

The foreign observers were watching the scene avidly from behind the grand duke's guardsmen, many straining to see past the broad shoulders and polished steel helmets.

The grand duke's narrow lips twitched slightly and he cleared his throat before speaking. "Eisengau respects harmony of home and hearth above all else. A high court justice would certainly have brought his stepdaughter up to tell the truth."

The tall, narrow man hesitated.

His wife elbowed him. "A high court justice!" she hissed in English.

"Yes, Judge," the grand duke drawled, his tones edged in a thousand years of absolute rule. "What do you think?"

Baumgart gulped nervously. "She can always be relied on for candor, Your Excellency," he admitted grudgingly.

"Excellent, Judge, you have reared a paragon." The grand duke snapped his fingers. "The parents of such a woman deserve to be rewarded."

"Oh my," sighed Mrs. Baumgart rapturously.

Greedy bitch. But if buying her off was the only way to take Meredith away from her . . .

"Guard, take these two back to my chamberlain at the Citadel. There's a vacancy on the high court for which I believe Judge Baumgart is already on the list."

"Of course, sir." The guard clicked his heels. Meredith's mother rushed into a profusion of torrid thanks, which died slowly away as her husband dragged her off down the corridor. The foreign observers muttered but said nothing of substance loudly enough to be acknowledged. Of course, Mrs. Baumgart's maternal affection hadn't been displayed strongly enough to command support for her.

Brian kept his smile fixed, despite its edge, and kissed Meredith's hand. She smiled up at him a little tremulously and her fingers trembled in his grip.

"I don't recall hearing of your engagement, Zorndorf. I'm sure any of my colonels would obtain my permission first, as regulations require," Grand Duke Rudolph remarked silkily.

Zorndorf flushed before turning very pale. His eyes darted around the impassive plaster walls but couldn't find an exit. He pressed his lips together and bowed jerkily.

"Quite so."

"I see no reason why Mr. Donovan can't have his own particular *friend*, when the other gentlemen's friends have already gone ahead."

Friend? Brian glared back at him. It didn't have the most polite connotations but it wasn't openly offensive, either. As long as nobody said anything rude to her, it should do.

"Since it's the Americans' first time here, of course. Is there anything else, Zorndorf?" Grand Duke Rudolph's tone dared his servant to mention anything.

He shook his head, his complexion mottled with red. A

cobra's declaration of eternal peace would have been more believable.

Boot heels drummed against the floor behind them and pounded around the corner. Sazonov burst into the narrow stretch of corridor and stopped, rocking back on his heels. Engineering students filled the hallway behind him, their gray uniforms and black insignia merging into the shadows like an army of young demons.

His eyes swept through the corridor, stabbing at Meredith where she rested in Brian's arms. "Miss Duncan!"

She flinched and Morro growled deep in his throat.

Son of a bitch, was he the one who'd been chasing her? Ice swept through Brian's skin, bringing every nerve to full alertness. His feet shifted, bringing him into guard stance but he kept his voice deliberately mild. "Glad to see you recognize my friend, Sazonov."

The Russian bastard took a quick step forward, rapidly assessing him for weapons.

Brian smiled faintly and waited hopefully. If he could provoke the other into attacking now, without any supporters, matters could be settled quickly and simply.

The grand duke coughed, eyeing the Russian with all the warmth of a Winchester rifle aimed at a rabid wolf. The guardsmen snapped to attention, clicking their heels like tigers' claws, followed an instant later by the students.

The blond foreigner seemed to shake himself then donned a barbed smile. Pity he'd recovered himself before the Eisengau soldiers could unleash their highly functional rifles.

"Your Excellency." He bowed, flourishing his hat over his heart. "How glad I am, to have joined you in time to depart on summer maneuvers."

"The pleasure, I'm sure, will be ours," returned his host and turned for his carriage, his guardsmen marching after him.

It would be Brian's, too, after that poisonous Russian snake was dead, of course.

Chapter Six

Meredith accepted another morsel of Sacher torte from the liveried footman, well aware she was using the chocolate delight to avoid looking at the far more tempting Brian Donovan.

Dear heavens, the nightmare of that last hour in the capital. Surely if she gave them some time, her parents would rethink their position and realize she'd simply needed to block any betrothal to Zorndorf. But if not—well, she'd cross that bridge when she came to it.

For now, she had to cope with Brian and the way her pulses skittered every time he came into the room. She somehow didn't think political conversations were going to help her dodge the effect this time.

They'd arrived at Schloss Belvedere late that afternoon, after a long train trip through the rugged countryside from the capital. She'd been shown to their private suite to change—good heavens, what clothes! And from where?—while Brian had spoken privately with that English captain. They'd rendezvoused in time to join the other guests for pre-dinner drinks on the terrace, amid the gardens overlooking the lake.

Late summer's heavy scents perfumed the air. Roses and heliotrope, hollyhocks and lily of the valley grew in abundance along the borders, sage invited touch, and hops' yellow flowers tumbled over arbors. A formal garden, full of neatly trimmed bright flowers and dark greenery, bordered by serpentine iron and impassive sphinxes, led to the pale yellow main house.

Grand Duke Nicholas I had built Schloss Belvedere for his mistress eighty years earlier with his profits from the Napoleonic Wars. Named for its superb views, it was sited high in the mountains close to Herzog Lake, near St. Nicholas's Pass and the source of the Eisenfluss, Eisengau's great river.

It was a bonbon of a royal palace, pale yellow and trimmed in white. Nor did it offer any aid to a royal work ethic. Carved red balconies caught and held the setting sun's rays, making it blaze like a birthday cake. A cupola at its center lifted itself to the heavens like a temple to revelry, and was flanked by two smaller domes at each end of the long, low building. An arched opening, the *porte cochère*, cut into its bulk at each end, framing the main building and providing a base for each little dome. They were large enough to admit carriages but no more; the palace's bedroom suites carried over across each gap. The attics were barely enough to store a little food and linens; all the servants slept elsewhere—which also provided privacy for the palace's master and his guests.

It had been built for summer pleasures, short-term affaires like the one she'd conduct with Brian starting tonight.

So why did she know exactly where he was? What every muscle and bone was doing? Whether he was lifting a wine glass or biting into a bit of truffle-topped toast? Why could she have told exactly how his big, scarred hands stretched to hold a plate or curved around a peach?

Why did she want to run away and hurl herself at him, all at the same time? She knew she couldn't. Or was she afraid she couldn't walk away from him, as she had from her first two lovers?

Her pulse skittered again and her chest tightened, heat thrumming through her veins. She dipped her head, wondering what on earth to do now.

Tonight a military orchestra offered lively waltzes from the upper terrace's corner, next to the palace. Liveried lackeys proffered hors d'oeuvres to anyone who stood still for a moment, while others circulated with bottles of champagne.

Thunder roiled the cloudless blue sky, every boom marking a cannon undergoing final preparations for tomorrow's demonstrations during the maneuvers. Men focused binoculars and telescopes on the resulting puffs of smoke and chatted near the palace, while waving cigars or wine glasses to emphasize a point.

Superbly dressed women, with bosoms threatening to tumble out of their décolletages, sauntered among the guests, laughing and cooing like a flock of tropical birds in their brilliant dresses and jewels. They strolled with each other or a gentleman, bright eyes darting about to mark their prey or cast languishing glances up at the current object of their affection.

The ladies of the demimonde had arrived, changing the previously sober atmosphere into one recklessly bent on pursuit of the next joke, drink, or disappearance into a more private place.

Meredith had never seen anyone like them. She was one of them for the moment, a private delight for the man beside her. It was an oddly freeing concept. She could do anything she wanted, so long as she pleased Brian.

She stole another glance at them from the lower terrace, fascinated by their absolute confidence. Brian had brought her down here after the cask of schnapps was rolled out, just before the grand duke had made his appearance.

And the courtesans' clothing! Not that she could say much about theirs when hers had also become so eye-catching. Her dress was pale pink panné velvet with a square neckline cut low across her chest, black velvet straps that barely managed to hold it onto her shoulders, and long tight sleeves. It hugged her waist and hips like a second skin before flaring out from an enormous black velvet bow just above one knee. Not quite a perfect fit, her maid had judged it-*her* maid?-but good enough to catch a man's eye.

Donovan braced himself against the balustrade and stretched, still carefully watching the lake. They were essentially alone, the other guests having drifted back to the palace. His white uniform highlighted his strong frame and lithe grace far too well for rational thought. Did he know she could glimpse the outline of his underthings through it?

And heaven knows the courtesans ogled him.

Morro had taken one look at her and Brian, accepted a scratch behind his ears, then settled down for a nap. It was the first time her watchdog had ever declined to accompany her.

Should she make an excuse and depart? But they shared the single suite, with nowhere else for either of them to sleep.

She had created this situation, too, when she asked him to ruin her.

Ruin. Back at the capital, that had sounded appalling. Here, it seemed decadent, perhaps enjoyable.

Donovan turned around to face her and stretched like a great cat, bracing his hands behind him against the stone, presenting her with a mouth-watering glimpse of effortless masculine grace. Muscular thighs, hips, shoulders, neck . . .

Her body clenched.

She rushed into speech. "That was quite a trip we had, wasn't it?"

She bit her lip, feeling like a fool. Drat it, she wasn't a virgin. She'd been shown to his suite when they arrived and she expected to share his bed. She could hardly back out now, even if she wanted to. Especially with Sazonov lurking back at the Schloss, desperate to get his hands on her and the cannon's plans through her.

"The views were spectacular, weren't they? The picnic lunch gave us some excellent opportunities to enjoy them, too."

"Eisengau is a very mountainous country, Mr. Donovan."

"That stuffy name belongs to my father when people are trying to butter him up." He grimaced. "Please call me Brian."

"If you'll call me Meredith." She flushed a little. Her brothers called her Meredith but neither of those one-night wonders she'd shared a bed with ever had.

"More champagne?" Brian asked. His dimple was much more apparent in this light when he smiled. He looked so lazy, stretched out against the stone balustrade like that. Yet he always knew when another lackey was approaching, even if they were coming up behind him.

"Maybe a little." Golden bubbles danced into her glass, filling it halfway. Later that evening, those long fingers of his would probably learn her body, touch her intimately. Could she allow him to? Would she want him to stop?

"Have you been here before?"

"Not here at the palace. Colonel Zorndorf and his staff lived at the barracks about five miles away, while I always stayed with the garrison commander's wife."

Another burst of laughter split the air. It was somehow more laden with intimate promises than the beer garden dances she'd been to, even the ones where she'd been intimate with a man afterward.

"Good," Brian muttered.

She blinked at him. He was staring at her mouth as if trying to memorize it. Oh my. Warmth shimmered across her skin.

Perhaps if she thought of this as simply good fun, the way her first two lovers had been, then she could go through with it. After all, she'd only be with him for a couple of weeks.

"Where are we located now, in relation to the capital?" He yanked his gaze away from her and studied the river drifting out of the lake.

"The capital is in the northeast and downriver of Herzog Lake. St. Nicholas's Pass is over there, almost hidden behind those very steep granite needles in the southwest."

She pointed, indicating a particularly sharp rocky spire. Herzog Lake lay below them, placid and brilliantly blue, with the Eisenfluss River spilling out of it. Railroad tracks were carved into its shores, arching over small rivers and climbing past unyielding promontories. A massive stone blockhouse, as much fortress as workhouse, stood high on a cliff, ready to disgorge spare rails or snowplows at need.

"Looks like a nasty climb," Brian commented. Somehow they were now only separated by an inch or two.

"Very much, plus the Upper Falls have been cutting into the trail for the past decade or so. But you can't see that stretch very well from here."

He whistled softly. "Sounds like a climb my cousin would enjoy."

Was family so important to him, that he'd introduce them into every conversation? She brought the subject firmly back to his original question, shivering at the sight of his firm mouth. Dear heavens, how his kiss had made her pulse pound.

"You can see the limestone mines from here, on the hillside beyond the capital, and the spires of Altstadt, the old city." She fought to keep her voice steady. Men shouldn't have long eyelashes over blue, blue eyes. "It's often flooded in springtime but it's a popular summer escape for workers and their families."

"It's beautiful." Brian leaned on the railing next to her, his shoulder brushing hers through her thin silk sleeve. "It reminds me of Montana."

"Is that where you live?"

"No, I'm from California. My family has a weekend house in Marin County, just north of San Francisco. We can barely see San Francisco Bay because we have so many trees."

"Braggart!" She pretended to pummel him, just to touch him. She could be his lover for a few weeks, long enough to escape Zorndorf and Sazonov. She was free to enjoy herself for a little while.

He laughed and trapped her hands, pulling her up to him. She came willingly, her eyes traveling over every detail of his face. "This is madness, Meredith. You deserve marriage with some proper young man."

Hardly.

"You promised to ruin me." She rubbed her cheek against his chest. How long had it been since a man was definitely taller than she was? "It's the only way to stop Zorndorf and Sazonov."

"I could sleep on the floor," he tried another tack.

"The servants would talk, especially that maid you found for me." He was warm and smelled wonderfully masculine, like a sun-baked herb garden. A dreadful thought occurred to her. "Or have you changed your mind?"

"Like hell!" He caught her shoulders. "But once you're in my bed, you won't climb out of it very quickly."

Her breath hung in her throat.

"Is that a threat or a promise?"

He gave a harsh bark of laughter, his eyes glittering. "You should be running away from me."

"Why?" She shifted her grip so she could explore the muscles in his upper arms.

"Lord, Meredith, do you have any idea what you're doing to me?" He shuddered, his lashes briefly veiling his thoughts.

"No, but I'm glad to learn." Her chest was very tight, her blood pounding in her ears.

"Are you a virgin?"

"I've had two lovers, for a total of," she paused to count up, "three hours."

He choked. "Are you always so precise?"

"I look forward to enjoying the benefits of your greater skills," she added demurely.

He hugged her, shaking. She couldn't read his expression but she didn't think he was angry. She wouldn't have dared to tease any other man this way.

"And thank you for my maid," she added primly. "I've never had a personal one before."

"You're very welcome. Captain Blackwell knew a, ah, lady who was traveling with two of them and was willing to temporarily part with one's services."

"Please extend both of them my thanks." She leaned her head against Brian's shoulder. Was a good girl supposed to stand between a man's legs? Who cared when it brought them so very close, even if she was wearing a corset?

He tilted her head back and ran his finger over her lips. Her tongue crept out to follow it, desperate for a taste of him—and he kissed her, teasing and tempting her. She moaned and pressed closer, stropping herself over him like a cat, trying to ease the ache in her breasts which lanced her core. She was hungry, so hungry, and his kiss only increased it.

He growled and rubbed the back of her thighs through her dress, where her thin silk skirts and petticoats clearly conveyed his demand into skin and muscle. She gasped and arched, lust strumming her from his fingers to his mouth, tightening her lungs and core, melting her cream. "Brian, oh please, more."

He boldly fondled her again, his breath rasping her throat until she shuddered. He licked and nibbled her lips and whispered explicit promises of how he'd enjoy her more intimate flesh the same way.

She kneaded his shoulders, sighing her eagerness. His cock was a heated bar against her belly, hidden behind his enticing white trousers.

Brian pulled his head back, his features harsh with determination, and slid her down off his lap.

She groped for him, unable to think beyond the frantic need driving her blood.

A man groaned nearby, closely followed by a woman's cooing reply.

What on earth was happening?

"Come, Meredith, darling." Brian kissed her cheek and turned toward the palace, taking her by the hand.

The groans came again, deeper this time and more regular. More passionate? Surely she could take an instant to satisfy her curiosity.

Meredith slid her fingers through Brian's and leaned back,

peering over the railing toward the staircase which led down to the lake.

A courtesan was on her knees in front of a guest, his glittering uniform wrenched open at the throat and his trousers shoved down to his knees.

Meredith stared at Brian. "She has his cock in her mouth!"

Brian nodded, watching her warily.

"Is that truly why those women came along?" She'd read some books but she'd never expected to actually see anything in real life.

He nodded cautiously. "You're not offended?"

"No, of course not, they've only been polite to me. This is a very wicked place—and he's enjoying it," she added. What a wonderfully decadent place this was, where such adventures happened.

Brian nodded again, much more vehemently, still eyeing her cautiously.

She considered him and everything he hadn't said. "Is it something very popular that's only learned with experience?"

"Yes, sweetheart, women need practice to master the art. But I've never heard of a man who didn't immediately enjoy it."

She stole another glance at the oblivious couple far below. The woman was smiling, her fingers cunningly twisting and stroking the man's privates.

"They don't care that we're here," she commented, fighting for breath. Her chest was uncommonly tight and her skin was crackling hot, despite the cool breeze. While her previous encounters had started at beer garden dances, they'd always finished privately in a hotel room. Was that a requirement here?

"Are you offended?" Brian wrapped his arms around her. She leaned back against him, her head resting neatly into the hollow of his shoulder—and found his cock rubbing her ass.

"No," she admitted and wiggled her hips, trying to move a little closer. At least she was wearing her marvelous new ribbon corset which only reached the top of her hips. If she'd been wearing one of her mother's preferred straight-front corsets, which covered her down to her thighs, she'd never have known his shape this soon. Oh my.

"Do you want to watch them finish?" He nuzzled her throat. "Or find our room? I warn you, I won't display my skills for you here."

"Have you done so in an *alfresco* setting before?" She tried to tease him. But it was so very difficult when he was trailing kisses over every frantically beating pulse point, while his hands guided her hips' rhythmic rocking.

"Of course," he purred. "Sunshine is a marvelous aid to lovemaking."

Oh. She'd have to remember to ask him about that—but not now.

Brian delicately nibbled her, shooting the most incredible fireworks through her breasts and into her core. She moaned and tilted her head, offering him full access.

He wrapped his arm around her waist and started walking, still kissing and nibbling on her. She went willingly, every cell focused on him.

They were so close together that their legs brushed, sparks leaping back and forth between his woolen trousers and her silk skirts, raising friction. Her petticoats swished and frothed around her ankles, enhancing the sensation tenfold. Or was it the lust sparking in their eyes and their entwined fingers, desperately seeking to touch any bits of the other available?

She couldn't have said a coherent sentence. They passed galaxies of courtesans, now intermixed with male guests, but she didn't give them a second glance. Men were loudly chanting, "One, two, three, *prost*!" in the ballroom. But the phrase sounded like encouragement to indulge in games, especially since it was followed by scrabbling sounds and laughter. And when Brian kissed her, her blood insisted that cheering and games had to mean bedroom sports, wonderful pastimes with a man like him.

He swept her through a *porte cochère* and in the tower's side door, pausing to kiss her yet again. She moaned helplessly, her head falling back against his shoulder, and clutched at him. Why hadn't she known before how enchanting it was to feel fragile next to a man?

He picked her up in his arms, making her squeak like a silly girl—how delicious!—and ran up the stairs. Their suite was only a few feet away from the top and he kicked the door in.

Morro sprang to his feet, growling.

Meredith closed her eyes, remembering exactly why her previous love affairs had been so very brief. She hid her face against Brian's shoulder and tried to calm down long enough to frame a command.

"Silence! Your mistress deserves her pleasure and you need your sleep," Brian ordered sternly. In Gaelic.

Morro rumbled something in a series of barks and yips that were barely loud enough to be heard. Then there was only blessed quiet.

Brian started walking forward. Meredith turned her head slightly and dared to peek out.

Morro was scratching and kicking his nest of pillows into shape, beside the outer door to the sitting room. He turned around thrice and flopped down, raising an eyebrow at her as if daring her to question his choice of activities.

He'd obeyed Brian. He'd accepted Brian's extremely close grasp of her, something he'd never tolerated from another man. She didn't want to think about the implications, not now, not when Brian was almost to the bedroom.

Sunset streamed through the lace curtains, gilding everything inside. The furnishings were deceptively simple, as if the palace's builder had wanted to play at wilderness life while still enjoying every comfort. The massive bed had been built in England decades ago and was draped in crisp white. A couple of chairs, a small table, a chest, an oriental rug—the room's openness was closer to Scotland's freedom than anything Meredith had encountered in Eisengau.

Her lover bumped the door closed with his hip and laid her on the bed. "Meredith," he purred and leaned over her.

"Hmm?" She stroked his arms restlessly, her blood catching fire at the look in his eyes.

He slid his hands up her ankles—under her skirts—and caressed her stockinged legs.

"Brian!" She arched upward, jolted by the fiery lance which ran from his fingers through her hips and pussy to her breasts.

"Do you like this?" He stroked and kneaded her calves, spreading her wider, easing her skirts up to her knees.

"Brian, I, ah." She tried again, made restless by a pleasure which seemed to have no purpose except to drive her mad. "Don't you want to do more?"

"Why? We have plenty of time." One hand found the back of her knee.

She flung her head back and drummed her feet on the bed. How could he tease her so much through silk stockings?"
"Brian, please!"

"Guess that means you're enjoying yourself." He opened her more and tossed her petticoats up, baring her drawers. "Lovely. I'll have to cable for more of these."

"Huh?"

"I like how they're trimmed with lace and ribbon—and how much I can see of you through their slit."

"What???" She tried to sit up. His strong hands pressed her back, the heel of his palms at her knees and his thumbs on the inside of her thighs. His grip's warmth and strength was like living iron bonds, flexible and perfectly matched to her legs. Made for her alone.

He fondled her again, his thumb rubbing over hidden places. Cream heated and pulsed in her core, eager for him. He kissed her breasts, plumping them above her décolletage. She moaned again and stroked his arms.

His hands slid up her thighs, teasing her until she couldn't think, couldn't do anything but feel his touch. She writhed under him, begging for more, needing more. Hunger pulsed in her blood, rocked her hips, made her muscles clench.

His broad, callused finger toyed with her through the slit in her drawers. "Nice," he drawled.

She whimpered and tried to drive herself down onto it. Her skin was so hot and tight, surely she'd fly apart if he didn't satisfy her soon.

"Pretty." He chuckled hoarsely and lifted her hips.

Pretty? Her?

He slipped off the bed, pulled her to the edge—and over his shoulders. He'd stripped off his coat, waistcoat, and shirt at some point—and she encountered bare, satiny skin, carved with muscles and tendons.

She gasped.

A hot, wet tongue swirled through her folds.

She climaxed, melting into a thousand swirling pieces laced with stardust.

Before she could think again, he ripped open her drawers and lifted her hips, sliding his fingers over her beautiful ribbon corset. He tongued her again, avidly seeking out every bit of cream.

And he took her up to the heights again and again, using tongue and fingers—and teeth!—until she was a writhing, sobbing, passionate woman.

When she lay hoarse from shrieking her pleasure through more orgasms than she could count, he looked up at her. Triumph was etched across his face, lined with a harshness she didn't quite understand.

"Meredith," he growled.

He stood up and knelt over her, shoving her back across the coverlet. Her skirts were a tattered, irreparable wreck but who cared when she'd finally have him? She dared to caress his hip. He shuddered before jerking off his belt and shoving his pants down his hips, grabbing up a condom from the packet on the bedside table.

An instant later, he was finally, finally in her. Big and solid and hot. Dear heavens, thank God he'd stretched her beforehand because she was surely tight now. And it was wonderful. She wrapped her legs around his, and savored him.

He rumbled something deep in his throat and rode her, hard and fast. Lust brightened every stroke, strengthened the current in her blood, intensified the sound of every wet slap between their bodies. Her hips rose to meet him, her breasts ached for his touch, her channel clenched around him.

And when he arched and shouted, jetting his heated come deep inside her, the added pressure shot her into yet another climax, like magma remaking anything in its way. She howled, shattering into a million pieces, everyone marked with a star.

Chapter Seven

As leader—and sole member—of a delegation, Brian rated a private carriage, ostensibly so he could see the fine mountain scenery and catch an early glimpse of the firing range. The road had been macadamized, giving it a solid surface which offered an amazingly smooth ride and could support very heavily loaded vehicles. Grassy meadows spilled into the distance, dotted with massive oaks and occasional stands of beech trees.

Water tumbled and frothed down the slopes, turning trickles into creeks and streams into rivers. The storm two days ago had been the latest in a very wet summer, filling the channels until crossing some bridges sent a misty plume flying up behind the carriage's wheels. Had his lover noticed?

He'd had little time to talk with Meredith this morning before departing the palace. There'd been the rush to dress and snatch breakfast, to say nothing of that all-too-strong stirrup cup offered to warm them for the journey.

He eyed their driver, impassive in his dark-blue Eisengau infantry uniform, and was reluctantly glad he wasn't making conversation with Meredith. Let the obvious spy attribute their silence to a night of frenzied lovemaking; God knows that was true enough.

He snorted privately. Only her inexperience had kept her enthusiasm—and his lust—from keeping them awake all night.

He also had the uneasy suspicion that only carnal diversions would keep her fine mind from following any inquiry to its logical conclusion—regardless of the consequences. At least she had Morro to guard her after he was gone.

His mouth tightened and he glanced sideways at her. She'd asked the driver to put the top down on their carriage so she could watch her beloved dog trot beside the carriage. The sturdy fellow was uttering happy little barks, no doubt delighted at the universe of new scents borne by the brisk morning air. She wore the fine tweed suit Brian had ordered for her yesterday, under its warm, matching cape. Her jaunty hat with its saucy feathers and ribbons left her expression open to his perusal. A smile played around her bruised lips, under her heavy-lidded eyes.

Something deep inside him sat up and purred, luxuriating in pure masculine triumph. His skin warmed and his cock swelled, climbing hopefully onto his thigh.

All the time and money he'd spent yesterday on ordering clothes for her, starting with Gareth's lady loves, then touching *modistes* currently encamped in Eisengau before finally reaching out to Paris and London—damn, but it had all been worthwhile, just to see her now. He hoped she agreed because he was counting the hours until he could have her alone again. No matter what his deal was with her—or the other fools' behavior around them—he wasn't about to enjoy her in public.

As if sensing his regard, Meredith slid her hand along the leather upholstery toward him. He caught it up and kissed her fingers, happy to look besotted. "Comfortable?"

"Very." She turned to him, glowing like a torch. "My clothes fit perfectly, even the corset. Thank you! How did you know exactly what size I am?"

He managed not to throw out his chest like a pompous politician. When had anybody ever looked at him like that before, especially since he'd grown up the second of four sons? He was loved, yes, by his family but hardly called infallible.

"A man of the world can tell these things," he pronounced smugly. He added more softly, "Besides, I'd kissed you thoroughly and my body remembered every detail."

He was still contentedly watching her blush when their driver neatly turned the carriage into a walled courtyard and stopped precisely in front of a cream-colored stone building. Strongly built with few doors on the first floor, its second floor windows provided comfortable views of surrounding area. The third floor offered classical bas-reliefs and the dynasty's salamander crest but few peepholes. All in all, it was stolidly militaristic and quietly functional, in complete contrast to the Schloss Belvedere's extravagance.

Pairs of hard-eyed young men strolled the courtyard in Eisengau's crack Rifle regiment's uniform, revolvers holstered quietly at their waist. A pair of their mates stood guard impassively at the front door, while another pair had exchanged salutes with Brian's driver at the courtyard's entrance.

Like the engineering college, this place knew what it meant to guard secrets.

A chill breeze slipped over Brian's skin, despite the courtyard's high walls. By the time his breath steadied on his next exhale, he'd assessed every sentry's position, weapons, and alertness while never looking directly at any of them.

He stepped down onto the smooth pavement, automatically gauging its decorative stones. Not macadamized so they didn't bring the truly priceless stuff, the heavy goods Eisengau was known for, in through this entrance.

There were motorcars and even a few new-fangled motorcycles mixed among the crisply parked carriages, none of which he'd seen earlier at the palace. Could they have come with the grand duke's notoriously conservative friends? Or was his heir sneaking in a few more modern thinkers?

"Meredith, have you attended summer maneuvers here? In the stands?"

"No, only from the outbuildings on the valley's edge. I was only present for practice sessions . . ."

"Not the real thing," he finished grimly. A few surprises were undoubtedly in store for them both.

A few minutes later, he and Meredith emerged from the headquarters onto the narrow balcony in the back. A row of leather armchairs marched along the balustrade, enough for the heads of delegations and a handful of honored guests. All in all, there was only enough room, sitting or standing, for a few people.

A military band was playing dashing martial airs from a flag-decked bandstand off to one side. Guests milled around, drinking coffee, tea, or something stronger, and finally assuming their proper role of foreign observers.

Some of the most top-flight courtesans were here, ornamenting the arms of the richest and most privileged attendees. Their tweeds were trimmed with luxurious sables and studded with diamond brooches. Their voices were low and melodious, their bearing that of queens. Men stopped to chat with them, then moved on.

Meredith's eyes widened and her fingers tightened briefly on Brian's arm but she said nothing about them. He patted her hand approvingly.

The headquarters' sides dropped steeply away to a bowl-shaped depression cut into the mountainside, where the morning fog's last few wisps were dancing in the sunlight. Tables in front of the balcony held long, straight, narrow objects, covered by cloths. An almost bucolic landscape was filled with grass and trees, except every knob seemed to feature a cannon—and every tree mourned at least one shattered branch.

He'd finally arrived at Eisengau's legendary test range.

He grinned privately and accepted a cup of coffee.

"Brian," Meredith whispered, "where will everyone sit? There isn't enough room on the balcony and the road doesn't go near the valley's borders."

"They won't, not here. Only the most important folks are allowed to see the demonstrations."

She frowned and rubbed Morro's head, while she considered his answer. Brian waited, curious to learn what her next question would be.

"But not every head of a delegation will make it here this morning, especially after all the drinking and, ah, everything else that happened last night. What happens then? Will the seats be empty?"

He shrugged and told the truth, doubting that lying would serve any good with her.

"Remember the chanting you heard last night? One, two, three, *prost*?"

"Or 'cheers,'" she agreed, translating the last word into English.

"It was a drinking contest, in which the winners get first claim on seats here."

She blinked. "How can they do that?"

"On the count of three, everybody shouts *prost!* and downs a small glass of hard liquor, in this case vodka. Then they march in single file to the head of the room and crawl under the tables back to their place. The winner is literally the last man standing."

"Who will have a very nasty headache in the morning to listen to these with." She indicated the cannons.

He nodded agreement.

"It seems silly."

He shrugged, having played far stranger games.

"But why vodka? That's not a spirit often seen in Eisengau."

"Sazonov provided it."

"Does anyone other than Russians know how to drink much of it?"

"Not many." He reluctantly gave her the truth.

"He must have wanted more than one of his men here." Her skin was pale from more than the weather.

He nodded slightly, wondering why his gut was looking for snipers.

"Miss Duncan?" The harsh accent smashed her name together.

She flinched and spun to face Sazonov, finishing against Brian. He raised an eyebrow at the fellow, observing only a well-dressed man wearing a very apologetic expression. Strange, very strange.

"Count Sazonov." Her tone was curt to the point of rudeness. Some of their neighbors looked around. He glared at them.

"May I speak to you for a moment, Miss Duncan? Privately but within eyesight of others. I assure you, you have nothing to fear."

"I cannot imagine what we have to say to each other."

"An apology?" Sazonov lowered his voice.

More people were staring. Meredith glanced at them then looked back at him. "Very well, if you swear never to accost me in public again."

"You have my word of honor."

"Meredith, you don't have to do this," Brian whispered.

"We can talk behind the previous grand duke's statue, away from the band. I'll take Morro and you can watch from the front of the balcony."

"No."

"He can help the workers," she mouthed, keeping her head turned so Sazonov couldn't read her lips.

Jesus, Mary, and Joseph, what wouldn't she risk for that damn cause?

But he couldn't find any holes in her proposal. He could be with her in three strides, while Morro could rip into Sazonov within an instant. If it would make her happy, it would have to do, although Sazonov's poorly hidden smirk made him very uneasy.

Meredith drew herself up, longing to hurl herself back into Brian's arms and demand shelter. Foolish thought; when had a man ever kept her safe?

But she had to talk to Sazonov. Maybe, just maybe, he'd changed his mind and was genuinely willing to help Eisengau's workers after all.

At least the plans were safe back in the capital.

"What is it, Count?"

"I must apologize for my previous boorish behavior, Miss Duncan. I should not have attempted to grab you."

Why was he being so polite? If only Brian was beside her. The warm wool Brian had given her wrapped her shoulders like a hug and she smiled faintly.

"But you are a beautiful woman and I lost my head. Please forgive me."

Sazonov was calling her beautiful? The bastard. *Liesel, oh, Liesel, I wish I hadn't been right . . .*

"You should be a princess, my darling, ruling a world blessed by loveliness and mercy."

What on earth was he talking about?

"And I can make you one. In your domain, workers will be treated fairly and honestly, while poets flock to sing of your fair face."

Was he mad? "My domain, Count?"

"Alaska, dear heart. The lowly peasants there are enslaved, forced to labor at canning salmon and curing sealskins. But after Russia regains it, you will be their great protectress, their goddess of mercy—if you help me *now.*"

"Alaska? Really." Where was this place?

"You will be revered for years, even decades!"

She nodded politely and wished she'd paid more attention to her few geography lessons. She was quite sure Alaska had never been part of the British Empire. It was an odd name, though—possibly American Indian?

"Aren't you worried I'll mention this to Mr. Donovan?" she asked, fencing for time.

"You'd never ally yourself with anyone who oppresses the common man." He snorted in disdain. "Donovan's father has owned silver mines for decades, building his fortune on the backs of unfortunate immigrants."

Could Brian's father really be that powerful—and callous? Oh, dear God, let her never linger near any family ruled by an autocratic patriarch. Those devils had no use for women with independent thoughts, and the law enforced their rights, no one else's.

And her father's memory was as much nightmare as talisman.

Sazonov's lips unfolded into a broad grin from something closer to a cobra's flickering watchfulness. That military band was enjoying a cavalry march, all fluting cornets and lively drumbeats.

"So you're with me?" He tilted his head, lifting his eyebrow in what he probably thought was a charming mannerism, and reached for her hands.

Morro growled and stepped between them. Good dog! She wasn't about to fall in with the jackal's plans, no matter how few the workers' alternatives were.

Sazonov automatically jerked away.

"What do you need first?" she inquired, keeping her expression mildly interested.

"The plans for Eisengau's new great gun, of course."

The ones he'd tried to force her to steal before, back at the engineering college.

Her jaw dropped. "That's ridiculous! The only complete set is back in the capital, not out here."

"Where only you and Zorndorf know the combination to the safe." His eyes were focused on hers, compelling her to obey.

"He's undoubtedly given orders to keep me out of the building," she protested. Just keep pretending they're still in the safe, Meredith.

"I'm sure you know ways around the guards, if you think hard enough." His gaze turned warmer. "You're a clever woman, Miss Duncan, who can do anything."

"He'd know in a moment who'd stolen it."

"But you'd be safe with me, my dearest." Was his expression what the cheap novelists meant by seductive?

"Think of the poor workers in Alaska," he coaxed.

"The plans should be used only to aid Eisengau."

Where was Brian? Pacing by the balustrade, exactly as he'd promised. Why was she looking to him for help? She'd always had to fight her own battles.

She pulled herself up a little straighter.

"But you always needed help to hide them from the grand duke's secret police." Sazonov's syrupy tone was an utter contrast to the violent penalties for her, should he fail.

"True. But you need my assistance now," she retorted, not about to say where.

His eyes narrowed and his breath hissed out. She braced herself, ready for a public fight.

The band crashed into a flaring trumpet call and thunderous drum roll, winding up the march. The conversational screen around Meredith and Sazonov died away as everyone involuntarily turned to watch.

"Gentlemen," called a trim colonel from the terrace's center. "Please take your assigned seats for Grand Duke Rudolph's opening remarks. Thank you."

Brian's shoulder brushed Meredith's and Morro's leg leaned against hers on the other side. Thank God, somebody cared about her, even if protocol reduced her to being an appendage to a man.

Sazonov glared at her, swallowed hard, then bowed. "I look forward to continuing our conversation later, Miss Duncan."

She responded with the smallest possible nod. Please, God, may the plans still be safely hidden.

"What was that about?" Brian whispered, taking advantage of the pause caused by a gaudily dressed *chère amie* being seated next to a stout old gentleman. Sazonov had long since bowed and elbowed his way through the crowd to reach the front row. If he'd lifted a finger against Meredith, the bastard wouldn't have lived long enough to draw another breath.

She used her lace-trimmed handkerchief to shield her words. "He tried to bribe me, if I'd steal the plans for a cannon."

He cast her an incredulous glance and she shrugged, her

mouth twitching slightly. He could have kissed her for understanding the need for discretion. "The bribe was to help workers in someplace called Alaska?"

"Alaska!" Damn!

He stopped dead in his tracks, causing vehement complaints
behind them. His blood ran cold at the implications. He murmured apologies to everyone nearby and nudged Meredith
forward, almost blind to where they were.

"Are you sure?" he hissed, hovering over her like a loon as
she sat down. With luck, everyone else thought she was sneaking him tidbits of information about Eisengau's equipment.

She shot him one incredulous glance but quickly pretended
to fuss over her tweed skirts' placement.

"Yes, I'm sure he wasn't lying. He mentioned after they *regained* it. Do you know what that means?"

"Russia plans to attack the U.S. and steal the Klondike
gold mines," Brian whispered in her ear, pretending to adjust
a woolen rug over her lap. "Though they're just over the border in Canada."

"British Empire?" Her voice started to rise, turning very
Scottish.

He clamped down on her wrist, thankful they sat near the
band's very enthusiastic trumpeters. She glared at him and
sat back. Even her hat's ridiculous feathers seemed to quiver
with indignation. She accepted a cup of tea from one of the
many servants and stirred sugar into it with unnecessary violence, sending her unique scent to tease his nostrils.

His body tightened immediately.

He claimed his own chair and pretended to study the excellent view of the test range. Sitting next to her was no hardship for anything except his cock.

Still, he was here on a mission. He wasn't a professional
soldier but he'd spent enough long days around them in Cuba,
mapping alternative attack plans, to have learned a few tricks.
Plus there'd been those hellacious battles, not to mention the
months he'd actually spent in Alaska.

His stomach plummeted, forcing restraint on his cock.

The other observers were chatting with each other, while they finished settling into place. Meredith dropped a bit of cheese between their armchairs for Morro to gobble up.

"He'll fail, won't he?" she whispered, her words hidden from anyone else by the others' gossip.

"Of course he will," Brian answered quickly.

She scanned his face and her eyes widened.

He'd been right: It did no good, whatsoever, to lie to her. She'd just see straight through the attempt.

Jesus, what a nightmare. There wasn't much anybody could do to stop a Russian invasion of Alaska. Right now, all that mattered was those Klondike goldfields and America held the sea routes. A few Coast Guard cutters enforced the law up there—but what could they do against the Russian army and navy? The miners had spirit but they weren't trained fighters.

And the British navy in Victoria wasn't even a handful of ships. They'd been fretting about a Russian invasion for decades but their so-called fortified positions wouldn't have held off a dozen drunks.

No, the Russians could just waltz right in and seize Alaska, plus the goldfields. The question would be what happened after that, when America and Great Britain came roaring back, determined to reclaim Alaska and the Klondike. Russia would need to fortify the ports very, very well or their second stay in that frozen wonderland would be damn brief.

That must be why Sazonov was here: He wanted Eisengau's best cannons for his jaunt to Alaska. Most European countries would buy their new guns from Germany's great Krupp family or perhaps France. But Krupp insisted on cash for all transactions, unless otherwise instructed by their empire's Kaiser. They'd probably refused to deal with them, since Russia was notoriously deep in debt.

France was very skittish about permitting its brilliant new guns out of its sight. They wouldn't even let routine maintenance be done by anyone other than a Frenchman. Alaska would seem like an unprincipled wilderness and probably too far away.

Should he tell anyone in Washington about this? He believed Meredith's judgment of Sazonov but would they trust a woman? Had his father ever successfully disagreed with his mother? Hardly. He snickered privately. Hell, he'd grown up knowing women had the last word, if they chose to take it.

No, he'd just have to deal with this problem privately. Find evidence if he could, harm Sazonov whenever possible, and keep Meredith safe at all costs.

That ridiculous military band fell silent, making the clatter of crockery and cutlery from inside the building sound like dynamite blasts.

"Gentlemen, may I present His Excellency, Grand Duke Rudolph."

Jesus, Mary, and Joseph, wasn't anybody polite enough to notice there were ladies present?

The vicious dandy strutted to the balcony's center. His polished brass helmet and multitude of buttons were almost blinding enough to distract from the crisply efficient grasp on his sabre. His young son Nicholas stood behind him, half a head taller and garbed in the sober dark green uniform of the Eisengau's legendary Rifle regiment. Zorndorf flipped through his notebook beside the headquarters' base, near the long tables.

"Welcome to Eisengau, my friends. Two and a half centuries ago, this very land defeated our enemies in the Battle of St. Nicholas's Pass, when a great avalanche crushed an invading army."

Brian studied the mountainside. If he rolled some big boulders off those granite needles and didn't much care what they damaged, he could start an avalanche now. He'd wager the ruler back then had been a ruthless son of a bitch, willing to ruin good pastureland and kill animals, if not his own people. But it had created a relatively flat space in this otherwise heavily slanted world.

"Every year, our army holds summer maneuvers here to remember our forefathers and to practice our own skills. We are honored to have you join us." The grand duke bowed repeatedly, smiling broadly as he answered the polite applause. It was the first time Brian had seen the old goat look genuinely happy.

"During these maneuvers, we will test the latest technologies from our armory. In this dawn of a new century, our foundry stands ready to build this equipment faster than anywhere else in the world."

"Sir?"

Everyone stared at Grand Duke Rudolph's previously impassive heir.

"What is it?" The autocrat demanded.

"As Master of the Armory and the Foundry, sir,"— Meredith's hand suddenly clamped down on Brian's wrist— "I am proud to have the traditional honor to co-sign all production agreements with you. Sir."

Grand Duke Rudolph's eyebrows beetled together above his narrowed eyes. He nodded shortly, his mustache points quivering. "Of course you do."

Meredith's breath hissed out, closely followed by several other men's. If Brian had read that byplay correctly, the heir had just announced nobody, even his father, could do anything in the foundry without his permission. Which meant increasing production of cannons in Eisengau would have to go through junior, not just the old man.

"With every consideration given to our people's health, of course," Nicholas added and became an impassive statute once again.

Brian wondered how long Nicholas's father would let him get away with that. Eisengau was not a place which welcomed change—except in weaponry.

Chapter Eight

Grand Duke Rudolph harrumphed and drew himself up once again, not looking back. "Today is an introduction to the maneuvers. We will start by showcasing the skills of individual men, plus our latest shotguns. After lunch, you will see our cannons. We have some mountains guns I'm sure you will like."

"And?"

Sazonov. Brian was sure that Russian accent came from Sazonov himself. None of his lackeys would have dared to speak.

"Did I not say cannons? Guns you can take into battle— and siege guns as powerful as any naval gun."

"Impossible!" The German representative smacked his fist into his palm.

"Very possible indeed, for men of intelligence with fine steel at their disposal. All the necessary patents already exist." Grand Duke Rudolph stroked his mustache, swirling its point into a longer spike. "Firing a shell more than eight times heavier at a range half again longer than the current greatest gun."

"Never," muttered the French observer.

The grand duke's tongue flickered over his lips like a satisfied cobra. He wove his head from side to side, assessing the other observers' stunned reactions. His lips curled, matching his heavy-lidded eyes' satisfied curve.

"We will enact scenarios whereby you can see how well all

of these work. You will help us choose from among the many options. In honor of the new century, the first scenario—and the first demonstration—will be chosen by the youngest here."

Brian frowned. By all the saints, there were enough old fools in their dotage here to make a mortician salivate. He'd guess himself, Gareth, and Sazonov were the youngest. But Gareth had seen more years than he had.

"Mr. Donovan, Count Sazonov? Please come forward."

Why both of us? Why not just one?

Brian rose. Meredith's fingers were digging into the armchair's upholstery hard enough to score the leather. She gave him a brief, gallant smile and folded her white hands in her lap, hiding them from onlookers. Morro thumped his tail on the hardwood floor, his all-too-intelligent dark eyes demanding a farewell. Brian gave him a quick scratch behind the ears and met Sazonov in front of Grand Duke Rudolph.

"Gentlemen, we are about to have a shooting competition between two very fine shots. Count Sazonov has killed tigers and bull elephants in India, while Mr. Donovan has been decorated for gallantry under fire."

Brian and Sazonov stared at each other, equally appalled for once. What the hell was the bastard planning?

Grand Duke Rudolph lifted his hand and two sergeants whisked the white linen cloth off the long table below, revealing a half dozen rifles, representing the top military rifles in the world.

"Each of you will select one rifle from those below. All of them are directly from the regular assembly lines, except the Mosin-Nagant which has been customized by the Tsar's arsenal."

That figured; it'd take some work to make such an ugly brute really smooth.

"Your targets will be teacup saucers from the set used aboard the trains into Eisengau."

Shit, shit, shit. Sturdy little devils, wobbling and leaping erratically like rabbits, impossible to predict and damn difficult to destroy with a small bullet.

"You must shoot it before it falls over. Twenty saucers for each of you, launched every two seconds."

Brian's jaw set hard, a muscle ticking in his cheek. He'd be lucky to hit two-thirds of them.

"What do we gain if we win?" Sazonov demanded.

"My artillery is prepared to conduct three scenarios this afternoon, Count. The first displays an entire squadron's speed in taking to the battlefield, while the second shows how our new mountain gun can be carried on mules. And quickly brought into action, of course."

Sazonov waved those off, his eyes glittering like a man with gold fever. "And the third?"

"A direct comparison of the French 75mm with our new 155mm. With the winner standing next to the gun commanders."

"Nobody has a six-inch gun except a navy!" exploded Gareth, storming to his feet.

Brian closed his eyes. Hell, 75mm was bigger than anything he'd encountered in Cuba. There they'd been damn happy to see anything larger than a rifle. But there was nothing to do now except play this hand out and see what Eisengau really was trying to sell. He blew out his breath and started considering his options for winning the match.

Five minutes later, he was standing at his mark with a Mauser 98 rifle snugged up to his shoulder. The Spanish snipers had used the same rifle to shred American troops in Cuba. He'd seized one and fallen in love with it. Later he'd bought a newer model and had it customized.

This one was six inches longer and heavier, not quite as smooth in action. But it could still feed bullets into the chamber more reliably than anybody else, and had damn good sights, too. All in all, it was the best damn military rifle in the world and he'd win with it.

Sazonov had chosen a Mosin-Nagant, of course, since he was probably very familiar with that rugged Russian bastard. Brian had never fired one.

Low barriers marked where saucers would soon emerge, rolling downhill, flinging themselves into the air like demented March hares. A faint breeze drifted across the field, then fell back, as unpredictable as the targets would be.

Brian folded his lips together more tightly and waited. Excuses didn't count, only results.

The formal audience had been swelled by Eisengau's uniformed military and the servants from within the building. Meredith stood near the balcony's edge with Morro at her knee. She'd given him encouraging smiles and was even making conversation with Gareth.

"Gentlemen!" The grand duke leaned on the balcony's edge, casually grasping his starter's pistol. "One last detail."

What else, you son of a bitch? Brian automatically clicked the safety on and spun to face the old devil who'd designed this hellish game.

"Now that you've chosen the finest two military rifles in the world, please lay them down on the table beside you. Then exchange places with each other."

"Your Excellency . . ." Sazonov started to protest.

"Yes, Count? If you don't like these rules, I can always change them. For example, I can display the new 155mm cannon to my guests one at a time, starting with those who've come the farthest. Say, from across an ocean?"

Sazonov's fair skin turned an ugly mottled red.

Brian very carefully laid the rifle down on the table and stepped back. While he hated to lose—and abhorred being manipulated—why the devil was Sazonov so extremely intent on winning this match? Wouldn't everyone get the same information sometime today, anyway?

But he added his own Gaelic curses when he picked up the damn heavy Russian rifle and tried to use the archaic sights.

Jesus, Mary, and Joseph, what battles did the Tsar really expect to win with these?

A sideways glance showed Sazonov quickly accustoming himself to the Mauser.

Brian bit his cheek, remembering some of Uncle Morgan's stories about stealing weapons from the Yankees as a guerrilla. He'd make do; he had to. Men had done damn good work with this rifle so he'd figure out how. He just had to do it fast, especially learning how to reload.

"Gentlemen, are you ready?" Grand Duke Rudolph called all too soon.

Brian held up his free hand and waited, the gun resting comfortably in the crook of his elbow.

"Ready!"

Brian brought the rifle up to his shoulder. *Come on, help me; you're the key to figuring out what that bastard is going to throw at my homeland.*

"Aim!" The Mauser was solid as a rock in Sazonov's hands.

Brian sighted down the Mosin-Nagant's long barrel and prayed it would shoot straight.

"Fire!"

The first saucer ducked out of the enclosure and sped down the hill.

BAM! Jesus, Mary, and Joseph, this gun was loud.

The saucer hit a tuft of grass, leaped into the air, and fell onto its side, entirely untouched.

The damn Russian rifle pulled left.

Pull the bolt back, eject the spent cartridge, turn the bolt back into position.

The next saucer was already whirling along.

BAM! The rifle's unusually violent slam into his shoulder was less startling this time.

He clipped the rabbit, but the sturdy china didn't break.

CRACK! CRACK! Sazonov shattered two saucers in a row.

Brian gritted his teeth and steadied his breathing.

CRACK! One saucer exploded into dust, praise God.

BAM! BAM! Did the china see the bullets coming and jump out of the way?

He reloaded as quickly as possible, feeding five more rounds in from the top with the stripper clip. The technique was faster than the American Army's insistence on individual rounds but nowhere near as rapid as the Mauser's box magazine.

CRACK! He'd hit that one dead on. He should do better now.

His gun jammed when the thirteenth saucer whipped out of the starting gate. Patience, just a little patience; Sazonov wasn't doing that much better.

He coaxed the bolt open, crooning to the weapon under his breath, watching white dervish after white dervish escape over the green grass from the corner of his eye.

Finally the rifle answered him. BAM! CRACK!

For a long, long moment, the range lay empty of anything except gently waving leaves, prostrate china, and flecks of white. Men were cheering somewhere far away.

Brian slowly clicked on the safety and set the Mosin-Nagant down on the table. It had served him far better than he'd expected.

"Congratulations, gentlemen," Grand Duke Rudolph called when both contestants faced him. "That was amazing shooting from both of you. However, I must proclaim Count Sazonov the winner, with ten kills to Mr. Donovan's seven."

Brian advanced to shake hands with his opponent but Sazonov was already running up the stairs to speak to the grand duke. Rude son of a bitch.

There was an appalled silence from the crowd before they clapped briefly and turned away. Poor sportsmanship was never rewarded in the finer circles.

Darling Meredith's face was white under her polite smile. But she still forced her way through the crush to meet him. He held out his hands to her, his heart racing faster than it should be for a summer love affair.

*   *   *

"I don't understand why we can't watch from your head-quarters," the German attaché complained querulously. "Surely we can see everything from its roof."

"Where the facilities are so much better," put in Gareth's boss.

"I'm sorry, gentlemen, but it was necessary to withdraw to this hostel for today's demonstration." Even the most unruly observer yielded to that steely tone and stepped onto wooden structure. The grand duke continued in a more cordial fashion, a glowing Zorndorf at his shoulder. "From here you can see the entire valley where we conduct maneuvers, from the railroad tracks over there to my headquarters farther down the mountain all the way to the lake at the foot."

The *entire* valley? Brian flicked a glance at Meredith. Like most of the foreign observers, she was standing on this rustic hostel's balcony, high on the mountainside just above the railroad blockhouse.

She'd never given a reason for why she'd had megrims after his match with Sazonov and he hadn't pressed her. Given that caprice, he also hadn't asked why she'd exchanged her very fashionable hat for such a plain straw boater on the journey here. The other women had kept their fashionable headgear. Some had even changed to more spectacular ones when they'd shed the morning's heavy capes.

Now Meredith glanced over at him and nodded definite agreement to the need for seeing the complete valley, all the while unpinning that boring bit of straw.

Other than Grand Duke Rudolph and Zorndorf, she was the only person present who'd encountered the cannons before. Were they so massively dangerous she wouldn't risk her headgear?

Morro was pacing between her and the railing, always watching the railroad tracks in the distance.

Brian decided to remain standing. If nothing else, the posture would let him order Zorndorf to stop leering at Meredith.

"Take your seats and let's have at it," the Frenchman called. "It's a beautiful day for enjoying great cannonades. We've already cheered the infantrymen's attack upon those paper targets."

"Now we consider those created by French genius." The grand duke made their representative a little bow, which was returned with a flourish.

"The greatest cannons in the world," the Frenchman agreed smugly and accepted a fizzing glass of champagne. "As you will all soon agree, even if you only see one of our guns."

"Oh, I assure you we have a complete battery," the old arms merchant purred, deadly as a hissing snake. "Gentlemen, in the scenario Count Sazonov chose, two attacking forces must break through a strongly defended position, marked by those two clumps of oak trees."

"Where?" queried the German sharply, shading his eyes from the sun.

"Below my headquarters, just above the lake." Grand Duke Rudolph was definitely enjoying himself.

Brian pulled out his binoculars and found the very healthy groves, filled with massive tree trunks and great branches which could block out the sky. Then he started looking for the cannons aimed at it.

Nothing. At least nobody standing around big lumps of metal, although he did find four interesting notches etched into a pasture a few miles away.

"Are you ready to begin, gentlemen? Very well." The grand duke fired a signal pistol, sending a puff of red smoke soaring into the brilliant sky.

An instant later, hundreds of men charged forward across the open valley floor from the headquarters, heading toward the first oak grove—and closely followed by a team of eight horses towing a heavy gun. With it came three other well-trained teams, all towing similar heavy guns.

All of the infantrymen were shooting rapidly at the man-shaped targets below the trees. They were moving across open ground, with nothing to hide them from snipers hidden in the trees or in the tall grass or along riverbanks. Smoke drifted into the air but offered little camouflage compared to the massive clouds from black powder.

"Get down, you fools, get down," Brian found himself muttering. Mother of God, how many men had been killed at Las Guasimas in the first few seconds without ever seeing the Spaniards?

The teams wheeled into position and came to a stop, placing their guns pointing at the oaks. Five men sprang down from each team's horses and went to work, heaving and shoving until the unwieldy steel rested precisely on each notch.

Gareth had his stopwatch out beside Brian.

A moment later, the first round appeared from its portable storehouse and disappeared into the breech.

Boom! Boom! BOOM! BOOM!!!

The artillery battery simultaneously fired its guns, shaking the ground beneath Brian's feet. Tree branches shattered and slowly fell to the ground. The acrid scent of cordite drifted through the air, mixed with a vagrant sweetness.

Well done! Damn, if he'd only had one of those in that hellish Cuban jungle!

The infantrymen continued to charge, their bullets slowly cutting apart the silhouettes before them.

The guns fired again a few seconds later, far faster than anything Brian had seen before. His fingers tightened, urging the soldiers forward against their inanimate opponents.

The bullets blurred into an explosively drilling sound, like an immense factory, punctuated by the deeper boom of the cannons. It beat through the ground, drumming against his feet and rattling the wineglasses.

Eventually the infantrymen shouted and punched through the targets' blasted remains, the cannons falling silent in their wake. They trotted into the shattered grove and carefully wended their way through the knee-deep chaos of collapsed branches and shredded leaves.

Brian was cheering, too. He snatched up a magnum of champagne to help toast the French observer, who was clasping his hands over his head in a victory salute.

The delighted warriors returned, every man waving a shredded bough over his head as a token of victory. The gunners ran forward to meet them and they embraced in the sunlight, their weapons' smoke disappearing like a bad dream.

Even the German attaché shook the Frenchman's hand.

Meredith straightened her jacket, tugging the sturdy wool down past her hips. Tonight he'd hold her close and they'd laugh together about this challenge.

There was barely a breeze, although dark clouds were starting to build over the peaks.

Grand Duke Rudolph said something under his breath to Zorndorf, which made the brute flush and stop watching Meredith.

Gareth checked his stopwatch. "Six shots per minute."

"Too damn fast."

"For my government's peace of mind, yes, especially when it's sending twelve pounds of high explosive at you."

"Its maximum range is actually six miles, not four," Meredith contributed under her breath.

How long would it take an army to march the same distance—two hours or so? Too far to just see it across a battlefield and grab it, should it become annoying. Oh hell.

The French observer was enjoying the crowd's acclaim, although he kept frowning at the complete artillery unit below. Washington had warned Brian they were secret guns, guarded by French police day and night, unavailable for sale even to France's allies. What was the grand duke leading up to?

"Gentlemen, the second half of this scenario will be conducted with the cannons emplaced inside the blockhouse," he announced in his most blandly imperious manner.

"What?" "Impossible!" "I must see the guns!" The observers erupted into a storm of protest, like children standing outside a candy store.

Meredith's mouth tightened but she remained silent.

Who among them would enjoy that sweet treat? The blockhouse was less than a mile away but only somebody inside it would know what was going on—like Sazonov. Damn, damn, damn.

"Today you will see what the Eisengau 155mm can do, gentlemen," Grand Duke Rudolph purred, gleefully holding all the cards.

"Ridiculous! Our view is completely blocked. We could only see your guns if we were on the lake," the German observer snarled.

"We can talk later if you wish to know more." The aristocratic jerk studied Brian, ignoring the shrill demands to immediately see his latest offering.

Brian tilted his head then rubbed his thumb and first two fingers together, using the traditional sign for money.

Grand Duke Rudolph smirked and twirled his mustache.

Oh hell, what wasn't for sale in this blasted country?

Meredith, Brian's heart answered.

"Gentlemen, earmuffs are available from the servants."

Meredith the unflappable was putting on a pair now?

"Why would we need them when the guns are hidden behind stone walls?" somebody complained.

No one from Eisengau answered him. Meredith gave a soft command, which sent Morro under the refreshment table built into the balcony, the sturdiest and quietest place nearby.

Brian acquired a pair for himself and offered another to Gareth. Cuba had taught him to take advantage of little things—like mosquito netting—if he wanted to live, not only the big, fancy ones.

A minute later, the grand duke fired his signal pistol again. Another wave of men roared out from behind his headquarters, charging at a new set of man-shaped targets in front of the second oak grove. They fired their rifles just as rapidly as the first group, the noise blurring into a distant staccato behind the earmuffs.

Gareth was counting down on his stopwatch, while Meredith edged away from the blockhouse. Brian caught and held her hand and she flashed a tight smile at him.

KERBOOM!!!

The sound blasted Brian in the face and roared upward through his bones from the ground, like a giant fist slamming into him. Wineglasses rattled and fell over. Somebody shouted in surprise.

Meredith staggered and Brian quickly wrapped his arms around her. Dammit, he'd learned how to cope with shockwaves in silver mines when he was a kid. He could protect her.

Far across the valley, the top of a giant oak slowly toppled and fell. It was a damn sight bigger than anything the French 75 had managed to destroy. A muscle in Brian's cheek jerked.

KERBOOM!!! The German observer grabbed for the railing, almost knocking down the junior delegate from France. The observers clapped their hands over their ears, or grabbed something, anything, for support. Somebody was yelling in delight.

The battery fired its second enormous volley. An ancient oak tree lost half of its side and slowly started to fall. The third volley toppled another oak tree and tore open the ground.

KERBOOM!!! KERBOOM!!! KERBOOM!!!

Brian's body rattled against his bones. The acrid scent washed over him, drenching his eyes and his throat like a victory tide.

He could have won Cuba in an hour with these. *Hip, hip, hurrah!*

The infantrymen's celebration was more emphatic this time, held at the edge of the giant crater where the oak grove had once existed. All that remained of them was kindling. The soldiers' leader clambered down into the pit and started to hunt for a branch larger than his rifle.

Jesus, Mary, and Joseph, if Sazonov had guns like that, what couldn't he conquer? Alaska would be a cakewalk.

Chapter Nine

The road back to Schloss Belvedere, the ducal palace, was full of open carriages and chattering foreigners.

Meredith leaned her head back against Brian's shoulder, grateful beyond words her lover had demanded a phaeton and chosen to drive it himself. She needed his warmth, the stretch and sweep of his muscles, his scent to overcome her usual melancholy after a demonstration. Dear God, to lose all those trees at once had made her stomach churn.

Morro drowsed at their feet, the cannonades' racket having left him exhausted enough to accept a rare carriage ride.

Even from its relative privacy at the back of the pack, she could hear the others' noisy plotting to gain an audience with Grand Duke Rudolph. The river frothing beside the road couldn't completely drown them out.

"Just pay him in cash, you fools," she muttered.

"What do you mean?" Brian asked.

She flushed slightly at being overheard but answered him honestly. "Our neighbors up ahead should know by now that all Grand Duke Rudolph cares about are power and money. They can't give him more power within Eisengau but they can give him—"

"Cash."

"Precisely." She couldn't help sitting up, alert and eager to talk to somebody who actually listened to her answers.

"Is that last gun—the Eisengau 155—the one Sazonov wants?" Brian asked quietly, his fingers long and competent on the reins.

"Yes, of course."

And America would want it, too. Even Brian's powerful father might pull strings on his country's behalf.

They crossed another bridge across the river, the horses' hooves striking dully instead of ringing sharply. The waters had risen so high recently they'd eliminated much of the usual airspace under the arch, cutting back any musical resonance.

Brian's jaw was set, turning his usually charming expression into the deadly warrior she'd glimpsed at the beer house. "How big are the shells for the 155?"

She hesitated, glancing uneasily at the carriages ahead of them. Foreign observers had to pay well for such information on each Eisengau weapon they were interested in and Grand Duke Rudolph had mentioned none of it yet.

But she'd promised to answer all his questions. Grand Duke Rudolph would surely be paid by everyone else to provide full details before day's end.

Brian promptly slowed the horses, opening up the distance between them and the others.

"Ninety-five pounds to the French 75's twelve pounds." She kept her voice very low and didn't look at the far mountains, where scudding winds hurled black clouds against the peaks.

Brian whistled softly. "One of those could destroy a small house. Or a lot of men, if you loaded it with shrapnel."

"It was test fired with shrapnel at sausages. The pictures are very impressive. And disgusting." Dear God, how she'd hated filing the test results, especially when Zorndorf was complaining about how much he'd have preferred to use live pigs.

"I'll bet," Brian muttered.

Her head whipped around and she stared at him. Warmth

touched her heart and she tentatively slipped her fingers into his coat pocket.

Clouds could build up without sending rain. Or instead deliver only a few drops that would quickly soak into the ground.

Don't think about that. It was easier to talk about man-made objects causing destruction.

"It can command a very large amount of territory, too, because of its unusual ability to lift and swivel the gun barrel. Altogether more than eighty square miles per gun."

"Jesus." He crossed himself. "And their maximum range is?"

"Ten miles." She glanced at him, gauging the impact.

"A half day's march for an army?" A muscle jerked in his cheek. "Hell, it almost makes every other weapon, even rifles, obsolete. It's a goddamn super-weapon and everyone will have to own one."

"Starting with Sazonov and Russia's plans for Alaska." And Canada.

"Yes, starting with that son of a bitch, pardon my language."

She forgave him easily. May she never again witness the pure hunger on Sazonov's face when he'd held that rifle—and Brian was helpless, his own gun jammed. Brian probably hadn't noticed because he was working too hard to extricate himself. But Meredith could still see every detail of Sazonov's expression—the glittering eyes, the curling lip, the tightness of his fingers, the slow turn toward Brian—only to stop when the grand duke shouted a warning.

She'd been so cold, she was shaking so hard she couldn't form words.

That loss of attention to the match was why Sazonov hadn't won by more shots.

The road whipped around a corner, exposing the steep slope down to the lake and the mountains beyond.

"It's also why the workers' party needs the plans," she added, seeing spirals of smoke rise from the blockhouse to join the low-hanging clouds. Inside it, men risked losing their hands—and their livelihoods—just to keep the trains running quickly to suit the grand duke's convenience. "Every country will crawl to Eisengau. Those plans are the only lever which could make him change their lives for the better."

Brian pulled the horses to an abrupt stop and turned to face her. "Do you honestly think that strategy will work?" he demanded.

"He paid a thousand marks for a mountain gun's model and this is far more important."

"He doesn't strike me as somebody who'd pay blackmail."

"Brian, we have to try and this is the only lever we have. I've gone to the foundry every week to watch these guns being made for the past three years. Do you know how many men I've seen burned to death?"

"Sweet Jesus, Meredith, how could they make you go through that?" A ferocious light appeared in his eyes and he covered her hands with one of his. She leaned toward him, hopeful that somebody finally understood the horrors that drove her. Then he spoke again.

"But every foundry has its dangers, Meredith."

She could have screamed. Was his family that callous?

Her struggle to speak calmly to the one man who at least conversed with her blinded her to the lightning flashing across the valley. "Have you seen men killed simply because they were exhausted from working seven days a week, every week?"

"No, but—"

She'd seen that overly patient look before on people's faces just before they walked away from Eisengau's workers. At least he was still talking to her, however patronizingly.

"Or worse, left crippled and begging in the streets from injuries which could have been mended if they'd been seen by a doctor."

"Meredith, you don't have to solve everyone else's problems."

"But I have to do everything I can." She glared back at him, equally adamant.

CRACK! Thunder boomed overhead, underlining their impasse. The horses reared, bugled in alarm, and bolted.

Storm? Thunderstorm—and Brian hadn't been watching his team? Meredith grabbed for the front rail, her heart pounding in her ears. If Brian lost control, they could overturn. Or roll down the mountainside. Or, worst of all, go into the river.

More thunder rumbled across the skies, even closer this time. It was raining, too.

Odd: Her knuckles were white and she was leaning against Brian, his big body warm and solid against her. They must be skidding through a downhill turn.

BOOM! The heavens slammed open overhead, hurling sizzling green light onto the road ahead.

Morro yelped and his claws scrabbled.

Must save Morro. Must. Save. Morro.

She leaned down and grabbed his collar, never leaving the comfort of Brian's side. Morro steadied and settled, nestled between two pairs of human boots.

Lightning cracked again, followed by thunder roaring like the ancient gods' artillery.

Her lungs were too tight and her pulse was racing. What had her old nanny taught her about breathing during a storm?

Brian braced his feet against the dash and pulled back hard, forcing the horses to slow down.

BOOM!

The team tried to leap forward again.

They had to get off the mountain and under cover, not just for her sake but for the horses and Morro. And Brian.

Where were they? She pushed her hat's feathers' sodden wreckage out of her eyes. Narrow bridge next to beech trees, steep drop beside waterfall—*for God's sake, don't look at that*—pasture on left side.

The thunder and lightning were almost happening together, sending the horses into a frenzy.

She craned her neck, looking for that low stone wall. "There, Brian! At the end of the wall, turn right."

She sensed, more than saw him nod. Thank God he didn't need to question her. There wasn't time for such frivolity.

He brought the frantic team hard around the stone wall's edge—and under a low-hanging roof, sheltered from the storm on three sides by more stone walls. Moments later, the horses were barely fretting, soothed by the dim light and quiet in their new enclosure.

Meredith reminded herself yet again that modern women didn't die in mountain storms and took her face out of her hands.

"How are you?" His voice was too careful. Could she fob him off with a social lie? Did he deserve that? No.

"I'm fine now." She hesitated, considering how much to admit. Could she stand to have him constantly watching her? They'd be sharing a bedroom once they returned to the palace. "My father died in a mountain thunderstorm, back in Scotland. Storms like this remind me."

She kept her head down, not looking at him.

He looped the reins over the rail, steadying the horses, and took her into his arms. "My poor darling, you must have been with him, to let another storm frighten you."

"Yes." She sniffled and leaned her head against his shoulder.

"But I'm sure he was a strong man, who'd be very proud of how you conquered your fear and found shelter for us today."

Father, strong? Oh yes, but what good had that done her? Images flickered behind her eyes. Father, who'd chosen the name for his first-born and hadn't changed his mind, despite the irritating arrival of a daughter. Father, pouring himself another neat whisky and ignoring her carefully practiced recital of a new foreign language. Father, always willing to depart early on a journey and leave her to follow with Nanny.

"Yes, quite." She disengaged herself and sat up, away from Brian's all-too-enticing body. She couldn't let herself give in. She'd been hurt once before in a storm like this. Could she survive another such disaster?

"Hell, I'm sorry, Meredith, if I raked old memories up."

"Brian . . ." She almost laughed. But she couldn't let him feel guilty. "Sometimes strong isn't comforting."

"What do you mean? Your father should be your biggest comfort and supporter, until you're married."

She could have laughed in his face. "Sometimes it simply implies selfish, especially when the world conspires to help."

Rain was drumming on the heavy wooden roof overhead, a reassuring sound now that she couldn't see water rising in the rivers and waterfalls. A few high, grilled windows pierced the stone walls. The floors were also stone, set with drains. It was a man-made cave but it was still almost a prison.

Brian's fingers entwined with hers. He waited but didn't demand any answers to his unspoken bafflement.

"We were on holiday in the Scottish Highlands when Father and I went hiking alone."

Brian opened his mouth, clearly outraged. She simply raised an eyebrow and waited for him to recollect her mother's highly citified ambitions.

"It was a wet year and the rivers were very full, in scenery much like this. We had a late start but managed to reach a famous overlook, high in the crags." She still loathed standing on cliffs, where one could see exactly how long falling to one's death would take.

She squeezed Brian's fingers, taking comfort from his strength, and he kissed her hands.

"The storm started on your way back down." Brian's voice was very tight. Morro pressed closer to her, whining in his throat. He always knew when she had nightmares.

"Yes." Maybe one day she'd sound relaxed, rather than

choked up. But not yet. "Soon we couldn't see more than a couple of steps away. Father shoved me under a ledge and told me to wait there, he'd bring back help."

She closed her eyes. Don't think about how dark it had been, the rivulets pouring in to become waterfalls, the chunks of rock falling down . . . He must have been doing his best.

"And then?" Brian's voice was soft as an owl's wing.

"I waited. And waited. The rain stopped after dark but the search party didn't find me until almost dawn. Apparently we'd wandered off the main path." She shrugged, trying yet again to convince herself help had come as soon as possible.

"What about your father?" She glanced up at her lover, startled at his tone. When Mother told this story, most people were very worried solely about her father's survival and stopped thinking about her, the little child who'd been lost. But Brian seemed almost angry, his brows drawn together as if he were second-guessing that night's events.

Maybe saying this out loud would help erase the agony. Besides, the tale wasn't a secret in Eisengau, thanks to the Judge's frequent claims of superiority over his wife's first husband. "They found him at midnight dead in a ditch, reeking of whisky."

"Maybe he was lost or heading for the first place he knew he could find people." The grooves by Brian's mouth deepened.

"He'd probably been drinking from the flask in his pocket, passed out, fell in, and drowned." He'd needed the whisky more than he needed to stay sober to find help to save her.

"Hell no!" Brian rubbed her hands against his cheek, his expression appalled. "It was only a brief lapse."

Dear God, how she envied his certainty because she couldn't share it.

"You may be right. But I saw hundreds of occasions where my father enjoyed the bottle more than my company or my mother's. And during the hours I spent among those rocks, my heart learned to believe that my father didn't care whether I lived or died."

"Meredith, please believe that not every father would do that. Mine would give his life to protect his children." Outrage blazed from his cobalt eyes, but she couldn't allow herself to lean on it, especially when he mentioned his sire.

"I'm glad for you." She shook her head at him. "You're twice lucky: You're a man and the laws are on your side. It's why I won't marry. If I can't trust my father, why would I give my life to another man who can do anything to me he wants to, under the law?"

His jaw dropped opened before he recovered himself.

"Meredith, not every man is like that. You must start believing in some men. Or come to America where the laws protect women."

She raised an eyebrow. Laws? What good were they when enforced by men like her stepfather? But maybe America might be different. "Equally? Including voting rights?"

"Well, no," he admitted. "But you could work to change that. It'd still be better than here."

He was undoubtedly correct—and physically tempting. She dared to smooth the frustrated lines in his cheek. "You're still trying to convince me to quit the workers' party. But I won't."

"Truce? At least for now?"

"Truce," she agreed. Why did he have to be so easy to talk to? Why couldn't he have been somebody who'd dismiss her thoughts—and let her walk away from him, too? A carnal night or two, not this yearning to hold hands and talk.

He caught her fingers and kissed them quickly.

She smiled at him but freed herself before she could be trapped by his skills and jumped down from the phaeton to stretch her legs.

"Where are we?" he asked. "There's actually a good deal of room here."

"We're above the private gallery connecting the railroad blockhouse and the big guns' emplacement. This was originally a snow shed but it was modified to hold private vehicles."

"That's why it's large enough to turn around in," he commented, suiting the action to the words.

She agreed silently, admiring his skill at the tricky art, especially in such tight confines. And his hands . . .

He loosely tied off the horses' reins and came to join her, looking around curiously. A small door in the far corner caught his attention. "That's definitely not the main entrance to the artillery emplacement."

The pure disgust in his voice sent giggles racing through her lungs and throat. She choked and yielded to them, glad to laugh, however near to hysteria.

"That was a very good joke, especially since I don't even know what it was. Care to share it?" He propped his hand on his hip and pretended to glare at her.

"Almost all the supplies travel using the railroad, and the railroad blockhouse. The troops come straight from headquarters and go directly to the emplacement itself."

"So this door is only for people."

"It was built for Grand Duke Rudolph but Zorndorf also uses it occasionally. There's an inspection port to the magazine behind it."

"Zorndorf doesn't use it often, I'll wager."

"No. Very important guests do, too, occasionally. It must be locked now, since there are no sentries posted."

Brian strolled a little farther forward, covering ground in a big cat's graceful prowl rather than a cavalryman's bow-legged strut. Her mouth went a little dry.

"What's that bit of white by the door?"

"A dropped handkerchief? A love letter for the chef?" She stayed by the main entrance, enjoying the open air. She couldn't see the river or any waterfalls from here, even if there was more rain than the watercourses could easily handle.

"A packet—or, actually two cigars wrapped in a piece of paper."

"Somebody will be very unhappy to miss their nighttime smoke."

"Mmhmm. Good cigars, too."

She chuckled at his purring anticipation.

"Wait, the paper has writing on it."

"On the wrapping paper, not the cigar itself?" She craned her neck, totally forgetting the storm for once.

"Yes. Two styles of text alternate. One line in the Latin alphabet and the other in a foreign language."

"What does it say?"

"The Latin text is random characters."

"Let me see it, please." The modern languages she'd been studying ought to be good for something.

He handed it over to her without a word and she held it up to the graying light.

"The foreign text is in Cyrillic, the Russian alphabet." Her skin was crawling.

Brian was as silent as a cat studying a mouse hole, ready to pounce at any second.

"It's not very grammatical," she complained, aware she was avoiding bad news. She cleared her throat and began, a block of ice expanding in her stomach. "Additional funds received today. Will use as instructed to buy cannons in time to meet General Staff deadline. Will acquire plans by any means. Sazonov."

Brian's mouth was a tight, hard line.

"Why is the Latin text such gobbledygook?" she whispered, afraid of the answer.

"It must be a coder's worksheet. First he writes down in plain language what he wants to say, which he transfers into the code. After that, he fair copies the coded version onto a telegraph blank."

"This is genuine?" Would that it wasn't.

"I'd say so. Can you recognize his handwriting?"

"I've only seen him write in French and English. But yes, I believe so." The scum truly did intend to capture Alaska with Canada's goldfields just beyond. How dare he take on the British Empire! "How can we stop him?"

"I'll cable Washington and hope they listen to me. And I'll ask Blackwell to do what he can in London, of course."

"Why wouldn't Washington listen?" She bristled immediately. "You're a decorated war hero and an officer!"

"I'm a self-made millionaire, who comes from an even richer family. I was reactivated for this mission."

Drat, he was being modest. He truly did come from a dynasty, wealthy and powerful enough to force his country to listen to it. What could they do to her if she disagreed? But that wasn't today's problem; Alaska was.

They had to stop Sazonov.

"I was recommended for this job by Colonel Teddy Roosevelt, who's a notorious warmonger and the current vice-presidential candidate. I have no official claim on Washington to do anything."

"But you did fight during the last war." She didn't make it a question.

"I finished as a major in the First Volunteer Cavalry, better known as the Rough Riders. A very young major."

"A very successful one," she retorted, having seen too many strutting old fools. "You'll succeed."

"If it doesn't work, we'll have to stop him here." His eyes were the same cold blue they'd been at the beer house, compelling her to listen and obey.

She stiffened her spine and looked him in the eye, wary of what came next. "You should be able to buy the guns instead of Sazonov, since you're so rich."

He bit off a half-formed curse and she kept her head high, waiting. She didn't know what he wanted yet but she wouldn't do it, simply because he said so.

"I can pay cash and I can purchase without permission

from my superiors, unlike anyone else here. But I can be out-bid if Grand Duke Rudolph starts accepting other types of payments."

"If he extends credit?"

"Or accepts some of the legendary Russian real estate in France, like those palaces in Paris and on the Riviera. Or equal access to their spies' secret reports. Or . . ."

"Surely they wouldn't give him that!" Those bribes would turn anyone's head, especially the grand duke's. She clawed for common sense as a counterweight.

"Probably not." Brian shrugged. "But they wouldn't have to actually deliver it, just convince him they meant to for long enough to get those big cannons out of Eisengau. And then?"

"Goodbye, Alaska and the Klondike." She sagged back against the stone wall, barely noticing the water rippling through the stone courses only inches away. "So we stop Sazonov from taking the guns, by either buying them or destroying them."

"And the plans."

"No!" Her eyes flashed to him. "The plans stay here, to help the workers."

"That won't work. The grand duke will simply make more cannons for Sazonov."

"Giving you extra time to convince Washington—and London—to fortify Alaska." She lifted an eyebrow at her lover. "I'm sure you can manage it."

"You're not yielding." He glared at her.

"Neither are you," she retorted. Why did this argument feel like tearing her heart out? "But I'm the only one who can steal the plans for you or Sazonov. You have to cut a deal with *me*."

He almost audibly gnashed his teeth and she could have purred. Any other man of her acquaintance would have hit her by now, instead of using conversation to convince her. Nor had he thrown their bargain into her face, which tied her to his bed.

Her throat was ridiculously tight and a little hoarse, as if she was about to cry.

"Mexican standoff?" she offered instead. "I can't leave town without you and you need me to get the plans."

"Mexican standoff, darling." An edged smile flashed across his face, full of anticipation for the fight ahead.

She managed a smile, hoping she'd win for the workers' sake. Or at least survive.

Chapter Ten

"What do you want to do after dinner tonight?" Brian asked late that afternoon in their room, manfully keeping his eyes on Meredith's face and not her décolletage. He'd do whatever it took to gain her cooperation and few women enjoyed being blatantly ogled, no matter how low their neckline. Or how beautiful their body.

She carelessly slung the velvet scarf over her shoulder, removing some of his distractions. Had he ever met a woman who cared less about her appearance, so long as she was tidy?

"Whatever you think best," she replied, idly turning over the paste trifles in her jewelry drawer. She'd look far better in real diamonds or rubies than those fakes.

"I heard there's a secret masquerade after midnight tonight. Did you want to attend?" She looked up at him inquiringly, all wide-eyed innocence.

He choked and coughed. She ran to fetch him a glass of water, which he accepted gratefully.

"Well?" she demanded, as soon as he could speak.

He frowned at her. "It's very scandalous."

"Zorndorf definitely wouldn't approve? Oh, we must go!"

"No!" He'd done many reckless things in his life but he'd never taken a good girl, like Meredith, to a party like that one.

"Explain to me why not." She folded her arms across her

chest, plumping up her bosom—and making his mouth go dry—and tapped her foot.

He closed his eyes briefly and prayed for continued self-control. "The men will be encouraged to wear dresses, and the women to wear trousers."

"Men in skirts?" Her voice cracked. "Impossible."

"Surprisingly common."

"I know the grand duke wears a corset—but dresses?" She snatched up his hands. "It can't be true."

"I've been to such parties before, Meredith."

"Not in a dress."

Her utter certainty made him grin. "Well, no."

"Of course not, you'd never squeeze into one."

"Sweetheart, a good *modiste* can work wonders," he drawled and began to kiss her fingers, one by one.

"Your shoulders are too broad." She trembled, watching his mouth.

"Is that a complaint?"

"Not for myself. But dressmakers might whine about having to drape silk over a stout paunch."

"Or consider it a challenge to their skill." He turned her hand over and started to tease the blue veins on the inside of her wrist.

She shuddered. "Perhaps," she whispered, her eyes drifting shut. "Are we going down for dinner?"

"Are you hungry?" He nibbled gently on her other thumb and she gasped, making his blood leap.

"Not after the enormous tea when we came back from the demonstration."

"Good, we're free to enjoy ourselves." Would that all duty was so pleasant and took him into such delightful company.

"You arrogant brute, that's not what I said."

He chuckled softly at her halfhearted protest and kissed the corner of her mouth. She moaned something, her lips sighing open. He slid his tongue over her lips, teasing her. She followed him blindly and caught his head between her hands, drawing him into a heated kiss.

He groaned, his chest tight, his blood running far too fast for this early in an encounter. He liked women, he loved sex, he'd been enjoying it with them for years. He knew how to do this—and walk away without a backward glance, leaving his partner smiling.

But accomplishing that demanded self-control and a certain deliberation. Not rushing to kiss or touch, not pulse pounding or lungs heaving.

He pulled away, fire darting over his skin wherever Meredith caressed him. She sighed again and reached for him. His lungs seized and his cock promptly lunged toward her.

Slow things down, Brian, slow them down.

He kissed her throat, finding the delectable pulse point under her ear. She trembled and sobbed his name, arching into his arms. He crooned to her and caressed it with his tongue, tasting her, enjoying the delicate hollows in her skin—and how she bucked against him, clutching his shoulder. How his own body tightened in rhythm with hers, heat sinking into his blood.

How could such a simple caress, which he'd performed so many times before, make him so breathless now?

He made love to her throat's strong tendons, grateful she wasn't wearing a high-necked style or one of the fashionable jeweled dog collars. Although placing a collar on a woman to tell other men to stay away was oddly attractive for the first time in his life.

She arched over his arm, sobbing his name. Thank God he hadn't put on his coat yet. Her fingers kneaded his shoulders as shamelessly as any cat, eager for more. His own hands were trembling a little and his cock had surged hot and full.

He moved lower still to find her breasts' creamy mounds. Too impatient for pretty words or smooth techniques, he quickly slipped them each out of their very revealing prison and paused to admire them.

"Brian!"

He ignored her protest, since her skin was heating under his hands.

Perfection, absolute perfection. Just the right amount for filling his mouth and driving his woman insane with lust. Any more might have been a distraction, however enjoyable.

He suited the action to the thought and swirled his tongue over one pale pink nipple.

"Dear heavens, Brian . . ." she gasped.

His blood began to run faster still.

He licked, he suckled, he nibbled delicately, he tugged, he drummed, he enjoyed himself—by all the saints, oh how he enjoyed himself. He slid her evening gown's straps off her shoulders, baring her to the waist except for her corset.

And Meredith writhed under him, clutching him and sobbing his name, caressing him and pulling his shirt open to find more of him. Until somehow his skin was raging hot and crackling tight, as if he'd burst should her nails rake his chest.

He unfastened her skirt without ripping anything, ironically grateful at least some of his experience was proving useful, and dropped it on the floor. He unbuttoned her petticoats and threw the frothy nonsense onto the chair with even less ceremony.

Now he could fondle more of her beautiful, strong legs, which he hadn't seen last night. She was panting, her eyes enormous with lust, her hips circling restlessly on the bed.

He ran his hand up her thigh and found cream—but wasn't overwhelmed by the scent of sex. She hadn't climaxed yet.

He caught her lambent gaze and slipped his fingers inside her silken drawers' slit, gathering her cream. Her eyes widened in shock and she instinctively rocked into his palm, seeking fulfillment, offering him everything.

He fought for control, bitterly glad of his fly's vicious bite into his cock.

"More, Brian, please."

He beckoned to her, drawing his thumb and forefinger through her intimate folds and pressing on her pearl.

"Brian!" She climaxed, drawing his fingertips into her, and she arched off the bed, her eyes wild with joy.

The absolute rapture in her eyes captured him—and ripped him into his own orgasm. His cock jerked, jetting his come into his trousers as if he were a twelve-year-old boy again, enjoying every taste of delight.

His heart spun like a wheel, sending him into a world where there were no cannons, nothing but him and Meredith and pure pleasure.

More than a week later, Morro had his nose down to the ground, stalking a rabbit who'd dived into a long border of vibrant summer flowers. Brian and Captain Blackwell were talking in hushed tones back at the stables by their horses, striving to look casual.

Meredith strolled along the path from the stables to the palace, twirling her parasol over her shoulder. She silently counted the number of revolutions, her private timekeeping method. He'd been given free run of the gardens so long as she chaperoned him and he didn't dig for too long.

Dear heavens, how Morro enjoyed it here at Schloss Belvedere, despite all the dangerous, underhanded games which kept him alert and close to her whenever they went out.

A shadow sliced the stonework ahead of her. "Miss Duncan." The interloper bowed.

She promptly lowered her parasol onto the pavement, placing it in the guard position toward him. "Count Sazonov."

"May I have a word with you?"

"It seems you're already taking it." There was nobody around to stop him, drat it. She looked down her nose at him, grateful for the courage granted by an excellent wardrobe.

"I bring a message for you from your friend—and mine— Franz Schnabel."

"Yes?"

Oh dear God, what now? She kept her expression immobile, well trained by long years in the Judge's house.

"He wishes to know when you will deliver the plans for the cannon so he can start the revolution." Sazonov's voice was silky soft and more deadly than arsenic.

Don't admit it's already gone, Meredith.

"Do you think I'd tell you?" She pounded the parasol on the ground. Morro looked up and started running.

"What choice do you have?"

"You will betray the workers' party in an instant, the same way you tried to kidnap me at the university so I'd steal the plans for Russia. Not for the party." She spat, wishing she could wring his lying throat. "You've flirted with me, betraying promises to Liesel."

"Misunderstandings only. She trusts me."

And Brian Donovan treats his paramour far better than you ever did, you treacherous fiend.

"Do you think Schnabel believes that? I've already given him money and supplies."

"Small change, coming from you." Morro arrived beside her, teeth bared and fur bristling.

Sazonov glared at the dog then continued to argue, a little wary but undeterred. "But more than anybody else has given him. More than the letter of support from Germany or the solidarity proclamation from France."

"He's not a fool." She tried to forget all the times he'd been more thinker than doer.

"I've given him reality—but you disappeared, only to reappear at the grand duke's palace, living in luxury. Who do you think he'll trust?"

She'd have to talk to him and the rest of the council as soon as possible. They needed to know how quickly Sazonov would betray anyone and anything to get those plans. "No matter what, I still won't give you the plans."

"You can make all of us happy." Sazonov started to sidle closer.

Morro growled, deep and raw, and braced his forequarters to charge. What if Sazonov was carrying a pistol?

Oh, if only Brian was here to stand by her.

Sazonov froze, clearly recognizing an imminent attack's warning.

"Speak your piece from where you are, no closer," Meredith ordered, making no move to curb her watchdog.

"If you gave them the true plans and created a set for me, everyone would be happy."

Her blood ran colder than any time before during this appalling conversation. "Create?" She managed to raise an eyebrow.

"Zorndorf says you can copy blueprints, as well as recreate them from memory."

Damn him! What else had the old goat said when he'd bragged about his staff? She waited, her mouth and throat an icy bog.

"Give the originals to Schnabel and another set to me. He can start his revolution, while Russia makes all the cannons we need."

Feet were running toward them from the stables. Dear God, let it be Brian.

"Certainly not. Schnabel's set is useful only if it's unique." Please, let him not see that she was bluffing.

"Unique? Of course, you're unique, darling," Brian drawled and slipped his arm possessively around her waist. "Count." An ice storm would have been warmer than his voice.

Blackwood took up his stance on Meredith's other side and Morro glared from beside her parasol.

"Donovan." Sazonov tilted his head, his fists clenching and unclenching. He hissed in a breath before recovering himself. "Shall I convey your compliments to our mutual friends, Miss Duncan?"

Brian's puzzlement was clear but he said nothing. She'd have to deal with it later, just as she'd have to deal with Franz and the rest of the council.

And think of something to do with the blueprints.

"Please do, Count. Good day."

Sazonov stalked off, barely bothering to favor Brian and Blackwell with a curt nod.

Blackwell glanced at them. "I believe I should stretch my legs in that direction, don't you? Wouldn't do to let him circle back. Until dinner, dear lady."

He departed, his long legs eating up ground remarkably fast.

Brian studied Meredith, wondering whether he should take her back to their suite immediately to soothe her after what had obviously been a nasty scene. She'd refused to discuss it, so it was probably related to her fellow revolutionaries, the only subject which silenced her quick tongue.

After the past days, he flattered himself he knew her pretty well—and he liked almost everything he saw.

Their Mexican standoff hadn't changed. Nor had he ever succeeded in twisting her to do his will through sex. His body was so interested in enjoying her, that he'd mostly given up trying to manage her in the bedroom.

Life could almost be called good. Almost.

"What did the cable from Washington say?" she asked. Trust Meredith to seek a distraction by heading for the intellectual.

Yes, that was a large portion of the *almost*.

"There's nothing in any reports from St. Petersburg to indicate an attack on Alaska."

She swung around to stare at him. Her hair was drifting deliciously over her temples, begging to be taken down further for a tumble among the sheets. "Do they expect an announcement in the newspapers?"

"Probably." Morro sat down to scratch.

"Arrogant old fools."

"It gets worse." He glanced around for an audience, found none, but still headed for a side path.

"How bad?" How could anybody this beautiful be so good at talking business—and playing in the bedroom? She'd be perfect for marriage. He grinned privately.

"We're instructed to let them handle any repercussions from the *so-called* cable."

"They don't believe it exists." She swung her parasol over her shoulder and spun it.

"London has it and they believe it's real. But they too ordered us to sit tight."

She paused, her parasol's silly ribbons fluttering around her beautiful face. "Is the British Empire that afraid to anger Eisengau?"

"London's bought cannons from the grand dukes for years," he reminded her. They undoubtedly hope for more."

"We're running out of time here. You haven't been able to buy the four examples of the new gun." She twisted the thin wand with unnecessary violence, her voice very tightly controlled.

"Neither has anybody else."

"You're very calm."

"The old fox is gathering bids, playing us off against each other—and the clock."

"Summer maneuvers end in four days."

"Exactly. That's when he'll probably gather the top two, maybe three, bidders together and try to wring us dry."

"Who do you think will make the final round?"

She was almost quivering, the same as if they were locked in each other's arms. He'd never met a woman before for whom an intellectual discussion was as exciting as making love.

"Sazonov, of course. He's spending far too much time whispering in Grand Duke Rudolph's ear. And me, I think."

"But you're not sure."

"No, dammit."

She grimaced and tapped her parasol briefly on the pavement. "Who else?"

"Everyone else is pretty much equal."

She shot him a speaking look. Her lithe body was poised against the parasol, ready for long bouts of arguments—or tumbling across the sheets. She'd be just as feisty about protecting her own children.

"God's own truth, Meredith. That gun would make any country in Europe either a conqueror or impregnable or both. They might not pay in cash but they'll offer him something just as attractive."

"We have to stop it somehow."

"We will." He'd already figured out how.

"You're too confident." She glared at him. "Those guns are locked up in a stone fortress, high atop a granite cliff, and guarded by some of the world's best troops. There are only three doors in, one of which is kept locked at all times. And—"

"Hush." He patted her elbow. "You're working up your color before dinner and people will talk."

"Gossip? I want them to do that!" She almost shrieked.

He didn't. He wanted the world to see her on his arm and envy him. While he didn't think she was the type of woman who'd only have her name in the newspaper at her birth, marriage, and death, he hated hearing the trollops here whisper about her.

Dammit, he wanted to take her to church with his parents. He wanted to see her swell with his babies and bounce them on his knee. And laugh to see his father carrying his grandchildren on his shoulders or teaching them to ride. Plus, there'd be the pure joy of making those little darlings with Meredith. Oh yes.

He'd always planned to marry first and provide the first grandchild to his parents, thus replacing the family his father had lost. It would also prove to big brother Neil that yet another responsibility wasn't a burden when performed with somebody you trusted.

They'd have a great marriage, just as soon as she agreed.

"Will you believe me if I promise to make sure Sazonov won't lay his hands on the guns?" he asked cautiously, bringing his mind back to their original quarrel.

"How can you guarantee that?" Lord, how he needed to kiss away the frown from between her brows. He wanted to see her happy.

"I'm here and I know Sazonov, the guns, and the terrain. Nobody else really has a chance. He means to conquer my country and I won't let him."

His tone had deepened into a growl, despite his attempts to keep it civilized enough for a lady's boudoir.

Her eyes widened and she nodded after a moment. "God help you."

He crossed himself automatically and went on. "Once matters start changing, we'll have to get you out of Eisengau quickly."

"Why? My parents should forgive me for breaking the betrothal to Zorndorf, since they know what he's like." Her voice broke briefly. "If they don't, then I'll go to Edinburgh."

She turned for the stairs to their suite, clearly ending the conversation.

Edinburgh? Like hell! He'd wrestle this out here and now, even if he'd planned to wait until they'd left Eisengau.

"Marry me and come back to California with me."

"Marriage?" She spun to face him. Her gray eyes, once so vibrant, were now narrow and cold. "Marriage? Why?"

His skin prickled. But he'd already said the big word. Stopping now would mean never bringing it up again.

"I'd like to introduce you to my parents and brothers, to start with." Buy a house close to his family. Thank God she was Catholic, not that he'd have cared if she was a Protestant. Definitely dress her in a Paris wardrobe. Oh, and introduce her to Teddy so she could tell him everything about the gun.

"Your parents? Do you mean your father, the patriarch? Never." She huffed and turned on her heel.

"Meredith, what's wrong?" He caught her by the shoulders and turned her.

"What will your father want from me for his dynasty?"

"What do you mean?" Brian frowned, caught totally off-guard.

"Will he want me to draw the big cannon's plans from memory so America can build one?" She was standing perfectly still yet she couldn't have been farther away.

"Can you truly do that?" Sweet Jesus, if she could, Eisengau wouldn't have such an infernal monopoly.

"You see, all you care about are the weapons!" Tears sparkled on her eyelashes. "You're just like every other man—you want me to live my life in your world, doing what you want, not what I asked for. Well, I won't do it."

Had he actually said that? Well, yes, he'd implied it. He tried a different approach. "Meredith, darling."

"Don't you darling me! We made a bargain and you can't change the terms in midstream."

"I asked you to marry me," he protested. "I'm trying to honor you."

"Take your so-called honors someplace else. I'm not clay to be molded, Brian. I won't turn meek and mild, I won't marry you, I won't go to America—and I won't draw the gun's plans for you."

"I'm trying to protect your reputation!"

"My reputation is already ruined, thank God—and maybe I'd like to grind it deeper into the mud." She poked her finger into his chest.

He reached for her. She flinched, almost flinging herself against the wall, so he tried to think of a bribe instead. "I could give you a superb library as a wedding present," he coaxed.

She shuddered. "If you think money makes you more acceptable, you have much to learn. The answer is still no."

"I'll keep asking you."

"You are certainly free to. I will maintain our original bargain but nothing more."

Hell, how was he supposed to enjoy a mistress who'd cold-shouldered him? Especially when he knew he'd missed something in their conversation—and he still needed to somehow destroy those damn guns and Sazonov.

Marlowe Donovan paced the Hotel Ritz's lobby, keeping a wary eye out for his twin brother, his father, and the hotel clerk, in more or less that order. Even though every palm tree in Paris seemed to have sprouted here, he'd have preferred rather more cover. The old man had an uncanny ability to know when his sons didn't want him around.

The hotel's maze of gilded walls, huge oil paintings, and overstuffed furniture under lofty ceilings, glittering mirrors, and enormous candelabra was superb camouflage. Had to be, given his London-made evening clothes. He wouldn't have worn them otherwise.

Hell, he wouldn't have come on this trip, unless he thought it would have helped big brother Neil, trapped in China with that crazy rebellion going on. The entire family had come to Europe to push for a united European army to rescue those trapped diplomats in Peking, where Neil had last been heard of.

Granted that, they'd settled back to wait for news of the army and Neil. And they prayed, long and often.

Even a blind man could tell Paris was the best place for Mother to be distracted from her worries. So here they were, in a two-year-old hotel, the fanciest place he'd ever seen.

But boring—until that very brief telegram this morning from Brian, the brother who'd taught him the better ways to cause mischief and get out of it.

He stepped behind another palm and eyed the front desk again. What was the telegrapher up to?

His oldest sixth sense warned him before the words came. "Any word yet?"

"No, no cable yet." He spun to meet his brother Spenser.

Blue eyes looked back at him and immediately relaxed, the

way they always did when the two of them got back together. Everything was always better side by side. Strangers couldn't tell them apart very well but family always did: Spenser had the quicker smile but Marlowe could move faster.

"Have you asked the desk clerk?" Spenser asked

"No. Where did you leave the parents?"

"A café in Montmartre. I told Father you wanted to show me a new brothel."

Marlowe stared at him.

"What's wrong?" Spenser frowned.

Marlowe grabbed his fifteen-minutes-younger brother by the shoulders and shoved him behind a potted palm.

"You dunce!" he hissed. "Do you honestly think Father will believe you walked out on a concert by two of the opera's top sopranos to visit some whores?"

Spenser knocked Marlowe's hands off. "Why not? I do it all the time."

"Yeah—but you don't interrupt good music for it."

"Oh hell." Spenser hesitated, their hands clenched in each other's starched shirtfronts.

"Cable for Mr. Donovan." The clerk's voice rang like a bell, the slip of neatly folded yellow paper enthroned on his silver tray.

"I'll take that, thank you," William Donovan announced and plucked the precious message off the tray. Hooded blue eyes considered his two youngest sons, while he fished for change in his pocket and used it to dismiss the previously bored clerk.

Marlowe pasted a polite smile on his face, reminding himself to breathe steadily. They hadn't done anything wrong— yet. They'd only done what big brother Brian had asked. Just because almost nobody pulled something over on Father was no reason to panic, right?

Then Mother glided up, looking remarkably young and pretty in her new Paris evening dress.

Shit. None of them had ever gotten away with anything around her, assuming she was well enough to observe them.

She rested her small hand on Father's arm. His attention immediately changed, shifting from his sons to his wife. "Shall we go up, sweetheart?"

"Who is the telegram from, dear?"

"I don't know; I wasn't expecting one." He glanced briefly at his sons before focusing again on his wife. Good; if Mother was around, his first concern was always for her comfort. "But I'm sure it's nothing for you to worry about."

Mother tilted her head, her tiny hat balanced like a bird on her curls. "How charming of the boys to present us with a surprise from Brian."

Marlowe choked.

"You cannot be serious, Viola."

She considered her sons then patted her husband's arm and freed herself. "We'll take coffee in our suite, while you read it to us, dear," she pronounced.

"Us?" Spenser questioned.

Marlowe didn't dare glance at his younger brother. How far was he willing to push the parents?

"All four of us, of course," she clarified. Her eyes swept over the two of them again, their deep blue almost impossible to read.

"Viola!" her husband protested.

"I believe all of the Donovan adults, William, should listen to whatever Brian has to say." She swept toward the elevator without a backward glance.

Mother was fighting for their right to hear Brian's cable? They'd never been regularly included in family councils before, Father being inclined to prioritize their college studies.

Marlowe took a few quick strides and offered her his arm. Spenser fell in behind, followed a moment later by their father. The senior Donovan's bristling silence filled the elevator cage, keeping the attendant's eyes darting nervously between them.

Their enormous suite overflowed with gilded chandeliers and mirrors, overstuffed furniture, and grandiose oil paintings. Marlowe eyed the fancy gimcracks and headed for the window seat, where he could pretend he was breathing fresh air. After they returned home, he hoped to spend a month in the Sierras, maybe two, and scrub Old World fussiness out of his skin.

Much more the diplomat, Spenser ordered coffee and tea, using the telephone.

"The message is from Brian," Father announced, pocket knife casually hanging between his fingers, "and it's coded."

He flipped the knife shut and shoved it into his pocket, its razor edge no longer needed to slice open the cable.

Coded? The hair on Marlowe's neck stood up. Neil and Brian had taught them the Donovan & Sons cipher. But he'd never personally used it on anything more important than lists of supplies.

"Decode it, will you please, Marlowe? I'd like to change my coat and I believe your mother may want to remove her hat." He couldn't interpret Father's expression.

His heart stuttered. "Of course, sir."

He was seated at the desk, still staring at the result, when they returned a few minutes later.

"Well?" Spenser demanded.

Marlowe cleared his throat.

MARLOWE AND SPENSER STOP MEET ME ST NICHOLAS PASS STATION EISENGAU TO-MORROW SIX PM STOP MUST DESTROY ARTILLERY BATTERY STOP VITAL TO AMERICA WE DO SO STOP BRIAN

"Blow up some cannons? Bully!"

Marlowe grinned wryly and continued to watch his parents. His twin usually kept his Donovan fighting streak much more deeply buried than the rest of the family.

"It's too far," Father announced abruptly. Why had Marlowe

never noticed the white at his temples? And he seemed to have aged another decade in the last minute. "I'll go instead."

"An artillery battery has four guns." Marlowe tried to be tactful. "Spenser and I can handle it, since Brian will need a lot of help."

"No, you're too young. This will take somebody with more experience."

"We'll all go." Mother set down her coffee cup.

"Viola!"

"Both of the boys must go and they'll need your aid, William. You have more experience with explosives than any of our sons except Neil." Her face twisted for a moment before she went on, "I'm coming, too."

"No, never, Viola." Deep grooves bracketed Father's mouth.

"You'll be working amid rocks and dynamite. I know more about that world than anyone here except you and we need everyone we can get. Plus, I can fit into places the three of you can barely even observe. If Brian is asking for help— saints preserve us, *Brian*—the need is dire."

"Don't ask me to risk your life, Viola." His harsh voice was barely a whisper.

Marlowe and Spenser glanced at each other, not daring to speak. Mother understood explosives? But Father didn't even like to let her go out into the rain. He'd never agree to have her come along.

"William." She took her husband's face in her hands. "My health has been excellent for years. You can't wrap me in cotton wool forever."

"I can't risk losing you, after we came so close to being parted." A muscle throbbed in his cheek.

"You never will, dearest." She kissed him gently on the corner of his mouth. He slid his arms around her and rested his chin on her hair, his eyes completely focused on her.

Marlowe's breath hung in his throat.

"Very well," Father muttered. "The entire Donovan clan will destroy those cannons. May God be with us."

Chapter Eleven

The once lasciviously cozy suite had become frigidly efficient. Meredith had even altered her wardrobe, shifting into neatly tailored suits, rather than the more daringly sensual silks he'd bought her. She'd just donned a wool version, which was so formidably conservative any passerby would take her for an upper servant such as a housekeeper. He couldn't even see her magnificent cairngorm brooch under it.

Morro whined softly from his bed by the balcony, clearly agreeing with Brian's opinion. Perhaps he could convince her to change clothes by persuading her to start a game.

Brian's cock, always half full near her, strengthened hopefully.

The rough-coated dog settled back down, paws thumping the silk cushion. He wouldn't openly argue with his goddess.

Brian cursed silently and started on his third silk tie of the evening. Living with an angry woman had to be easier than going to war, which he'd already successfully accomplished. Hell, last night he'd even slept on the floor.

"A note came for you earlier," he remarked, finally achieving a result he could live with.

"Really?" She'd probably have displayed more interest in a conversation about Chinese women's voting rights, or lack thereof.

"It's on the table."

She accepted the spectacularly respectable hat from her maid with a curt nod and picked up the innocuous envelope. Good; he'd managed to prick her attention about something.

The Frenchwoman slipped out the door silently, discreet as ever.

Meredith considered the plain white envelope for a long minute before opening it. An instant later, she snorted loudly and threw it into the fire.

"What is it?"

"Colonel Zorndorf offers me his hand. He's convinced that a course of hard work and religion, plus rigorous discipline, will bring me back to the path of righteousness."

"The self-righteous son of a bitch!" Brian's hands closed into fists. "What the hell was he thinking of?"

"Oh, he's very clear he wants me to become his secretary again." Bittersweet laughter touched her voice.

Brian lightly brushed her shoulders and she jerked away from him.

Red mist clouded his eyes, the hunger to destroy every man who'd ever harmed or failed her. "Meredith," he croaked.

Damn but he could do better than that. He'd always been able to have any woman he wanted. For that matter, any prize he'd ever hungered for.

He cleared his throat and tried again. "Meredith."

She straightened her shoulders, setting herself halfway across the room from him. She faced him with a false smile stretched across her lips.

His stomach spiraled into his boots, faster than rotten fish falling off a fork.

"I have to go to Altstadt tonight, at the other end of the lake, to visit a sick friend," she announced, her eyes meeting his briefly before sliding away.

She was running away from him? His pain was so deep he could only grunt acknowledgment, while his brain tried to work. He had no time to think about where she was going before she continued.

"I've arranged for a seat in the servants' launch, where Sazonov will never look for me. And I'll take the servants' stair down to the quay so he won't see me. Please convey my excuses to Grand Duke Rudolph for missing the gala aboard his yacht. You can say I'm inclined to seasickness, or whatever the freshwater equivalent is."

Brian cast her a disbelieving look. "I hadn't planned to take you. It will be little more than an orgy by sunrise when the yacht finally docks again."

"But everyone else is going." Comprehension flashed into her eyes and she blushed hotly.

"I would never take my fiancée to such a party." There, he'd mentioned her nightmare subject again.

Her expression, which had been almost friendly for a moment, turned shuttered again. "I will not marry you or anyone else, Brian. I would never sign my life over to a man's control."

"I swear our marriage wouldn't be that way, Meredith." Brian took a step toward her and she flung up her hand.

He stopped in his tracks, a knife twisting into his gut.

"Will you be my friend, Meredith?" he asked when he could trust his voice.

"Would you agree to marry another woman if I say yes? If that is all I let you become?"

He gaped at her. "Hell, no!" rocketed out of his mouth before he could stop himself, surprising him more than her.

"You're too damn stubborn for your own good," she remarked.

He shrugged, wondering when the devil she'd come to matter so much. Never before had there been a woman he couldn't walk away from. Oh, he'd been furious when Mary FitzAllen had left him at the altar but he'd regained his equilibrium within a month. He'd even ultimately been wryly amused she'd misjudged his income so greatly as to run off with another man.

Would he sleep well again if Meredith's hair wasn't tickling his shoulder? No, God help him, he probably wouldn't.

Perhaps if he seduced her? God knows she always went up in flames the minute he kissed her. He should be able to keep her for days—weeks, months?—longer with a little, highly enjoyable effort.

He knotted his fingers into his trousers seam. No, God damn it, he wouldn't.

Meredith wasn't just another pretty face and a useful body. She had a brain, too. He wanted all of her or nothing—even if it meant she used that brilliant mind to leave him in the end.

Shit, he was in this far too deep.

He'd have to let her go to Altstadt because he was off to blow up those damn cannons. She'd be safer at a bourgeois town among friends where Sazonov wouldn't look for her, than staying in this decadent palace alone.

"Our bargain stands until summer maneuvers are over," Meredith said slowly, obviously calculating the least she was required to give him.

"And after I've taken you back to Eisengau or Scotland, if you need an escort out of the country," Brian added quickly, determined to gain the most.

"That will not be necessary," she snapped. "Mother will take me back."

"Or will she continue to seek the advantage to herself and her family?" Brian wasn't sure anyone could humiliate that mercenary bitch enough to make her yield a long-sought goal. If Zorndorf didn't take Meredith back—well, may the Blessed Mother help Meredith, because her own mother probably wouldn't.

"That's not true! She's my mother and she'll understand." Meredith was almost quivering, clearly desperate to convince him—and possibly herself. "She's always said Zorndorf was a brute and she'll realize I had to use any possible method to stop his pursuit."

Brian inclined his head, not trusting his voice.

Meredith cast him a suspicious look before nodding. "Very well. But I'm only agreeing so you'll stop fussing at me."

A muscle throbbed in his jaw. God help her if he was right.

Brian lay on a small knob in the mountainside with his family, letting them study the blockhouse through their binoculars. They were well concealed behind some boulders edging a clump of ash trees, far from the summer palace or the headquarters. The landscape here was similar to that around the headquarters for summer maneuvers: wide stretches of pastureland edged with trees or narrow hedgerows, and spotted with occasional groves of trees. The long vistas were helpful for watching others, if one took care to be discreet.

The massive stone blockhouse was actually two round buildings linked by a long bar into the shape of the letter "I," stretching out along a cliff above the lakeshore. The northern tip of the letter was where the four cannons—the artillery battery—were placed, while the base was the railroad blockhouse where the railroad line to the palace and headquarters ended. It was also where all the railroad supplies were kept, near the river flowing out of the lake.

The Citadel's famous fireworks would be visible from here in a few hours, beyond the same rugged hills which had taken him hours to travel by train. Flickers of light revealed the tiny villages stretched along the rivers and lake, all of them set behind Eisengau's rippling white line floodwall and low bluffs.

Meredith—dearest, dearest Meredith—was in Altstadt, an hour downriver from here and a decaying holiday spot for the bourgeois. If he put a note in a bottle and tossed it into the lake, it could reach her. Folly, purest folly.

Remember your mission, major, not the woman. Think about destroying those guns and protecting your country.

His family was here on an old-fashioned raiding party, such as their ancestors would have recognized. The stationmaster must have thought they'd come to hike, given their sturdy tweeds and stout boots. Lord, how he'd gulped when he'd received the cable saying the parents were coming. But when he'd seen Mother, with her plus fours neatly tucked into her high-topped boots making the woolen trousers almost as baggy and respectable as bloomers—that was when he'd realized she too had come to fight, not just hold the horses.

Father had brought three immense carpetbags, filled with an assortment of deadly tricks. Brian had another one, loaded with toys he'd lifted from Eisengau's labs. Their horses waited just beyond the rise, patiently grazing in the eternal calm. After all, it was centuries since anyone had last gone to war inside this country's boundaries.

"Interesting," Father pronounced at last. "Your small door is in the center under that snow shed?"

"Yes, sir."

"We're not carrying enough cordite or dynamite to completely destroy the gun turret."

Brian could almost feel Marlowe and Spenser's quivering interest. But they were steady enough to stay in place and quiet.

"Of course not, sir. But the magazine is under the long gallery running from the battery toward the railroad blockhouse."

"Ahhh," Mother breathed, swinging her glasses around to view the far end. "If we put enough charges in there—"

"The entire bottom will drop out of the turret, letting the guns drop into the lake," Father finished her sentence as always.

"How deep is the water there?" Spenser asked.

"Nobody knows." Brian grinned savagely. "They sent a diver down once but he couldn't touch bottom."

"So there's no hope of salvage." Marlowe was almost purring. Good lad.

"Where are the magazine's doors?"

Brian hesitated.

"What's the problem?" snapped the founder of Donovan & Sons, whose motto was, "Risky freight into risky places."

"I only know of two entrances."

"Well, of course, they wouldn't build many—they want to minimize accidents. Go on."

"One is the main entrance from within the battery itself. The other is through a small inspection port off the long gallery." He swallowed and met his father's eyes squarely. "A teenager might get through it but I'm too big to manage it, sir. Nor could you or the twins."

"Pity. How did you plan to attack?" the senior Donovan asked. Mother shifted restlessly, sending a few rocks skittering down the slope.

"The three of us would take out the sentries, trying not to kill them. The enemy is Russia, not the Eisengau people, after all. If the door was still locked, then the twins would help me climb in through the gun port."

"Simple and probably effective, given the rough terrain and the sentries' over-confidence." Father was visibly counting uniformed bodies.

"What if one of them sounds the alarm?" Mother asked.

Four heads snapped around to stare at her. She shrugged. "Wouldn't they be trained to shout or whistle or something?"

"What are you thinking of, Mother?"

"Wouldn't a silent attack be best?

"Viola . . ." her husband protested.

"I'm a petite woman. If the alternative is attacking a gun turret, I can certainly squeeze into a powder magazine by myself, William."

"Do you have any idea how dangerous it would be? One false move and you could be blown to smithereens. If you died . . ." He stopped, too hoarse to continue.

"I won't die, darling." She kissed her fingers and reached out. Father turned his head to meet them, tears glistening unashamedly on his lashes.

Christ, if he thought he and Meredith would ever have anything like what his parents shared, he'd move mountains.

"What's your plan, son?" his sire asked a minute later.

"Eisengau has very few artillerymen who can work these

guns so they only come up here when there's a demonstration scheduled. It's empty the rest of the time, with sentries keeping watch on the outside."

"In that case, we definitely go in after dark. Viola slips into the magazine through the inspection port and opens the door into the battery for the rest of us." Father's fingers twined restlessly around Mother's. "Then we place enough charges to send the guns sliding down the hill and get the hell out. Simple, sweet, and hopefully effective."

"Exactly," Brian agreed, ice slivering his veins. This could work—if Mother stayed safe.

"Not much time to get into position, if we're to pull this off after nightfall, boyos." He kissed his wife's hand one more time, then rolled over and started squirming back toward the road. She followed him an instant later, then Spenser and Marlowe. Spenser was whistling under his breath, while Marlowe was moving faster and cleaner than ever before.

Brian came last, trying for the first time to see his father as an outsider would. Arrogant, successful, brilliant. The Irish street tough whose advice was now sought by presidents, even J. P. Morgan. The patriarch who'd do anything for his God, his family, or his business in that order—and the law would back him. A man whose word was his bond.

But Meredith had never known a trustworthy man.

Even her own father had chosen alcohol over her own life and her stepfather would sell her in a moment for political gain.

She'd probably view William Donovan's self-confidence as a threat, an attempt to push her into the cubbyhole of no more than His Daughter-in-Law. And he had the power to succeed.

Cold climbed through Brian's body, despite his double woolen socks, heavy leather trousers, and tightly woven jacket.

If he wanted Meredith, could he live close to somebody who upset her, especially a high-handed patriarch since they'd always ruined her life? He knew he could trust his father but she didn't. Could she ever learn?

Dammit, all he'd ever wanted was a big, happy family to

share with his parents and brothers. Now he'd found the woman of his dreams.

Did he have to choose between her and his family?

How much would he have to give up to gain Meredith? Arguing politics with Father while Mother played the piano and tried not to laugh? Plotting investments with Neil? Rescuing Marlowe and Spenser from their latest folly while Father could still pretend he didn't know?

Or maybe he could just put some distance between them and his family—but how far would he have to go before she'd relax and stop seeing him as an excuse for his father to grab her? The other side of San Francisco Bay, God willing? Or Southern California? Maybe Denver with half a continent between him and family laughter? Or, saints preserve him, somewhere on the East Coast?

But if she did, he'd have Meredith at last. Meredith with her wicked smile, and her glowing eyes when she argued for what she believed in, and her clever tongue with the insatiable appetite for his skin. Meredith of the slow, satisfied glint when he held her close after they made love.

Meredith, who'd do anything and everything for those she cared about.

His mouth tightened.

He quickened his stride, joining his parents and brothers for what might be the last time.

"Blackwood!"

"Sir?" Gareth pivoted on the upper hallway's intricate parquet floor and waited none too patiently for the British ambassador to join him. Down below at the quay, Sophie and Emilie, the wittiest two brunettes present, were boarding the official Eisengau yacht for tonight's grand gala. They'd promised to save him a seat but he needed to arrive before another gentleman claimed their rather fickle attentions.

"How long have you known Donovan?" Sir Henry's sharp

blue eyes scrutinized him from within deep wrinkles. His body might be shrouded in fat but his brain wasn't.

"Four years, sir. His family firm had sent him out to deliver some engineering supplies required on the Northwest Frontier." A very nasty jaunt for both of them, not that he could speak of it. "We traveled together on the ship back to London from Calcutta.

"Became friends at once?"

"We had a great deal in common, since we were the only two bachelors in first-class, sir, other than the ship's officers."

"You must have been chased by all the fishing fleeters who'd failed to catch a man in India," Sir Henry snickered.

Like Mary FitzAllen, who'd all but thrown herself into Brian's arms. He was still amazed Brian was interested in her, since he'd been so hard-headed about every other female.

"No wonder you became friends."

"And I'm still free as a bird, sir." He'd happily poured whisky down Brian after the tart left him for old Baron Giffard in Alexandria on two days' acquaintance. Twenty thousand pounds a year plus a title probably seemed a fortune to an Anglo-Irish chit who didn't understand the American propensity to shower wealth on all their children, including second sons. He'd be astonished if Brian didn't have at least ten million dollars.

The yacht's deep steam whistle hooted once, a mere formality. It would never leave until every high ranking guest had boarded.

"Excellent, excellent. You're just the man to get straight answers out of him."

"Sir?" Answers to what?

The older man glanced around, eyeing a centuries' old suit of armor as if it might contain a modern spy. He jerked his head and Gareth obediently followed him to a niche carved into an immense marble fireplace. "The negotiations have all but broken down, leaving us unable to buy the guns."

"Damn." If the Boers' allies bought those cannons for them, they'd never put down that rebellion. His friends would be massacred every time they showed their face in the field. "We have to get our hands on those guns."

"Quite so, quite so." They understood each other perfectly. "Only Donovan or Sazonov is still in the running, according to the grand duke's secretary. You must find out if Donovan has bought the guns."

"Very well. And if he has?"

"See if he's willing to let us look at them. It's not much of a chance but it may be something." Sir Henry brooded, running his fingers over an intricately carved stag.

"And if the Russians have bought them?"

"They're diplomatic property. In that case, we steal or copy their plans and you must locate Miss Duncan."

"You're joking!"

"Hardly. Zorndorf may be an obnoxious braggart but he's a damn efficient genius. He'd never tolerate a secretary who wasn't up to his standards. If he said she can create blueprints from memory, then the lady can do it."

"Why would she help us when she's constantly around Donovan?"

"Appeal to her patriotism, man. Remind her of Wallace, the Bruce, of all the great men who fought and bled and died to protect Scotland."

"She's Donovan's *chère amie*. What if she's hoping for something . . ." He groped for words to describe what he'd seen in Brian's eyes.

"She's a Scotswoman and they imbibe pragmatism with their mother's milk. I married one and I know." Sir Henry chuckled. "No, ask Donovan first. Then talk to Miss Duncan no matter what he says."

"Very well, sir." He could tell Brian the truth, at least, since it would hardly surprise him.

"We have to move quickly, man. All the junior diplomats are on the hunt now."

"Didn't they go to the capital for young Nicholas's informal party at that beer garden?"

"Excellent excuse, wasn't it, whether or not they actually attended?" Sir Henry shook his head. "No, they're out there now, trying to find a way into the engineering college's safe for those plans."

"*All* of the juniors, sir?" Gareth asked carefully. Good God, how many people and countries would be chasing her?

"Every foreigner who didn't make it onto the boat is now trying to lay his hands on the plans. It will be the greatest treasure hunt in Europe by dawn. But we'll have the golden goose, thanks to Miss Duncan."

"Quite."

Pyotr counted flower pots under his breath, listening for the tell-tale clip-clop of a secret policeman's hobnailed shoes following him. Every month, he had to pick up his spies' reports. They arrived on different days, at different places, some of which rotated, thanks to Eisengau's irritating paranoia. He'd have preferred to pay the bureaucrats off and accept the reports at his office or a local tavern, the customary practice elsewhere. Then he could have attended Grand Duke Rudolph's charming gala tonight, instead of skulking through this back alley behind the cathedral.

Five, six . . .

On the first of each month, a sizable sum was deposited into that Swiss bank account, whether or not there was anything here. It was how he'd learned of that magnificent gun before anyone else.

At least Grand Duke Rudolph had agreed to sell him the four existing cannons, although he wouldn't part with the plans.

Damn foreigners.

No followers so far.

Nine, ten.

He slid the eleventh flowerpot aside and plucked the coping stone underneath out of the wall, exposing a sizeable hollow. His two fingers neatly scooped out the packet hidden there, neatly wrapped in oiled silk. It disappeared into his pocket, while at the same time he smoothly replaced the coping stone and flower pot.

He'd have time to celebrate at his favorite brothel before heading back to Schloss Belvedere. They must be lonely for creative, aristocratic patrons with stamina.

He grinned.

Chapter Twelve

The last sentry dropped in his tracks, as silently as the others.

"Three," noted Spenser in Gaelic, the family's private language. He wasn't even breathing hard.

"Well done," applauded William, honestly impressed. He'd have expected as brilliant a job from Brian, or even Marlowe for whom he'd have added some extra praise for the skill shown at such a young age.

But Spenser? Yesterday, he'd have described Spenser as the sickly pup who'd nearly died a dozen times before his first birthday—and almost cost his mother her life. Now he was looking at a real man, a fighting Donovan like his other three sons.

"Very well done indeed," he added. "Let me show you a trick to tying this fellow up before we meet your brothers and pick that lock."

"Will you show me how to pick the lock?"

William paused, just about to throw the first loop around their captive's wrists. None of his other boys had ever really been interested in learning the more disreputable arts.

But his grandfather had always enjoyed the more outlandish skills best. He seemed to hear that old devil whistling somewhere.

"Aye, boyo, I'd be glad to. You can watch this time and I'll teach you more when we get home."

Meredith trod carefully along the causeway's uneven blocks. She'd always been amazed at how attached people were to their summer homes in Altstadt, the old medieval capital, despite its hazards. Only a massive flood had finally forced moving the capital to the higher site five centuries ago, where a small river joined the Eisenfluss just above St. Martin's Bridge, providing a natural port. Even so, many families still came every year on holiday to this now fading riverside resort.

Located on the widest tributary of the Eisenfluss, Altstadt prized its water views and called it Lake St. Charles. They'd fought against building the floodwall which protected the rest of Eisengau from the river's springtime fury, together with the natural bluffs. Franz's family had even used their traditional connections with the church to completely avoid having the stone wall on their property at all. Unlike any other house on the promontory, it could only be reached by walking out onto the floodwall, then following a very fragile causeway which wound along the lakeshore.

Even in the moonlight she could see where the floodwall's edges had been torn away by storms over time, leaving stone blocks scattered across the uneven path.

A dark spot shone in on the pavement, undoubtedly wet. But how deep?

Morro barked brusquely at it and jumped over.

Meredith shook her head, a reluctant smile curling her lips. She'd once thought such travails were romantic. Now she wondered why Franz couldn't take care of basics. She gathered up her skirts and followed her canine friend, her passport brushing against her shirt in its accustomed suit pocket.

When she'd first seen Franz Schnabel's family home shortly after arriving in Eisengau, it had looked like a fairy castle, thanks to its tall chimneys and dozens of candle flames reflecting in the waves. Now it resembled a decrepit old house, whose owners couldn't afford to provide modern heating or lighting. Tonight the once magical causeway seemed to have more holes in it than a political argument.

Meredith bit her tongue and castigated herself for even considering such an analogy. She was coming to a long-planned, friendly meeting. The central committee gathered here every month on the full moon, since they could watch for the secret police and then take precautions.

Tonight all the lights were on, including the safe signal.

Judge Baumgart's vacation cottage was barely visible through the trees beyond, a dark shadow against the silvery sky. She'd spent years slipping out of it and trekking over to visit her friends.

Morro turned, sniffing the air, and spun again. She fought the temptation to do the same and rang the bell far more firmly than usual.

Gerhardt opened the door, sending a burst of laughter dancing out over the water. Shock washed over his face. An instant later, his eyes were shuttered and harder than the mathematical formulas he loved to solve.

What was wrong? Yes, there'd been a little argument the last time they'd met. But they'd had more vehement ones before.

"Who is it, Gerhardt?" Franz peered around his shoulder.

"Good evening, Franz. May I come in?" Meredith tried to sound normal.

He frowned. "Well, I suppose."

He stepped back, holding the door completely open. "But only because you've come so far—and you'd probably cause a scene if I said no."

What? Why was he treating her like this? She preferred logic to emotion during central committee meetings, when discussing a topic. Her skin tried to crawl off her bones. "Thank you."

She and Morro followed him inside. For the first time ever, Gerhardt didn't offer to take her coat and she chose not to take it off.

The others silently watched her enter. Even Erich and Rosa stopped cuddling each other in order to study her like a poisonous snake.

"Good evening." Meredith smiled at her old friends. Please, she'd known them all for so long and they'd been through so much together. Surely they could fix anything that was wrong. "How are you, Liesel?"

Liesel straightened up from the armoire she'd been leaning against. "That's a very beautiful dress. Did you trade the cannon's plans to the Americans for it?"

"No!"

"But he asked for them, didn't he?"

Caught completely off guard, Meredith flushed. The others gasped.

"So Sazonov was right all along, Liesel: she's been selling herself to the American. Bah!" Gerhardt spat.

"I have not!" Meredith spun on him. "He asked but I refused. And he didn't press me. It's Sazonov, the Russian, you should worry about."

"Don't be ridiculous. He's always been our friend, unlike you." Liesel hunched her shoulder and turned up her nose.

"Me? I've fought for the workers and the revolution for years." She stared at her old companion, baffled by the accusation.

"You're a foreigner and you're sleeping with a foreigner. How can we trust you?" Liesel sneered.

"Give us the blueprints and we'll forgive you," Franz leaned forward, his eyes far too eager.

Instinct gagged her tongue. Why would she need forgiveness?

"We have much more to fight for now," Erich said softly. "Sazonov says . . ."

"We must be trained."

Training? What did Eisengau need from Russia?

Liesel cast Franz a brief smile before glaring once again at

Meredith. "In Russia, where they understand how to do such things well."

"Russia? What about the workers?" People like Meyer and Brecht and their children, who need help *now* before anyone else was crippled or died?

"They can wait." Franz waved such trifles off.

But he'd always been the first one to argue for haste! Meredith clenched her fists.

"The election isn't very important, as long as we have the blueprints, according to Sazonov."

Franz truly was writing off the revolution. In that case, the same to him. A debate's welcome chill settled into her veins.

"No, I'm afraid not." She crossed her arms over her chest.

Silence blanketed the room, backed by hostile, glittering eyes. Meredith cursed the honesty which had led her to tell the unvarnished truth. Morro growled deep in his throat.

"It's the American." Why couldn't somebody here believe what she said—and have that person be Liesel?

Meredith slammed the door on one part of her past and kept fighting.

"No, it's because of the workers. Can't you see Sazonov and the Russians only want the blueprints, not us? Not a new government in Eisengau?" She choked back the lump in her throat. "The minute they have them, they'll drop all interest in Eisengau—and the workers will be worse off than before. I can't do that."

"Ridiculous. They can buy the guns, as they always have." Gerhardt shook his head.

"He tried to seduce me into giving him the blueprints," Meredith countered.

"Liar!" Liesel shrieked. "Jealous bitch!"

Meredith slapped her, knocking her oldest female friend onto the floor.

All the times they'd studied, or shopped, or giggled together—destroyed by one vicious epithet, and everything she'd said before. Meredith had once called Liesel the sister of her heart. Tonight's loss ran too deep for tears.

Silence caught the room, broken only by Liesel's gasping sobs. Meredith turned around slowly, hoping somebody would try logic.

"You're wrong because Sazonov has always told us the truth. You're blinded by your foolish feminine lusts." Franz dismissed them with a wave of his hand. "We're willing to forgive you, if you bring us the blueprints like a good girl."

He was the male leader of their little clan but all he could offer was a demand for feminine subjugation. He should have known better after twelve years.

Rosa helped Liesel onto her feet and they clung together, backed by the men.

Meredith spoke between gritted teeth. "I think I'd best be going now."

"If you leave now, don't bother to come back. Even if you brought a set of plans, we wouldn't believe they were genuine."

"You foolish, strutting cockerel." She shook her head. "I hope you soon learn just how little you truly mean to Russia. Come, Morro."

Brian refused to pace. Mother had to be alive, deep in the blockhouse's bowels. No, inside the magazine by now. Just as Meredith had to be doing well. His heart would know in an instant if its reason for living had ended.

Instead he ran his hand over the great cannon and stared out the narrow firing slit to the lake. The wheel alone reached his shoulder. Three other guns loomed behind him, every one more than double his height. But the cavernous stone vault swallowed them up and even provided a balcony to admire them from.

God help the fellow who went to war against these devils.

Outside, the grand duke's yacht was circling the lake, while its orchestra played an endless collection of tunes from Viennese operettas, the grand duke sang, and Zorndorf conducted the orchestra. The passengers were openly engaged in drinking, fornication, or both. Brian had been warned the grand duke occasionally used the pictures for blackmail. Thankfully, he hadn't seen Gareth there. At least his friend was safe from that nightmare.

"Five minutes," Father announced. He looked up from his pocket watch, his face ghastly in the silvery moonlight. "Are you sure your map of the ventilation shaft was accurate?"

Brian's breath hissed out, like a dying balloon. "How can I be sure since I couldn't check it? It's what they told me when I paid to observe a full day's effort here. But I'm too tall to know for sure. Only Mother—" He stopped abruptly.

"You were right: only your mother could slip inside the inspection port." His father swallowed convulsively.

Brian closed his eyes then turned to watch the lake again. He hadn't seen Father wear that expression since Mother was desperately ill after Marlowe and Spenser were born. He gave his stomach ten seconds to stop flopping like a landed trout before he spoke. "We know she entered the magazine and didn't get stuck in the magazine because she untied the rope from her waist. So all we have to do now is wait."

"Marlowe and Spenser can handle everything outside, no matter how long this takes."

"They're doing very well," Brian agreed, eager to remove at least one source of anxiety. His own worries about Meredith would remain private. At least she had Morro with her and that dog could fight off a platoon.

He glowered at the tumbler lock on the door, which neither he nor Father could open. If it had been designed differently—if they didn't need Mother to open the door from the unlocked inside—she'd be waiting safely back with the horses.

Scratch! Scratch! The door sighed once then swung wide.

"Sorry I'm late, darling." Mother fumbled to turn off her lantern. "The magazine was much more crowded than I expected."

Brian grinned, a band loosening around his heart.

Father swooped her up into his arms. Somehow her light landed upright, despite her complete disregard for it.

Brian picked it up, careful to stay out of his parents' way. If Neil had been here, they'd been placing bets on how long it would take before Father carried Mother upstairs to bed. But that wasn't an option tonight.

He had another, more urgent question to answer: Why had she said the magazine was crowded? She knew explosives well enough to guess what four great guns would need for support.

He stepped into the great vault his mother had just come out of and began scanning it with the lantern's beam.

"Jesus, Mary, and Joseph." He crossed himself.

"What's wrong, Brian?" Father had come alert again.

"The shells are stacked to the ceiling and the room looks as tall and wide as this one. The racks are very close together." He swallowed, his skin growing colder and colder. "How far back do they go, Mother?"

"Farther than where I came in. My guess is they reach almost to the railroad blockhouse." She shivered and pressed closer to her husband. "There's another storey beneath this one, too, which reaches deep inside the mountain."

"They must store all the ammunition for both the Eisengau 155s and the French 75s here," Brian muttered, appalled. It was more than twice as much as he'd expected.

"Sweet Jesus," Father murmured. "How much of the mountain will go when we blow this up? Are we sure there's nobody working on the railroad side?"

"Yes, I'm certain. I veered into that direction and listened."

"Well, nobody will raise these four demons from their graves when we're done, lad." Father chuckled humorlessly. "Fetch Marlowe and Spenser in here; we'll need their help if we're to wire all of this before the first shift arrives for the railroad. We'll also need to move the sentries someplace where they can escape at the proper time."

"Aye, sir." He saluted instinctively.

If—when—he survived this, he was going to find Meredith and tell her he loved her. He'd been a fool to forget that before. Then he'd spend the rest of his life protecting her, whatever that meant and wherever it led him.

Because life wasn't worth living without the one you loved. Anybody who doubted that could ask his parents.

Meredith blinked back another round of angry, foolish tears. Maybe she should have known Franz and Liesel and the others were better at talk than action. But she'd hoped for so much more to help the workers. Now she'd have to do what she could.

She took another turn along the trail, instinct and long habit driving her, and emerged between two high fences. Trees whispered over their tops, almost obscuring the moon.

She'd have to reclaim the blueprints first, since she was only a few miles away from the capital where they were. And she'd have to figure out how to get them out of the country . . .

Morro growled deep in his throat.

Meredith came to an abrupt halt, her heart leaping into her mouth. Maybe there was another option.

Her mother and Judge Baumgart stood in the small alley, watching her with equally hostile expressions.

"If you're here to ask for forgiveness, you're knocking on the wrong door—unless you come as Frau Zorndorf, young lady." Judge Baumgart patted his wife's hand. "Correct, my dear?"

"As ever, my love." A chill breeze brushed Meredith's shoulders and shifted the trees, brightening the street. Her mother's eyes were crystal-clear and diamond-hard. "She is no daughter of mine."

"But Mother! You always said Colonel Zorndorf would

be an impossible husband for any woman. Don't you understand I did what I had to, in order to stop the betrothal?"

"I know you refused to help your family."

"Mother . . ." Meredith bit her lip against a whimper.

"If you marry him, we'll be received at court. A post as high-court justice is splendid but the American gave that to us, not you."

No, this wasn't warmth. Brian had showed her what that meant. He'd always supported her, even when she'd argued bitterly with him. She did not have to accept this.

"You're saying that unless I prostitute myself, I'm worthless."

"Prostitute? Now, see here, young lady," the Judge tried to interrupt.

"If that's your definition of a daughter, then I'm glad I'm not one. Goodbye."

She spun on her heel and headed back the way she came, refusing to run until she'd rounded the corner. Morro followed her, walking backwards and barking. He was finally free to express his opinion of his old enemies.

She didn't answer her parents' shouts.

Maybe someday she'd stop crying when she remembered the good times—her mother singing her to sleep as a little girl, or laughing when she fell into a flowerbed, or beaming when she recited a poem for one of Father's fellow professors. Because who knew how many tears she'd shed before she saw her brothers again? It might take months, or even years, but she had to believe she would—even though her throat was tight and raw.

Morro shoved his nose into her hand, whining softly. She choked and stooped down to wrap her arms around his neck. He leaned closer, lending her the strength of his steady heartbeat and understanding, while she trembled.

At least she still had dear, darling Morro to remind her that love was unconditional.

"Good boy, Morro, good boy." She rubbed his sides and

he licked her eagerly, wagging his tail and bringing a slow smile to her face.

She rose and turned for the trolley to the capital, the only transportation still running at this late hour. Thankfully, Brian had given her pocket money in case she missed the launch and had to take the train.

She had to fetch the blueprints and do something to help the workers with them. They were Eisengau's treasure, nobody else's; they needed to be used for Eisengau's benefit.

And then she'd find Brian and beg him to hold her.

The fuse stretched across the path like a snake, warning all comers not to tread on it. The moon was fading behind the mountains, dimming before the coming dawn. There was nobody else around. Even the small animal noises had faded to silence in the pre-dawn hush. Perhaps they'd read the humans' intentions and fled.

But the orchestra aboard the grand duke's yacht had been replaced by a brass band. It was now loudly—and badly— playing a possibly military march, erratically guided by Zorndorf using a saber for a conductor's baton. The grand duke was the center of one of the orgies' more salacious groupings.

Mother and the twins were hidden a mile away uphill, near the train station.

Brian finished tightening the fuse and shut the cover, lifting the handle. When it connected again, all of the charges would go off, sending a complicated signal inside the magazine and triggering every shell to explode.

Had anyone ever detonated that much firepower before?

"Care to make a guess how much of the mountain we're going to lose?" he asked, trying to sound casual.

"We'll have a loud bang. The blockhouse will be gone. Maybe not just drop into the lake—but gone."

All of that heavy stone disappear? Jesus, Mary, and Joseph, they certainly would have a very big noise.

At least they'd hauled the sentries well beyond the railroad blockhouse, carrying them over the horses' backs like sacks of grain. They were sure to be discovered there, when Eisengau's army came to investigate.

"After that?"

"Who knows?" His father shrugged. "The entire cliff underneath goes into the lake? The hillside above as far as that knoll? Maybe to the ridge line on the south? Or . . ."

"You're joking."

"Care to make a bet?" Father shot back promptly. "Dinner for two at a restaurant of my choice against . . ."

"Dinner for two." The family had always settled arguments by gambling with food, usually dinners in Chinatown. But he couldn't claim that for Meredith. He might be eating sausage in Europe for a long time to come.

He hoped his smile looked like a cocky grin. "Care to set it off?"

"Your job—and then we'll both run for our lives."

Brian nodded curtly, not trusting his voice, and stood up. He wrapped his hands around the metal handle, flexing his fingers until he was certain he had the best possible grip. He rolled his shoulders, ensuring he'd pounce solidly on his enemy at the right time.

These guns had to die so the Americans in Alaska would live.

"Thanks for being here." Brian looked back for a moment at the man who'd given him life.

"I wouldn't want to be anywhere else, son." William Donovan gripped him on the shoulder and gave him the thumbs-up.

Brian took a deep breath. "Five, four, three, two, one . . ."

He slammed the handle down, firing the charges.

BOOM!

Light rippled down the fuse and into the blockhouse, almost faster than he could see, despite a lifetime's experience.

BOOM!!! KERBOOM! KERBOOM!!!

Light blasted out of the blockhouse's window slits. Cordite's acrid stench slammed into his face and drove into his lungs. The ground shook underfoot, staggering him. Rocks rattled and boulders heaved.

Sweet singing Jesus, how long could an explosion last?

His father grabbed him by the elbow and heaved him into motion, hurling him sideways. Their feet skidded on the suddenly slippery pavement.

KERBOOOOOMMMMM!!!

The blast roared upwards from the mountain's roots through Brian's spine and out his skull.

He froze.

Father caught him around the waist and hauled him forward, heading not uphill but for a narrow finger of rock on the side. "Run, you damn ox, run!"

Brian staggered again but obeyed, his legs gradually moving faster and faster.

The mountain thundered again. Dust exploded into the air, covering the trees and sky.

They leaped onto the granite and rolled across it, taking shelter on the other side like children hiding from an ogre.

Brian peered through the swirling clouds of gray ash, choking and coughing.

CRACK!

The cliff split away, taking away the blockhouse above it—and undercutting its parent mountain. SPLASH!

The mountain trembled.

CRACK, CRACK, CRACK! Great lines appeared in the hillside.

KERACK!!! The hillside collapsed upon itself and slid, accelerating faster and faster until it fell into the lake.

SPLASH!!!

Water leaped high, three times as high as a man, and raced across the lake. Grand Duke Rudolph's yacht rolled over, emitting a wild burst of brazen cacophony. Only its hull could be seen and the waves pounded it mercilessly, shattering the fragile wood against the cliff. It sank in a blur of splinters and roiling waters, without trace of human hand or voice.

The white-edged waters raced around the shore, ravenously seeking for prey. They smashed trees, dislodged boulders, swept back to the blockhouse's original site—and found an outlet.

"No!" Brian ran to the rib's edge and peered out, straining to see all the way downriver to the capital.

The Eisenfluss River's narrow channel rebuilt the wave. It hurled itself forward, faster and faster, wiping out the few trees which had braved its rocky cliffs. It burst into the capital's wider waters and spiraled outward again—seeking and finding the tiny entrance to Altstadt. A tall oak swayed and fell into the torrent, just before the angry waves disappeared.

Not Altstadt, please, not Altstadt. Brian crossed himself, his lips moving in a frantic, silent prayer. *Mother Mary, please keep Meredith safe. I don't care if the capital looks to be mostly unharmed, thanks to centuries of preparing for floods. If Meredith is alive, I'll do anything. I'll leave my family. I'll . . .*

Meredith rested her chin on her palm, her eyes shut. Morro was a warm comfort against her knees, while the cable car's brakeman hummed peacefully up front. The other two passengers were riding in the open half, allowing her to hear the steady whir of the cable pulling them forward. They'd just passed the foundry so they still had a long way to go before reaching Market Square.

She'd have too, too much time to think in this working class neighborhood, full of boarding houses and very small businesses.

She scratched Morro's head.

BOOM! BOOM! BOOM!

The little car shook, hurling her against the opposite bench. Morro yelped and started to slide away. She grabbed him quickly, holding desperately onto a brass pole.

The other passengers shouted. The brakeman cursed un-apologetically and started squeezing, forcing the cable car to halt. Strangers' hands helped her down and she joined families with coats hastily pulled on over nightshirts and night-gowns, wearing slippers or barefeet.

She picked Morro up in her arms, hugging him close for a few seconds' reassurance.

"Where did it come from?" somebody asked, a suddenly clear voice amid all the hissing speculation.

"Far—not the foundry."

"Headquarters of those summer maneuvers, then."

"We've been hearing cannonades from there for years. There was a big one, only last week," a woman agreed.

Sazonov. Meredith clenched her teeth. He must have blown up the guns to make sure Brian didn't get them.

The—the beast!

A man spat on the pavement. "I always said they'd taken too much ammunition out there."

"Must have been big for us to hear it from this far away, with the mountains in between," another man commented. "An entire magazine, perhaps, full of shells?"

"Oh no!" The crowd gasped as one, even the older children, silencing the dozens of small conversations.

"God's will," a woman said finally. "God's will."

Meredith turned to look for who'd spoken, startled by her acceptance. But this was a soldier's country, very superstitious and long accustomed to working with high explosives.

A silvery glint in the fading moonlight caught her eye—and she gasped. Oh no!

Water pulled itself up in the river until it stood far taller than a man, covered with foam and black specks.

Others turned to follow her.

The river roared like a thundering train and leaped forward, plunging past the capital's high floodwalls and shipping basin, diving under St. Martin's Bridge—and heading for Altstadt.

That massive wave must have come from the lake below Schloss Belvedere, under the guns' emplacement—where Brian had gone cruising with the grand duke.

Brian. Dear God in heaven, *Brian*. Was he safe? Was he even alive?

She closed her eyes, shaking. She was cold, so very cold.

Morro licked her face, whining. She hid her face in his fur for an instant before she put him down.

Look for some hope somewhere. Do something, anything. She bit her lip until it bled, forcing the tears back. She would not cry in public.

How could she help Brian, especially since no boat ran to Schloss Belvedere at this hour? How did the living aid the dead? Was time truly of the essence? If the only service she could offer was identifying his body and making sure it reached his mother safely—well, that could wait until the morning.

She shuddered. She could not, would not believe all his bright laughter had gone out of this world. Yet what hope was there?

But she might still be able to do something for Franz and the others if she moved quickly.

Her throat was so tight, it was amazing she could breathe at all. "Come, Morro," she croaked.

She picked up her skirts, edged her way through the crowd, and started for Altstadt, with Morro at her heels.

Large waves were still rolling across the lake when she arrived. The rocks along the shoreline were full of debris, mostly tree branches until she came closer to Franz's house. Crippled furniture and shredded fabric danced in the trees. People, dressed in their nightclothes, were hunting in the shoreline and dragging large, heavy items back to the shore.

She couldn't see Franz's house but all of the others looked well, including Mother's.

She started to count the corpses, trying to discreetly check who was there.

Rosa was still identifiable by her red hair. She was in Erich's arms, as united in death as they'd been in life.

A woman was sobbing. "I shouted at them to run but they laughed. They laughed!"

"Hush, hush. They were young and foolish, probably drunk," another woman soothed her.

Franz and Gerhardt still wore identical seal rings, antique black onyx cameos from their college.

"But to lose six people . . ."

"Surely not all."

Ernst's watch still lacked a second hand.

"No, we just found the sixth," a man said heavily, clumping past.

Liesel's blond hair straggled over his arm, the only part of her skull that wasn't a battered mess of red blood and white bone plastered to the thin shirt wrapped around it.

Meredith bolted for the nearest tree and some privacy, in order to be very, very sick.

"And Droysen, the telegraphist, says Grand Duke Rudolph died, too, on his yacht."

"Ah! So the Devil has finally claimed his own," the second woman comfortably pronounced sentence.

Meredith shook, bracing herself against the rough bark. Grand Duke Rudolph dead? But that meant Brian was surely dead, too, since he'd been leaving for the gala aboard the yacht the last time she saw him.

Brian! She wrapped her arms around herself and rocked, the pain so agonizing it seemed as if her heart was ripping the bones out of her chest one by one.

How much was life worth now? Very little.

She had to return to the capital and retrieve the plans. Eisengau's workers still needed her, at least.

Chapter Thirteen

"No, you have to board the dawn train for Switzerland," Viola's normally rambunctious second son repeated stoically. He'd been using the same monotone ever since they'd blown up the guns almost an hour ago. "I'll take the express back to Berlin like an ordinary diplomat."

She didn't think he was grieving for the orgiastic partygoers on the overturned yacht. He'd grown to be a rowdy man with strong carnal appetites, as befitted someone with Donovan and Lindsay blood. Not that she was supposed to know that, of course.

Besides, he'd barely given the boat's wreckage a second glance. Instead, he kept staring downriver—to somewhere past the capital, if she guessed aright.

The train station down below showed few signs of life under the setting moon. Designed as a watering stop, it would also pick up any hikers exhausted by the steep St. Nicholas Pass.

William frowned. "You must come with us. They'll know who blew up the guns and be looking for revenge."

"We're not the only ones the Russians beat out in the auction for the guns. Eisengau will look at other countries to see if they did it. I have to go to the capital."

His voice roughened and stopped, like a saw grinding through heartwood.

Knives clawed at Viola's skin. Of all her sons, he was the

most like the men of her family, the famous golden Lindsays, for whom everything always came very easily—except finding and claiming the woman of their heart. Brian had been successful far too young at sports, in business, with women—anything and everything he set his hand to. Even that aborted engagement he rarely spoke of didn't seem to have soured his temper.

To hear him turn laconic, sharp-edged with hard emotion . . . Well, she'd always wanted him to grow up and take matters a little more seriously.

But it still hurt to know she couldn't hug and kiss him and take away the pain.

"Besides, you need to take Mother to safety," Brian finished more quickly.

William hesitated. "Well . . ."

Viola wrapped her hand over his wrist, under cover of darkness. He jerked slightly in surprise, although long practice had taught him not to show the boys when she cued him.

"They'll undoubtedly arrange a fund to help the injured," she commented. "The sooner we're over the border, the easier we can contribute to it anonymously. Even if we call our deeds the fortunes of war, some of the dead were innocents."

Even in this poor light, she could see Brian flinch.

Ah! So he had risked somebody he cared about. Poor, poor darling.

"The railroad company won't bother us," Marlowe drawled. "Dirty as we are, they'll believe we're just simple hikers—"

"Not world-class spies who'd blow up cannons," Spenser finished his twin's sentence. "This is the last stop before the border and they'll be in a hurry to keep steam up. They won't want to cause trouble for us, especially with a woman like Mother around."

"Very well. If you did come with us, it'd be as good as a signed confession, anyway." William yielded abruptly and folded his arms over his chest. "But the whole place reeks of conspiracies so we won't go far."

"Father . . ."

"We'll come back over the pass via horseback in two days. Consider it a tourist's excursion to look at pleasant scenery."

"Sir, that's not necessary. I can handle this by myself."

"You should be able to reach the capital and leave the country within one day. Two is more than generous." William must be terrified, judging by how he was snapping out orders.

"Cable us if you depart early," Viola suggested, hoping it would happen. She twined her fingers with William's to give both of them courage. It was bitter enough to acknowledge they couldn't rescue Neil. Knowing they couldn't help Brian was hell on earth.

"I brought your trunk with us from Paris and it's waiting in Switzerland. I assume it contains items you could find useful?"

Viola held her breath, very conscious of the twins doing the same.

Brian harrumphed then pulled his watch out of his pocket. "No wonder J. P. Morgan enjoys doing business with you, Father. He can't count on winning all the time." He stripped a key off the fob and slapped it into his sire's waiting palm.

"My customized Mauser is in there, plus some other toys. Traveling with them may risk your life."

"Don't you remember the Donovan & Sons' motto, Brian?"

"Risky freight into risky places," five voices chorused.

"The Donovan family can surely pull it off for one of their own," William said fiercely and hugged his son.

Tears touched her eyes, since none of them could rescue Brian's heart.

Dawn brushed the icy peaks high above the valley floor but shrank away from Altstadt's dank groves, laden with shards of the young lives torn apart. Sodden books were mashed into the causeway and flattened against trees, bright cloth wrapped around muddy bushes, shattered crockery led the way to torn gate hinges and gaping windows.

Nothing lived here, nothing.

Her mother's cook had quietly told Brian that if Meredith was anywhere in town, she'd be at Franz Schnabel's house. Then she'd burst into tears and refused to say more.

He might have accepted Meredith's return to a lost lover if it had meant she was alive. But this?

He took off his hat and shoved his hand through his hair, refusing to let his knees buckle to the ground. *Meredith, oh dear God, Meredith* . . .

"Excuse us, sir." Two men approached, carrying shovels and brooms over their shoulders. "Would you mind stepping aside, please? We want to start cleaning this up for the archbishop."

"Archbishop?" Brian moved out of their way automatically.

"He owned the house but his nephew lived here. A terrible tragedy, losing so many young lives at once."

Brian couldn't control his flinch. "Do you know who they were?" His voice was too hoarse, but he couldn't help that, either.

"Gerhardt Hagen, of course, with the nephew. Plus Erich Schulze and his girl Rosa." The laborer set down his shovel and broom so he could count on his fingers, his seamed face settling into deeper lines.

"And another young man with a broken watch," the other fellow spoke up for the first time.

The first man nodded agreement. "Plus the blond girl."

Brian staggered. Meredith!

Dear, sweet, Meredith was dead—and he'd killed her. No matter what the reason, no matter how accidentally.

A silent scream ripped out of his gut and into his brain, blinding him with a wall of pain.

Nothing was left now but duty and family.

He needed to find the plans so he could leave this hell.

* * *

Another cart rattled across market square, setting off echoes which would have been disappeared at a later hour. Milk cans rattled ferociously in its back, protesting their ride over the stone paving.

Meredith yawned and beat her fists together. She was leaning against a door embrasure hidden underneath one of the colonnades ringing the square. It had been a long day and a worse night. She'd already relaxed once and barely stopped herself from sliding down the wall. If she did that again, she might fall asleep—and dream of Brian's death.

No, no, no.

She bolted out of the darkness and began to walk along the line of square pillars. In a few more hours, she could retrieve the plans and then find a hotel. Dearest, darling Brian had hidden cash in her purse before she'd left him.

She bit her lip and tried to find something interesting in the meager traffic occasionally drifting through the square.

The excitement of the grand duke's death had died down, at least for the moment. Only the few deliveries necessary to keep businesses alive happened now—from country farms avoiding heavy traffic, to early-rising bakers, and so on. The real rush would start in another hour when vendors started flooding the square, prepared to sell their wares.

Even the supposedly all-night activities had disappeared in these last few hours before dawn. The capital's honest cops were back at their station houses, finishing up their paperwork before going off duty. Even the churches' regular bells were reduced to striking hourly rather than on the quarter-hour.

Meredith rubbed her arms, wishing she had something— anything!—to do, other than think. Morro was diverting himself very well by hunting for mice, or perhaps rats. Of course, nothing spoiled his appetite, let alone his joy in the hunt. She'd have to eat soon, but not yet.

She walked faster.

A tall, blond man raced out of the colonnade's shadows at her. Sazonov!

She instinctively flung up her arm to protect herself.

He whipped it behind her, spinning her against him. She opened her mouth to shriek for help.

His hard forearm crushed her throat and lifted her onto her toes. She dangled, helpless, barely able to support herself. Blood rushed into her ears, cloaking the noise of her heels being dragged over the cobblestones and under the colonnade. Sparks flickered before her eyes, fading in the blackness.

He loosened his grip slightly and she choked in a little air. She clawed at his arm but it didn't move any farther. Damn him.

"Such an unexpected pleasure encountering you here, on my way back to the palace. Thank you for still wearing that very bourgeois hat."

The roaring in her ears faded, but that brought little hope. She writhed and kicked. But her skirts were so tight around the hips and full around the ankles, they only muffled the few strikes she did manage to launch.

If she couldn't call for help and Morro didn't notice her plight . . .

"Your lover destroyed my cannons but he went to hell with that bastard of a grand duke."

The hole in her heart gaped too wide for him to open it farther. She waited, biding her time. There had to be something she could do, sooner or later.

"As his survivor, you owe me for them and you're going to give me the plans. If you don't, I'll take your ear."

He chuckled, his arm tightening around her throat.

"What?" she gasped, barely able to speak, let alone imagine what he meant.

"Slice your ear off—with this."

A wickedly sharp blade scraped her cheek.

"First your right ear, then your left should you prove exceptionally intransigent. After that, we can discuss your fingers."

She didn't dare move. Sweat trickled down her forehead. If that knife slipped and knicked the vein frantically beating in her jaw, she could die—without doing anything for the workers.

Her ear? The blade crushed her skin until a hot trickle of blood slid down her cheek and over her jaw. He was serious. What could she do?

"Now, Miss Duncan, which . . ."

A solid black piece of shadows suddenly displayed ferocious white teeth. Morro!

Meredith tried to scream a warning but Sazonov cruelly tightened his grip. She sagged against him, her vision graying.

Morro leaped silently and accurately for Sazonov's elbow, sinking his teeth into the arm holding Meredith captive.

Sazonov staggered back but he still managed to keep hold of Meredith.

She writhed, kicking and clawing at his arm. But he ignored her, cursing her champion in Russian.

Morro circled and came back, still deadly quiet. Sazonov turned, trying to keep him in sight—and Meredith went completely limp, forcing him to support her not-inconsiderable weight. He automatically glanced down at her, his blade slipping upward to rest against her hair.

Morro struck again, biting deep into Sazonov's knife hand.

Sazonov shouted in agony and shook himself frantically. Meredith twisted away, her jaw snapping cruelly back in that desperate bid. She staggered, barely able to stand given the roaring in her ears.

The black dog, barely visible in the darkness, charged at Sazonov and took him down, destroying her enemy's ability to chase her. The Russian kicked and lashed out, cursing in his native language. His knife clattered onto the pavement and his bowler rolled away.

She panted, air searing her lungs but grateful she could

hear again. Morro had saved her life; now she had to do the same for him. But how?

The wicked blade gleamed evilly on the pavement. She caught it up and tried to hold it in a fighter's grip. But her hand was shaking too much to use it, even if she'd known how. She kicked it into a drain and it fell, bouncing and clicking and dying in a cascade of watery echoes.

No, all they could do was run—and hope her valiant rescuer had bought them both enough time.

She backed up, glad nobody had come to investigate. Yet.

"Morro!" She whistled the emphatic recall Frau Masaryk had taught her years ago. She'd never honestly thought she'd need to use it.

She picked up her skirts and waited, praying harder than she'd ever prayed before. Would he come to her?

Morro immediately released Sazonov, as if he smelled of foul meat. He raced proudly to Meredith and planted himself in front of her, his stumpy tail thumping the paving. "Good, good boy!"

Sazonov lurched to his feet, his face bloody—but that could have been caused by minor injuries. He took one step after her, then another, his gait moving more and more smoothly with each one. His boots must have protected his legs from any serious harm.

She gulped and ran for the corner, as if the devil was at her heels. A doggy woof caroled into the dank sky from beside her, celebrating a battle won.

Tears touched her eyes but she somehow ran faster, desperate to protect her small family. Heaven help them if Sazonov had servants anywhere around.

"Meredith!"

She slowed for a moment then speeded up again. Surely her mind was playing tricks on her, making her believe she heard Brian's voice.

"Meredith!"

Morro exploded into a chorus of rapturous barks and left

her side. She turned around warily, trusting his instincts more than her own.

She stood in the hotel gardens where, with Brian, she'd once spied upon an amorous couple. A few feet away was where he'd kissed her for the first time. Surely that heated memory was enough to conjure up this phantom.

Morro ecstatically bounced up and down, shouting his joy to the skies. Brian patted him on the head with one hand, his other hand brushing his hat over his leg. His face seemed harder, almost careworn in the hesitant light borrowed from the hotel's environs.

"Meredith," he said again. "Dearest, dearest Meredith." His voice broke and he took a step toward her.

She flung herself into his arms and they closed around her like heaven on earth.

For a moment, they simply held each other and she savored everything about him—the rapid beat of his heart, the heavy wool of his coat, even the stench of cordite.

Brian was alive.

She looked up at him to tell him something, anything about how much she cared, how much he mattered, how much she needed him more than life.

His mouth came down on hers. She yielded, melting into him for the first time without thinking, just letting herself be a part of him.

His tongue caressed her lips, their breath sighed together. He rumbled soft praise when he nuzzled her face before he kissed her again, this time more deeply, more ecstatically. She twined her arms around his neck, the fire flashing down through her lungs into her veins and lower. He tugged gently on her lower lip with his teeth and she moaned softly, her head falling back against his shoulder.

"Meredith, darling, I love you." He plunged his tongue into her mouth, possessing her, mimicking the way they'd soon make love.

She threaded her fingers through his silken hair and pulled

him closer. "Yes, please," she murmured, blushing a little at what she'd just confessed to.

He lifted his head and stared at her. "What did you say?"

"Yes. Please." Her color deepened. Morro was briskly scratching behind one ear, obviously allowing them all the time they needed to sort their affairs out.

She ran her fingers gently down his cheek, nervous at what she was about to clearly admit. "I want you to love me."

Brian gasped.

"Because I love you, too," she finished in a rush.

His arms locked around her so tightly all the air whooshed out of her lungs. "Meredith, my love!"

He lifted her off the ground and swung her around as if she was a featherweight, both of them laughing like fools.

"When will you marry me?"

Drat. She hesitated. "I didn't say that."

"Why not?" he asked carefully. Dawn was coming and she could see him much more clearly now, know he was trying not to show how much she'd hurt him. She had to speak the truth.

"If I commit to marriage, then all the power is on my husband's side."

"I would never abuse it."

"And with his family's patriarch. Even if I trusted you not to abuse your rights with me . . ."

He brushed his lips across her knuckles, silently reassuring her.

"How can I trust the weapons' plans to your family, knowing I can recreate them at any time? What happens to Eisengau's workers?"

He was silent.

"Can you understand that, Brian?" Her heart was making agonized flutters in her chest.

"Yes, of course, I can. I can even admire your dedication, while I hate the penalties."

He seemed to have grown older, looking at something far away.

"I'd like to live with you in California," she offered. "As soon as possible."

"You would?" He stared down at her.

She nodded shyly. "I don't know much about it but I'm willing to learn."

"You're a brave woman, Meredith." He hugged her, shaking a little. "Come on, let's get all of us into that hotel so we can wash up and eat."

"Maybe have a nap?" she suggested hesitantly.

"Are you sure the plans are safe where they are?" he demanded.

She nodded, covering her mouth against a sudden yawn. "For another month, in fact."

"I can hardly wait to hear this explanation," he said drily. "Come on, honey. Let's get you and little Morro some food and shuteye before you fall down on your feet."

"Shuteye?"

"If you're going to live in the West, you need to start learning the lingo." He tucked his hand under her elbow and headed toward the hotel.

"Lingo?"

"You're the linguist, honey. You figure it out."

"Wretch."

He chuckled.

Brian wrapped his arms around Meredith and started counting her pulse again. Her soft hair tickled his shoulder with every breath she took, reminding him she truly was sleeping with him willingly. No bargains this time, just the reservation about not getting married—because she was afraid of his father.

Father! As if William Donovan would ever harm a woman, or make her do anything against her will.

He snarled instinctively and Morro lifted his head from his cushion near the balcony. Sleepy dark eyes met his enquiringly and Brian shrugged a little sheepishly.

Morro yawned and relaxed again, resting his chin on his paws. He must have worked damn hard for his lady yesterday, to be so calm today. Brian still didn't like thinking about how thoroughly she'd checked the little terror's body over for wounds last night.

Damn Sazonov. He'd take a very personal pleasure in destroying that bastard, the minute he saw her to safety. When he'd seen that cut along the side of her face and heard how she'd received it—well, all he could think of were some of the older tales of how Indians took revenge.

But she was alive and that was enough for now, her slender fingers curled over his hip and her legs twined with his. His lady, his love, his life—her breath warming the skin over his heart before they caught the night train to Berlin.

At least she'd agreed to live in California. She probably wouldn't be comfortable in San Francisco, since his parents lived there. But a house in Los Angeles would only be a day away, close enough to visit and have Mother coax her into relaxing.

She shifted, sliding her leg higher across his thigh.

His breath hitched in his throat. Warmth swelled from everywhere she touched, dancing across his skin like a thousand delighted fireflies. His pulse heated, thudding through his veins in slow, steady anticipation. He wasn't about to think about those damn weapons, not when his cock was snuggling up to her hip.

He smiled and began to trace small circles on her shoulder. Meredith would love his mother; everyone did. Or if they didn't, they were smart enough not to mention it in front of his father. And there were his aunts and uncles, too—Hal and Rosalind, Morgan and Jessamyn, Lucas and Rachel—plus his adopted sister Portia and all his cousins. Surely somewhere in that great gaggle was somebody Meredith would want to visit often.

She nuzzled his chest. "You're thinking."

"I'm enjoying myself." Thank God he'd been retracing the

route they'd run to escape the police, trying to stamp every memory he could into his brain. Otherwise, he wouldn't have seen her and he might have lost her forever.

Bright sunlight sent brilliant shards of light dancing through the stained glass and over her hair, like a crown.

"We'd have found each other again somehow. Surely we would have known somehow that each other was alive." She swirled her tongue over his nipple, making him gasp.

"Probably when we bumped into each other, fighting for the blueprints," he choked out and rolled her under him.

"I doubt that." She shook her head, her gray eyes full of mischief. "You'll never guess where they are."

"In Zorndorf's safe, of course."

She sniffed and kissed him passionately on the mouth. Her long, slender fingers stroked his shoulders, awakening little devils in his muscles. He scooped her closer, hungry for her taste, savoring her scent with its heady overtones of musk.

She broke away, panting. His eyes lingered on her rapidly rising and falling breasts with some satisfaction, despite his cock's aggrieved complaint.

"Too obvious," she retorted. Her tongue slipped out to glide over her swollen lips.

"In the city?"

"Are we playing a game?"

"Perhaps we should." He cupped her breasts and bent his head to one, tracing a single blue vein with his tongue. Surely if he waited long enough before tasting her beautiful nipples, he'd regain his control and make her beg for mercy.

Maybe.

On the other hand, they could play this game again after she'd retrieved the plans. That would permit him to simply enjoy himself now and save tricking her for later. If he could trick her.

"Nice try at deceiving me, mister." She pulled his head closer, sliding her fingers through his hair and kneading his scalp.

"Mmph," he muttered. Warmth burned brighter, flashing between his lips and his chest.

She wrapped her leg around his hips, rubbing herself against him like a fierce little tigress. His lady.

Hunger pulsed between his lungs and his groin, surged into his crotch, built deep in his blood. His cock swelled stronger, reaching for her alone.

She rubbed her foot restlessly over the back of his thigh, rocking her hips against him. Her breasts were honey to his lips, her nipples' aching tips the finest candy, the delicate blue veins like the finest wine because they led to intoxication for both of them.

"Roll over, mister."

"What?" She wanted to have a conversation at a time like this?

She rubbed her thumbs over his cheekbones. Her eyes were glinting with laughter under their heavy lids, her lips bruised and swollen.

His mouth went dry.

"If you give me a condom"—Of course, he would!—"And let me be on the top, I'll show you where the plans are."

She gave him a lascivious wink and slipped her hand between them to gently cup his balls. His eyes crossed from sheer, liquid pleasure and he fought not to come. Why had he taught her how to do that?

So she could do it again, after they left Eisengau, a faint bit of sanity answered.

He managed to nod agreement.

She smiled happily and he grinned. What wouldn't he have pledged, to see that look on her face?

He grabbed a condom from the stash in the bedside drawer, while any logic survived. His checkbook had made the hotel staff very helpful when they'd arrived. A moment later, he'd applied it to his rearing cock and lay back down.

She sighed, making him grin triumphantly in private, and knelt beside him. She reached out tentatively, her eyes enormous with hunger.

"Anything you want, my love," he encouraged.

"You're so beautiful," she whispered.

He flushed scarlet but his cock swelled even more. She believed that of him?

She circled her palm over his chest, her fingers diving through the matted hair then into the line leading lower. Into, out of his fur, her fingertips explored, always going farther down—taking his breath away—until they lightly glided down his cock.

He jerked upward, throwing himself at her mercy. His pulse pounded in his ears and his veins. His skin was so hot and tight, the slightest spark would make it explode.

She brushed her hair over him and kissed his cock. He couldn't breathe, couldn't think. He gripped her shoulders, aching to pull her upward. But if this was what she wanted, he'd give it to her.

"Brian, my love." His heart stopped beating.

She came astride him. His hands slid down her shoulders, to her thighs, always staying in touch.

She squatted and guided him into her, slowly, slowly, wet slick channel sucking fiery aching stalk. Deep muscles grabbed him and sweetly hauled him in, every agonizingly steady inch.

But he couldn't scrabble for patience among the bedclothes. He flung his head back on the pillow, fighting not to bruise her sweet thighs. He reached for the bedclothes, aching to shred something so he wouldn't snatch her onto his chest, roll over, and drive himself into her like a crazed fool.

She wobbled, nearly falling over. *She isn't a trained courtesan, you damn fool!* His hands shot back to her, faster than a heartbeat, to steady her and protect himself. She needed his help—and he'd give it to her, no matter what.

She sighed in pleasure, her eyes shuttering in pure bliss, when their bodies finally meshed. Any agony was worth that expression on her face.

She closed her legs firmly and circled her hips experimentally and he moaned, the exquisite, unique sensations driving into places unused to such intense pleasures of body and mind. She repeated the motion but tilted her hips forward slightly.

His eyes crossed. Sweet Jesus, perhaps they should argue about weapons more often!

How many ways could she find to enjoy each other? A dozen? Two dozen?

His hips rocked against her, his seed a fiery explosion barely leashed next to his spine. Cream slipped down her thighs to meet his cock, easing the eager glide of their bodies over each other.

She was gasping for breath, rising and falling above him. Meredith chanted his name, her face taut with desperation.

Brian pinched her nipple, giving her one last, sharp stab of pleasure and pain.

She arched, sobbing, and finally climaxed. The great spasms racked her body above him, around him, and through him. Fire shot down his spine and out through his cock, ripping his seed from him. He shook again and again, his ears deafened by his pulse exploding through his bones.

Somehow he caught her and rolled her under him, aching to hold onto his one true anchor.

She was still resting against his heart when the world came back into being afterward.

"Couldn't stand to be underneath for very long, could you," she teased, a little sleepily.

"Couldn't stand to be very far away from you," he corrected.

She let the silence stretch for a moment before she answered.

"Sweet words won't change my mind about what to do with the plans," she said gently.

"Did you truly think I'd ever let you out of my sight again?"

"No, thank God." Her voice broke on a little sob and he held her closer.

"We can solve anything together, darling. I don't know how we'll manage to make both of us happy but we'll do it somehow."

"Together." She kissed him gently on the cheek.

Chapter Fourteen

"First, we need to regain the plans." Brian tapped his forefinger, his face lost in thought under the very Germanic woolen hat. They'd both acquired local costumes at the hotel, which wasn't a hardship. She didn't want to ever see again the clothes Sazonov had recognized her in. Hers had the delightful—and pragmatic—advantage of hanging a few inches off the ground.

Plus, he was wearing a map case, whose long narrow shape would be perfect for carrying the plans.

"We can do that very easily, so long as it's daylight." She studied the university's back entrance. They were standing in student lodgings across the street, which were vacant for the summer. The small room was minimally furnished, although its usual rent was exorbitant.

The cathedral was ringing the passing bell again for Grand Duke Rudolph, calling the faithful to pray for his soul. She suspected more would answer the joyous carillons at Grand Duke Nicholas's coronation than this steady, dolorous call.

"Second, we have to catch the train for Berlin," Brian went on, after only a moment's pause.

She smiled at him. It was time to start showing her hand. "Actually, first, we need to obtain the materials to destroy the plans—should affairs go wrong and Sazonov lay his hands on them."

"Are you sure, Meredith?" Brian stared at her.

"After last night, I know Sazonov will do—anything to obtain them. The workers would gain nothing but America and Britain would be, ah, greatly damaged." She wasn't used to fumbling for words, let alone changing her mind.

"Hence, the university."

"Exactly."

"Where we can kill two birds with one stone."

He grinned.

Not exactly. She opened her mouth to correct him.

"After which, you can show the plans to a member of Her Majesty's Government. Or, if you're feeling generous—or exceptionally paranoid—you can give them to us for safe transport out of Eisengau in the diplomatic bag," a crisp Welsh voice interrupted them.

They spun to face the door. Brian's young British friend propped his shoulder against the doorframe and watched them.

"Gareth. I should have known." Brian's mouth worked but he didn't spit.

Morro growled and Meredith silenced him with a single hand signal, warning him to caution.

"Don't look so furious, old man. I come as a friend, not a foe."

"How did you know we were here?" Stall, Meredith, stall. Maybe Brian would think of a way to escape.

"If I was trying to break into the university, this is exactly where I'd spy on it from. Assuming I had a lady present, that is." He bowed to her.

"What do you want?" Brian asked coldly, his earlier flash of temper entirely muffled. She'd have felt better facing the fury.

"What every other diplomat in this town wants: the chance to copy those plans. They're all hunting you, y'know."

Meredith looked back and forth between the two men, trying to judge where friendship began and ended.

"Where are they?"

"Eisengau is a steep mountain valley, for pity's sake. Every

road, every railway station, even the barges on the river—
they all now have at least one paid spy and probably more.
Secret police are fairly efficient but you can usually bribe them."

"But not this many spies."

"Even you couldn't buy off all of them with such an enormous
prize at stake." Blackwood shook his head. "Plus, they're bringing in the big guns from Switzerland and beyond to hunt you."

"In case she's gone to ground." Brian's tone was very flat.

"Exactly. They'll flush her out, no matter where she goes
or who she's with." Blackwood cautiously straightened up.
"If you give us the plans, all will be solved."

"No."

"Why not? You don't have an embassy here to provide
sanctuary."

"Because she wants the chance to use them for Eisengau's
workers."

"You've gone mad. Those cannons are needed by the U.S.
and Britain, not a gaggle of backwater peasants."

"I suggest you reconsider your opinion." A knife slid into
Brian's palm, light glinting on its razor-sharp blade. Meredith
squeaked faintly.

The air was suddenly too heavy to breathe.

Blackwood frowned, his eyes narrowing. "You wouldn't
use that, would you? Not over this?"

"Not unless you force me to. But Meredith gets to make
her own decisions as long as I'm around."

"She's a woman."

"So?"

"You've lost your mind." Blackwood marched over to the
room's sole chair, sat down, and thrust his hands behind him.
"Best make it look good when you tie me up. My ambassador's a canny old bird."

The sharp blade disappeared back into Brian's sleeve.
Meredith gulped and started to hunt for clothesline.

"Anything else we should know?" Brian asked.

"Rumor says the Russians have the biggest organization

here, other than ours." Blackwood warily eyed the dog sniffing suspiciously at him then brought his attention back to
Brian. "Supposedly they have people scattered throughout
the capital and outside it, as well."

"Bully for them." Brian finished tying him off, his long fingers moving almost too quickly to be seen. "Thanks for the tip."

"And please . . ."

"Yes?" They looked back from the door.

"Send me an invitation to the wedding."

Meredith gaped at him. "There won't be one."

"I beg to differ, miss. Good luck."

She managed not to slam the door. She would have preferred to throw something at him.

"Where now? The university?" Brian asked, considering the
dreary alley with its row of trashcans. Marlowe and Spenser
undoubtedly knew exactly how to break into such places,
given their proven ability to escape from every school the
family had ever sent them to. And get excellent grades at the
same institutions, too, which his own boredom had always
hampered.

"Yes, of course." Meredith was listening to the bells again
and he fought back his impatience. The last one tolled and
she nodded briskly. "Now we can go. The guard should have
just finished his round inside."

Brian raised an eyebrow at her reliance on Teutonic efficiency
but followed her down the squalid passageway. He choked
when she produced a key ring from her purse and began to
quickly flip through it. "Do you have keys for all the doors?"

He leaned against the wall, keeping an eye out for any
passersby. Morro was beside him, doing the same.

"A master key for most of them, yes. Zorndorf enjoyed
calling his staff in after hours." She held up a key to the single
shaft of light, nodded, and shoved it into the lock. A quick
twist and the door silently opened.

Brian caught the knob out of her hand, provoking a glare.

Good Lord, the chances that woman had been about to take, stepping into a dark building without a second thought.

He poked his head inside and looked around but saw nobody. "Come on."

She sniffed and followed, Morro at her heels as always.

"Where now? Upstairs?" he whispered.

"No, the supply closet."

Supplies? Had she hidden the plans in the one room many people were likely to go in and out of?

"Turn left and go to the end, then take a right to the first door," she hissed.

The hallways were deserted, the only sounds those of gossip over clattering coffee cops and footsteps crossing floors overhead. Morro was silent, his head up but his ears relaxed.

She produced this key faster than the last one but he still gripped his knife the entire time. She grabbed the lantern and disappeared inside, emerging within seconds and carrying a sturdy wicker basket.

"Those aren't the plans," he commented, heading for the door.

"No." She chuckled. "Let's just say we absolutely don't want to mix its contents with any water."

He regarded the nondescript parcel with considerably more interest but didn't stop to ask questions. They had very little time if they wanted to catch the evening train to Berlin.

She led him to another street, filled with closely packed, gold and orange stucco and brick buildings, topped by red tile roofs. She was far more cautious here, always keeping a wary eye out for any watchers.

He eyed the stiff set of her shoulders, glad for his knife. Dammit, he'd have preferred his Mauser, little though that suited a polite district.

A gleaming white church rose out of the fog and rain, fronted by elegant white pillars. Above it gilded pediments raised a cross to the darkening sky and a single bell rang mournfully. A few black-clad women rushed out of it, bringing bursts of organ music and lifting umbrellas as if warding off the devil.

Meredith lingered by the café across the street, eyeing them.

Why the devil was she going to church, someplace guaranteed to have watchers?

He frowned and wrapped his arm around her waist. "Where's the back door, love?" he whispered.

"Around to the right. But I don't have a key and the organist will notice me."

"And Morro."

"Oh, dogs are common enough not to attract much attention."

Morro wagged his tail, recognizing his name, and Brian harrumphed under his breath. Even for a sentimental Germanic country, Eisengau welcomed its canines more than most.

The flow of churchgoers ebbed, leaving a lull in the traffic.

Brian immediately gripped Meredith by the elbow and raced across the street. He shoved her inside the door and closed it quietly. Whoever the builders had been, all those centuries ago, they'd done very, very well.

Morro slipped through on their heels, silent as a well-bred cat.

Meredith tugged Brian's sleeve and half-pushed, half-pulled him into the closest pew. Morro settled at her feet, barely visible against the black and white marble floor. He'd clearly been here before.

Brian sat down, determined to be inconspicuous, and took stock of one of the fanciest churches he'd ever seen.

The place of worship was all cream and gold magnificence, with an immense pair of paintings towering behind the ornate, gold high altar. Great white pillars, topped by embossed gold curlicues, upheld a ceiling composed of magnificent frescoes. Black and gold pulpits stood tall, to enhance the speaker's authority. Sunlight crept into the great hall from immense semicircular windows between the frescoes and the pillars, bouncing between the white surfaces until it became a glowing ball and the paintings seemed to float.

A quiet warmth enveloped its sanctuary, as if its golden light had sunk into its bones. A few old women knelt in prayer among the pews, their soft words a reassuringly familiar hum from the few times he'd been an altar boy. Even the bells which tolled loudly elsewhere for the dead grand duke were muffled here.

Brian instinctively bowed his head and crossed himself, taking comfort from old joys.

Two black-robed priests whispered urgently amid the columns to the side.

"If the new grand duke is coming here for matins tomorrow morning, I must have time to practice before then. Not on the piano—but on the organ to be played for the service!"

"I'm telling you all must be cleaned first. It is the archbishop's order."

Meredith gasped and Brian stared at her. She'd turned very pale.

"Not everything . . ."

"The organ screen tops the rear balcony. All of it must be perfect for the grand duke. This is a great honor, do you hear me?"

Meredith closed her eyes. She tugged at Brian's sleeve, her hand shaking, and left the pew through the center aisle.

"A century has passed since a grand duke has prayed at the people's church." The organist shook his head. "It is good Grand Duke Nicholas who is bringing back the ancient tradition—but must he make me look like a fool?"

Brian glanced back but the two men were facing the high altar, their heads close together.

"You are the greatest organist in all of Eisengau. It's impossible for you to appear anything but brilliant."

The organist sniffed and folded his arms across his chest.

She swallowed hard and began to move faster, Morro matching her every step. She headed for the rear of the church, moving with the assurance of somebody who had every right to be there and totally ignoring everyone else.

He frowned and followed her, hoping her strategy would work and nobody would raise the alarm.

An instant later, she left the sunlight behind and passed into the shadows under the deep balcony. She headed unerringly for a doorway, identifiable only by ripples of wood carved into a broad pillar and a thin metal strip for a handle.

"Let me try it first, sweetheart." Brian wrapped his hand around hers.

She started but didn't scream, thank God. Instead, she stepped back and allowed him to lead the way, her white teeth gnawing her lower lip.

The narrow staircase inside was steep and full of turns. A teenager could have defended it against an army but Morro went up it fearlessly.

They emerged into blinding light, the sun having finally broken through the rainclouds. Complicated carved screens loomed on every side, filled with great pipes, in a great symphony of art and frozen music. Four great keyboards rose, one above the other, begging to be played. Rows of wooden plugs murmured suggestions about loudness and softness. Dozens of pedals stretched across the loft, beneath the widest bench he'd ever seen.

Brian gaped at it. Despite his escapades in later years, he'd been born the son of a very fine pianist.

"How many organists do you need to play it?" he queried, barely remembering to keep his voice down.

"One can manage the basics." Meredith set her basket down and silently ordered Morro to guard it.

He shot her a disbelieving look and demanded a better answer, without saying another word. Her mouth twitched.

"Two are more common—and I've seen four."

Four? He mouthed the number.

She nodded rueful agreement and went to her knees before the bench, careful to dodge the pedals' protruding edges behind it.

He eyed it suspiciously from his guard post in front of the

door. It was long, shallow, and solid wood, lacking even an upholstered top. Its legs were superbly carved, curved and cross-braced to support the seat. Maybe it held the key to where the plans really were.

She sprang up to her feet, holding a tawdry, brown roll of fabric, as long and as thick as her arm. She clutched it and spun, chortling.

"Meredith!" Brian hissed. By all the saints, if anybody happened to glance up here or if Morro disobeyed her order to be quiet, they'd be spotted immediately.

She glanced at him inquiringly. Her eyes widened and she stopped immediately, flushing. Then she winked at him.

He shook his head but had to grin back at her. "How did you find that that drawer? Or is it a ledge?"

"Ledge. It helps cross-brace the bench's legs." She knelt to tuck the damn plans inside his map case. "My best friend studied organ and once dropped an earring between the pedals. While hunting for it, we spotted the shelf and used it to pass notes."

He'd have done the same with his brothers.

"Now what?" she asked, standing up with a neatly fastened case.

"We have just enough time to catch the afternoon train to Berlin and Paris." Thank God his intellectual darling always kept her paperwork with her. He didn't know which would have been worse—try to bribe a Prussian customs inspector or persuade her to marry him so she could travel on his passport.

"We can't take the plans out of Eisengau." Her lovely jaw was locked tighter than a steel vault.

He glanced over the railing, settling the map case diagonally across his chest. The priest and organist seemed to have become closer friends. "Let's talk about this somewhere else."

"*Not* on the train."

"Not *here*." He jerked his head toward the scarlet carpet flowing toward them below—and the two men still arguing there.

"I believe the processional must be more eloquent, rather than a strictly traditional piece," the organist stated, clearly determined not to add "*dolt.*"

"For a prayer service like this . . ." the priest began.

The organist sighed grandiloquently. "If you'll let me fetch my music, I can show you what I mean."

Meredith cast a horrified look at Brian. "Not here," she agreed.

They tiptoed out, doing their best to appear ordinary citizens.

The moment the great doors opened onto the street, Meredith turned to Brian. "Altstadt," she said firmly.

No words came. Instead, his hand brutally gripped her shoulder and shoved her toward one of the pillars.

"What on earth?" She rubbed her aching muscles and looked to see what had provoked him.

"*Entschuldigung, mein Herr?*" a very smug man inquired.

Oh, drat and double drat. It was Chief Inspector Grebing, who'd led the raid on the beer house—together with Sazonov. He'd always been willing to take bribes, if it didn't interfere with Grand Duke Rudolph's orders.

The big, brutal beast smiled at Brian, exposing a row of sharp, crooked teeth.

"Good afternoon, Donovan." Sazonov chuckled, his face obscured by a bloodstained bandage wrapped around his forehead. "Let me introduce to my friend to make sure you realize which one of us is master." He briefly flourished an ugly revolver before putting it back into his pocket.

Meredith gritted her teeth, her stomach sinking toward her boots. Should she pray for somebody to come along so they could send help? Or would Sazonov shoot them, too?

Morro snarled deep in his throat, warning he too could attack.

"How did you know we were here?" Brian asked, neither voice nor attitude betraying any discomfort.

"It's where the girls always spent the most time. My spies sent me word the moment you showed up."

She'd remember that the next time she had to hide something. But, oh, she didn't want Brian to die for her mistake.

Morro bared his teeth, his rumbling roar deepening.

"Now have the girl bring the map case and the basket to the steps."

She blinked. He didn't know which one held the plans.

"No, I will," Brian said softly. "If she comes, the dog does, too."

Her lungs seized—but she didn't argue. Brian must have something in mind.

"Very well," Sazonov agreed.

Brian advanced onto the wet marble steps, his suddenly nervous smile making him look remarkably young and foolish.

She eased out from behind the white marble column to see him better, nervously aware of the windows rising around them. Morro growled vehement objections.

"If you please, sir," Brian suggested.

"Yes?" Grebing took a gloating step closer toward him.

Brian slung the basket over his shoulder straight back at her.

If it crashed to the ground, they'd all die.

Terrified beyond rational thought, she dived forward and caught the flying missile only inches above the ground. Shaking and gasping for breath, she clutched it to her chest and sat up.

"You fool!" Sazonov snapped.

Brian ignored him, eyeing instead the crooked policeman.

Morro arrived beside her, clearly willing to do battle. She steadied him with a single quick pat and chanced a quick look at her new location.

"Why did you do that?" demanded Grebing, who must sometimes still remember how to be a policeman.

Brian punched him in the nose, using the back of his fist. Blood spurted, spilling crimson over the other's far too expensive clothes.

The crooked cop lost his footing on the slick paving and went down, sliding into Sazonov.

The Russian's pistol fired, sending echoes ricocheting off building after building.

Meredith sprang to her feet

Brian snatched up the map case and dropped it over his head. In the same smooth movement, he caught her by the hand and hauled her into motion, barely giving her time to get her feet under her. Morro galloped alongside, quiet as a lion on the hunt.

A shot whizzed after them. Meredith flinched but Brian only moved faster, dodging a bit from side to side. Oh dear Lord, Sazonov must either control the police or have nothing left to lose, if he was willing to try to kill them where so many people could see.

And if one of his bullets nicked the basket, causing it to explode . . .Her heart was pounding far faster than the windows being thrown open around them.

Saffron and gold walls rose around them, filled with windows and topped by dozens of different spires. Where could they escape Sazonov?

BAM! BAM! Plaster chips burst around them, scouring their arms and spitting dust into the air. Their enemy was coming closer.

"Turn just past the second building—where the balcony is upheld by the two eagles."

Brian didn't bother to nod. At the last possible second, he dodged sideways into a narrow passageway under a broad arch. A dozen immensely dark steps led to a sharp left hand turn and a long passageway between blank brick walls. The floor was drier here than the street outside, a tribute to its original builders' skills.

Unfortunately, only a single pair of feet ran past them. She'd have preferred to hear a pack, hunting Sazonov down like a beast. Instead, he'd probably come back more slowly to sniff them out.

Chapter Fifteen

"Now will you let me go?" Meredith demanded, her fingers aching from where he'd gripped them so ferociously.

"Yes, of course." Brian released her slowly, panting but still in control of himself.

Morro's ears were pricked forward as he listened to something outside. Then he relaxed and came back to her, strutting a little, to deliver the good news their enemy had gone well past them.

"Where are we?" Brian ran his hand over the smoothly plastered walls.

"Underneath the national library. Today is a national day of mourning so it should be closed."

"Librarians didn't build this." He pulled her into an alcove, lit by borrowed light from a garden above.

"No, it was the Catholic university three centuries ago. Spanish Jesuits designed it."

"Jesuits." His mouth twisted ruefully. "They always did have the most creative thought processes."

"My friend Liesel rarely came here so Sazonov shouldn't know about these passages." Hopefully, one of the day's lessons would prove useful.

"We still have a few minutes to catch the train." He kissed her fingers.

She frowned at him. "Are you trying to encourage me? Spur me into a mad dash across the market square?"

"Well . . ." He shrugged

"Won't Grebing have warned—or bribed—all his fellow secret policemen to arrest both of us?" she demanded.

"Yes."

"Don't conceal the truth from me again." She started to stomp her foot but thought better of it. These passageways could produce very strange echoes, possibly enough to be heard outside, even though they were talking softly.

"You could make it onboard if I diverted them."

"And they'd grab me five minutes later." She trailed her fingers over his jaw. "No, love. Our lives are at stake now. We do this together or not at all."

"If we made it to a neutral embassy . . ." Brian frowned.

"Whose? Switzerland hasn't bothered to maintain one here for decades. Everyone else wants the cannon's plans for themselves."

"If Sazonov was guarding your friends' favorite retreat—at the church—then he'll definitely watch my only friend's sanctuary."

"The British embassy." She followed his thoughts readily and he nodded grimly.

"The answer's Switzerland. But the country, not the embassy, and we'll have to walk."

He kissed her forehead and she allowed herself to lean against him for an instant. "My father . . ."

Father? She stared at him, her breath frozen in her throat. What would that autocrat demand from her?

The dark walls began to tighten around her. But bright light still shone high above, echoed in Brian's smooth drawl.

"My entire family, sweetheart, is coming over St. Nicholas Pass tomorrow afternoon with horses and supplies. Once we meet them, all will be well."

Roses perfumed the air, as reassuring as the warmth in

Brian's blue eyes. He genuinely believed this. She needed to do so, as well. Somehow.

"Your family?" she questioned, kneading Brian's shoulder with her free hand.

"My mother will be there, too."

Surely a woman wouldn't let Mr. Donovan be too impossible? Ochre bricks faded into saffron plaster, allowing air to seep into her lungs again. Brian nuzzled her cheek, offering her comfort and time to accept the brutal necessity.

After a few moments, she kissed him gently on the mouth. His lips curved and they pledged themselves silently to each other.

She forced herself to focus on practicalities, after he lifted his head. "Very well. We can't take the passenger train to Switzerland, even though the customs post there is lightly manned. There are so few trains, we'd be caught in a moment."

He nodded agreement, his dear face brightening. There had to be at least some good people among his family to produce somebody like him.

She'd have to make sure they wouldn't be seen by anyone on that hike to the border, lest the police shoot or arrest her darling.

Dratted police.

But perhaps they could be seen by some people.

"How much money do you have?" she demanded.

"Sweetheart, when you've broken a chief inspector's nose, no amount of cash will stop the police from venting their wrath on you."

"Not them, darling. I think I know somebody who can smuggle us onto a train out of the capital. But we'd have to pay for any supplies."

Brian spun around, staring at her. A moment later, he shook his head and a gleeful smile dawned on his face. "I might have known you could pull something like that. Let's start moving, darling. Sazonov could investigate this hole in the wall at any time."

* * *

An hour of dodging through narrow passages, steep stairs, and dank basements gave Brian new respect for the workers' party's ancient roots and widespread support. They were rarely aboveground more than a half dozen paces before disappearing into another colonnade or opening a nondescript door to discover a steep stairwell.

He'd always prided himself on having a teamster's nose for direction. But Meredith's route through dark, twisting tunnels, that never seemed to find the same level twice, would have baffled a gopher.

"How do you know where we are?" he demanded once, enjoying a rare glimpse of sunlight while they waited to cross a street unnoticed.

"I was the courier, since I carried messages for Zorndorf at odd hours across the city. He was a demanding master so I learned quickly." She smiled briefly. "Truly, we haven't gone that far. We're mostly taking a very obscure route . . ."

"To avoid meeting any cops," he finished her sentence.

"Correct." Traffic finally satisfied her and she dodged across the cobblestoned gap, jumping a puddle on the other side. Morro accompanied her, ears swiveling alertly.

Brian shook his head and followed his lady into the less reputable sections.

Finally she stepped boldly onto a street and turned left into a square. She walked calmly here, clearly expecting to be recognized and greeted.

Sweet Jesus, what a risk! How many secret police were there in Eisengau? How long would it take before one of them saw her?

Brian took two quick strides and caught up with her, letting Morro escort her on the other side.

This neighborhood wasn't nearly as pretty as the others Brian had seen in Eisengau, although it was just as immaculately clean. Stone had been husbanded carefully here, starting with its usage in only a few buildings' lower levels to protect against floods. Most buildings were made entirely of the cheaper bricks. No smooth stucco walls existed to be embellished with fancy curlicues or plaques, bragging of their makers. The few arches were strictly functional to protect windows and doorways against winter snows. Even the roofs' simple tiles had been replaced again and again, leading to a patchwork quilt of chipped, uneven surfaces and different colors.

The light was thin here, filtered by the late afternoon mists rising from the great river. It was as tenuous as the scent of dinner drifting from open windows, of stewing cabbages barely enlivened by pork and a little sausage.

The children studying them wore clothing that was too old and had been darned too often, their bodies much too thin. Their parents' eyes were too watchful and their hands too ready to snatch up their little ones.

Brian had seen places like this in Pennsylvania and Colorado, company towns where the employer himself wasn't trusted. But there were no police anywhere in sight, no skin crawling over his scalp in warning.

Then Morro woofed in greeting. The residents grinned and waved at him, their faces lighting up as if they'd spotted a long-lost relation. The little kids danced out to play with him, their mothers called out affectionately to him, and the men stopped to offer compliments.

"Why is Morro so special here?" Brian whispered after the fourth such conversation.

"He's from a local breed—peasant stock, not blue blood. They're highly valued as watchdogs and ratters."

"But not by aristocrats or social climbers." Like Meredith's mother and stepfather.

She stiffened but didn't look at him. "No, not by folks like that. He came from a lady who took me under her wing shortly after I arrived."

"And he proves our bona fides as friends of the people."

"Hopefully." She paused to smile at Morro being hugged

by two very small little girls. "I haven't visited my friends at home before. I do know that police never come to this neighborhood. They didn't dare do that even during the great 1848 demonstrations."

"When all Europe was ablaze with revolution," Brian filled in. "And the aftermath was bloody."

She nodded and moved forward again.

Two men waited outside a broad archway, watching them approach. One wore a respectable suit and hat, while the other had a mismatched jacket and trousers, plus patched boots. A boy stood next to them, possibly twelve years old, wearing an oversized straw boater. His bare feet and shins were badly nicked and bruised.

"Herr Mayer," Meredith bobbed a respectful curtsy to the suit-wearer. "Herr Brecht." She repeated the courtesy. "How are you, Anton?"

"Very well indeed, Fräulein Duncan, thank you." Brown eyes, which had been scrutinizing Brian suspiciously, blazed into radiance when they dwelt on her. "Thank you for everything."

"Yes, indeed." Brecht dropped his hand onto Anton's shoulder, underlining their strong likeness.

What had she done for the family?

"May I introduce you to Brian Donovan, from America?"

Mayer gripped hard, obviously trying to grind Brian's bones together. It wasn't the first time somebody had misjudged him by his face. But he'd learned this game on the West's roughest trails.

Brian squeezed back, giving as good as he got.

Mayer grunted and broke the handshake first. Brecht's hand was far rougher but Brian gritted his teeth and refused to back down. He was still relieved when Brecht released him.

Meredith's eyes were very wide but she was smart enough not to say anything.

"You're not a student," Mayer stated.

"No, sir. I left at sixteen, after I finished high school, to work for my father." He wasn't about to shake his hand to restore the circulation, no matter how much it hurt.

"Miner?" Brecht asked.

"Sometimes. I spent a winter in the Klondike and I've worked the high Rockies. But mostly I'm a teamster." Better stick to the public stuff, not the risky freight which the company only discussed with the client.

"Driving four-horse teams for drays and trucks? Your hands are stronger than that."

"Those are popular for city work, Herr Mayer. Donovan & Sons carries a good deal of freight across the West's wide-open country. So I can also drive a sixteen-horse hitch." Why were they asking enough questions for a job interview?

"Impressive," muttered Brecht. "Not many men can stand up to my grip."

Meredith choked.

"Please enter, Fräulein Duncan, fellow worker." Meyer stepped back, allowing them to pass. "Warn us if they're followed, Anton."

"Of course, uncle." The boy ran off, after one more beaming smile at Meredith.

The tiny apartment was painfully clean and filled with an odd assortment of old, sturdy furniture. Vivid posters covered the walls, advertising art gallery openings.

A silent woman produced coffee for all of them and promptly disappeared, while Mayer shut the windows. He leaned his hip against the sideboard, upsetting a stack of papers.

Brian promptly grabbed for them and came up holding—a certificate from Grand Duke Rudolph? He promptly schooled his face into urbanity.

"I'm a foreman at the grand duke's foundry." Mayer took the gold-stamped parchment from him.

"He's the man responsible for overseeing all the special castings from the engineering college," added Meredith.

"Like Zorndorf's designs," interpreted Brian.

"Exactly," she agreed. "He's the best foreman at the foundry."

Mayer gave her a horrified look and hastily gulped his coffee, hiding his face. Brian sympathized with the need to avoid acknowledging a woman's praise.

"Herr Brecht is his brother-in-law. They married sisters," she added.

"You saved my son's life." Brecht leaned forward, his big shoulders and arms enveloping the room's center. "Whatever we have is yours."

"That's not . . ." She tried again, her gray eyes enormous. "That's not necessary. Anybody would have done the same."

"Shouted a warning? Which could have broken everyone's concentration and destroyed a very important casting? While the secret police were there?" He slowly shook his shaggy head. "I think not. If we have it, it is yours."

He sat back, folding his arms.

She gaped at him, utterly silenced for once.

"What do you need, Herr Donovan?" Mayer asked briskly. "You are a worker; you can express these things in practicalities."

"Travel to Switzerland without meeting the police or anyone else." Brian dragged his gaze away from his flummoxed darling. The sight would undoubtedly become a treasured memory, if only for its rarity.

"Every spy in the country hunts you, according to beer hall gossip," Brecht remarked conversationally. "They are like locusts, trying to eat everything we create."

"It will add sport to the game, to finally tweak their tails." The two men saluted each other with their coffee cups.

"So you'll do it?" Brian asked eagerly.

"Yes, of course." Brecht frowned at him. "We would have done far more than that."

"We couldn't put you in further danger."

The men ignored her by unspoken agreement.

"There's a train leaving late tonight for Italy, traveling through Switzerland and carrying some of our older cannons." Mayer clicked his tongue. "Our police won't stop them. But Swiss customs inspectors will—and the two posts are very close together at the border. You will need to disappear at a watering stop before then."

"It will be our pleasure." Brian bowed.

"There's a separate boxcar for the more fragile gear, which have been painted with their insignia. You should not be disturbed in there but there won't be any comforts for Fräulein Duncan." Brecht rubbed his chin, visibly disturbed.

"I won't break." Meredith sniffed and sat up very straight.

No, but she'd be trekking into the Alps, over a very steep, difficult pass, immediately after strong rains, making a boxcar the least of his worries. He didn't want to contemplate coaxing her through a granite fissure, while a torrent rushed past their feet. He'd rather face Sazonov than do that.

At least they still had the plans for that damn big cannon so they could keep the Russians out of Alaska.

Meredith grumbled, rolled over, and stuck her elbow into living human rather than featherbed.

"Oof!" Brian grunted but he didn't push her away.

She shot upright, appalled. "I'm sorry. I forgot you were here. I mean, that doesn't sound quite right."

Blue eyes regarded her quizzically in the faint light from the running lantern outside the door. "I'm glad you were able to sleep that well."

"I'm sorry I woke you up."

He shrugged and pulled her back down onto his chest, tucking the threadbare blanket around them. They'd only allowed Mayer and Brecht to provide the minimum of supplies, despite heated protests.

Wheels clickety-clacked rhythmically underneath them. The forest of boxes around them rattled continuously, despite being fastened to the floor. Far worse was the constant clatter coming from the boxcars next door where the Italian cannon traveled. They rattled, creaked, and groaned, every metal part banging endlessly and randomly against another. The box-cars themselves complained about their heavy load, the frames groaning and the wheels shuddering as much as clacking. She and Brian almost had to shout at each other, in order to be heard.

Morro had spent his first half hour aboard pacing the box-car's perimeter and sniffing every sealed object. Finally he'd curled up and gone to sleep, apparently satisfied the mechanical demons had temporarily taken over guard duty.

"Would you like some more cheese? Or bread?" Brian offered.

She shook her head and shifted into a sitting position. Now that she was awake, the unpredictable drafts and jostling made it impossible to relax again. "What time is it?"

"A couple of hours before dawn." He drew himself up to talk to her more easily. "We've been pulled over several times for fast trains."

"Troop trains?"

"Possibly. From what I overhead, I suspect we're maybe an hour from the border."

She frowned, trying to calculate where they were.

The brakes screamed, a harsh cry that echoed through the walls and the wheels underneath. Next door, metal banged loudly and shattered. Somebody yelled a profanity.

The boxes around them rattled hard and hurtled toward the boxcar's rear. Morro woke with a howl. Meredith's hips slid out from under her, sending her straight for a stack of falling equipment.

Time suddenly stretched until all she could see was Brian's face, all she could feel was her pulse slowly beating in her veins.

Brian grabbed both her and Morro, his fingers locking like bracelets around her wrist. He braced his feet against a pair of wheels bolted into the floor and held grimly on, his jaw set in an unspoken challenge to fate.

The boxcar shuddered, shaking and wavering on its wheels.

The basket shot past them—but she didn't care if it exploded, not if she had Brian.

The train finally stopped, its overtaxed metal complaining vehemently to the end.

He released her immediately, a silent question in his eyes.

She nodded her all-clear. She was well now, since he was. Morro gave her fingers a quick lick, making her smile a little tremulously. The rogue had probably enjoyed that wild ride.

Italian voices rose in bitter complaint from the railroad cars behind them to be answered by men tramping alongside the train.

"Accident ahead?" Brian whispered.

She shook her head, listening hard.

"The police then." He tossed her the map case and she caught it automatically, silently questioning him. "Sazonov won't hurt anyone who's carrying it."

She reared up in immediate outrage and started to hand it back. He needed the protection more than she did. But he shoved her hat into her hand before she could move.

"Besides, it could get in my way. Now hurry up."

She glared at him and dropped it over her shoulders, twisting it so the precious cannon plans rested over her back. She pinned her soft hat on her head with more violence than necessary and snatched up her fragile basket and the staff Brecht had insisted she take.

Morro glanced back from the door he'd been sniffing. The footsteps were moving forward along the train, heading for them.

"Ready?" Brian was standing by the other door, calm, deadly, utterly poised.

She nodded to her warrior, an echo of his calmness sinking into her bones.

Mayer and Brecht had arranged for a false lock to be placed on their door. If it still worked . . .

Brian pulled the well-oiled latch back, taking the lock with it, thank God. He jumped silently down and Morro promptly stuck his head outside to inspect their surroundings.

Her lover jolted in surprise then waited.

Morro looked back at him an instant later, ears pricked forward, and chuffed softly. An instant later, Brian had brought both her and his canine cohort onto the ground.

He silently closed the door behind them and grabbed her hand. Even after the dimness inside the boxcar, the outside night was bitterly black and she could barely see the mountain-side's rocks and trees.

"I do not care if these cars are protected by diplomatic immunity. These criminals tried to kill a policeman." Sazonov's voice broke through the confused blur of men's voices.

Meredith's fingers tightened around her lover's. How typical of that Russian to exaggerate in order to gain what he wanted.

Brian tugged her forward, moving unerringly into the forest. "Wait here."

"But . . ."

He was gone.

She seethed at how he'd blocked any objections. She fretted within an instant, unable to see him. She'd already once watched Sazonov hold a gun to his head; must she do that again?

Morro's ears came forward and he snuffled happily. A darker shape loomed up against the night, announcing Brian.

"I should slap you for leaving me alone," Meredith hissed.

He kissed her cheek. "I'll buy you a Paris wardrobe," he offered.

She sniffed. "And a week in bed at a good hotel."

He spluttered and lifted her to her feet.

"Why are we following the railroad tracks?" she asked a minute later. "Assuming you did something unkind to the train . . ."

He didn't answer.

"Do we want to stay near it?"

"How better to reach the pass?" he countered. "We're higher on the mountainside than the army's line, which ran to Schloss Belvedere and the summer maneuvers."

"There's an old cart trail just ahead. If we use it to veer even farther up the mountain, we should be able to find one of the great horse farms. The mountain meadows are highly prized for fodder."

There was a thoughtful silence.

"We'd still have to come back down to cross into Switzerland."

"If we continue to swing away from the railroad, we'll come to Old St. Nicholas Pass, the one used by the Romans and Napoleon. It's not the one suggested by the railroad to tourists."

Why was she even mentioning this? Because it was the route least likely to bring Sazonov.

"Is it very dangerous?" His voice sharpened.

"It's barely maintained now. But it is the steepest and the fastest route." She had to take Brian away from the Russian before his recklessness brought him into more danger.

"It's the most frightening for you." He paused but she couldn't disagree. "The railroad will suit us."

"No! I can manage the hike, truly." She caught his sleeve. "Brian . . ."

"Sweetheart."

His hand closed over hers.

Down below, wheels began to rumble very slowly. Somebody shouted a warning, followed by other men's loud objections. Metal began to move, pounding its rhythm across the ground. It roared into motion, thundered down the line— and slammed into a solid wall of more metal. It tumbled over and over down the mountain, every monstrous thud echoing through the ground.

The very trees shook. Men shouted and cursed, their words dimmed by distance. Meredith staggered but Brian's strong arms kept her from falling. Morro barked loudly, jumping up and down to emphasize his objections.

She silenced him, stooping down with her beloved to soothe her oldest friend.

"Now we're definitely taking the old pass," she announced when she could trust herself to form sentences again. Thank God for Brecht's foresight in providing them with gear.

"Why?" He glanced over at her.

"I don't know how you sabotaged Sazonov's train . . ."

"Cut the brake lines on ours and pulled the pin between two of the front cars. But they took longer than I expected to start rolling."

"I won't ask who taught you that trick." She stood up and briskly brushed out her skirt. They definitely needed to leave this area.

Brian chortled softly.

"But I'm certain that Russian fiend will chase us twice as hard and fast because of it. I refuse to go anywhere except the Old St. Nicholas Pass."

"Are you certain? It appears the best route but not if it will cause you problems."

"I'm certain I'll be fine."

No matter how bad it was, it would be better than giving Sazonov a better chance to kill Brian. And surely it would be no worse than unpleasant. Surely.

Chapter Sixteen

Dawn swirled over the mountains high above, hiding Old St. Nicholas Pass in a brilliant panorama of light and shadow. The Iron Mountain's ancient gray cliffs closed in tighter and tighter on the trail. Water trickled out of its sides and bounded into waterfalls. It danced over the rocks and swept into the Eisenbach, the stream which bordered the path.

Meredith had come here last year with her brothers for a picnic. The boys had hunted for a long time to find someplace to swim. But today? The Eisenbach almost swept over the road, instead of six feet below it, and small waterfalls misted passersby every few minutes.

But this morning, she threw back her head and laughed, determined to enjoy the temporary freedom of a good horse under her. Her tweed skirt bunched and shifted across the sidesaddle under her, unlike the smoother comfort of chamois breeches and a crisply tailored riding habit. She'd brusquely declined to ride astride as being even more awkward, since she was wearing the ordinary drawers which lacked a crotch.

Brian's head snapped around from where he'd been watching their back trail to assess her. He relaxed quickly and tossed her a two-fingered salute, his blue eyes glinting under his soft-brimmed hat.

Riding with him anywhere at her side was a foretaste of

heaven—no matter who was following or how much her bones ached. Even Morro thought so, judging by his happy yips from where he trotted alongside.

It hadn't taken long to find a horse farm after they'd left the train and arranged to borrow these horses. But that had been the largest establishment they'd encountered. Now the thread of green meadow was narrowing behind them, edged by trees and towering gray cliffs. Up ahead, a slim steeple marked a tiny mountain chapel, dedicated to climbers who'd lost their lives among these peaks. A barn beside it provided cover for curing hay, the sole crop grown here. Thank God, the grand duke hadn't strung telegraph wires through here yet.

"How far do you think we can take the horses?" Brian asked. He didn't add that the trusting beasts were starting to tire.

"Not even half a mile," she admitted, casting an unhappy glance at the sharp turn immediately past the chapel.

"We'll dismount here and let them drift home," Brian decided.

"Of course." The railroad's route for tourists allowed packhorses throughout it. "Do you know which route your family will take?"

She couldn't bring herself to refer to his father.

He shook his head and her heart sank. But if she'd been the first one to tell Brian about the old pass, how could his family plan to use it?

"We'd best hurry." Brian jumped down off his big gelding in front of the chapel and rapidly began to unbuckle the satchel Mayer had provided.

Meredith swiveled in her saddle—and blanched. A heavy dust cloud was forming over the road at the narrow little valley's entrance. It had to be Sazonov, together with the secret police.

At least her beautiful little mare should have a pleasant journey.

*   *   *

Meredith leaned her head forward against the rocks, panting too hard to care whether she was in sunshine or shade. Thank God she was wearing the lightweight modern corset Brian had given her, which allowed her to drag deep gasps of air into her lungs, unlike the more fashionable versions.

Brian had set a brutal pace but she'd matched it, desperate to save him. Sazonov might keep her alive to recreate Zorndorf's masterworks but he'd undoubtedly kill Brian without a second thought.

Only the felt-soled boots Brecht provided had kept them ahead, since their enemy was using more fashionable footgear on the treacherous ground.

The cliffs were streaked granite blocks here, as if giants had decided to play nursery games and gone home without cleaning up. They towered to the sky in all directions, drowning the light and trapping ice and snow among their crevices and narrow spires. The route through the old pass was really a series of ledges, linked by steps cut into narrow chimneys, next to the fast-moving mountain stream.

In dry years, artists competed to paint it. In wet years, waterfalls ripped boulders out of the walls.

Thank God for the alpenstock Mayer had shoved into her hand at the last moment. That wooden staff with its pointed metal end had saved her balance more than once when the path slipped away under her foot.

"Steady, boy, steady," Brian crooned.

She wiped the sweat out of her eyes and leaned back to check on Brian and Morro. Morro was their leader, his prerogative due to his uncanny ability to sense weak ground. Brian came next, as the strongest climber.

Brian lifted Morro to his shoulder, pointing him toward the next section.

A boulder had fallen out, undercutting the path to a shelf where the trail started again. The result looked like a ladder cut into stone and she'd need both hands for it.

Her alpenstock had a leather loop which she could drop around her wrist. But the basket? It was ordinarily used for shopping, which meant it couldn't be slung over her back or hooked over her shoulder, not if she wanted to climb that wall.

"There they are!" Sazonov shouted. Echoes swirled through the canyon, stabbing into her bones like knives.

She peered around the corner. A thunderstorm was brewing among the peaks, an eerie reminder of her father's killer. But that was an old peril, not today's.

Sazonov was close, too close, about fifty feet below. He was in the lead, as ever, with his big, ugly rifle slung eagerly over his shoulder. A dozen men trailed him, some also carrying guns.

On a city street, the route might take five minutes but here? The trail was so steep and the intervening turn so sharp, she might have ten minutes before he arrived.

Meredith gnawed her lip. How many choices did she really have?

She set the basket down and began to hastily unpack it. By the time Brian turned around with Morro safely deposited on the trail's next segment, she'd tucked her vials of explosives amongst the plans for the world's greatest cannon. She slung the sturdy, fabric map case along her back, silently vowing to be very careful about leaning against the rocks.

"Ready?" she asked brightly.

"Always. Are you sure you don't need the basket anymore?"

"Completely. But you must go first."

He frowned, his brows drawing close together in the shadows under his hat. "What was in the basket, Meredith?"

"We don't have time to chat, Brian." She glanced desperately over her shoulder. She'd stolen the plans; she'd take the deadly risk of carrying this, not him.

"Sazonov could have shot you for catching it, back at the church. But you risked your life." He took a step toward her and she backed away from him, her hand outstretched against the wall.

"Don't come near me!" Her voice caught flight among the rocks.

"Me, me, me . . ." they sang back to her.

"Explosives?" he whispered.

She nodded desperately and shooed him away with her hands.

Morro barked unhappily from up above.

"Miss Duncan?" Sazonov called. "Please believe I want only the best for you."

"I won't move until you're up there." Meredith folded her arms across her chest. She was startlingly calm.

"Meredith." Brian gritted his teeth.

"There's no time."

His beautiful eyes promised painful retribution later but he turned and ran. She'd gladly accept his punishments, since it meant he'd be alive.

One, two, three, four, five grips—and he swung himself up beside Morro. "Come on, Meredith!"

She took one last, quick peek around the corner and flinched.

Sazonov and his men were unlimbering their rifles to shoot at Brian.

Like hell she'd allow that to happen, no matter what it cost.

She slipped the map case over her shoulder and ran around the corner.

"Meredith, no!" Brian shouted. Morro exploded into barking.

She took a few more steps, winding her arm as her brothers had taught her, and hurled the map case end over end at the path below. Her momentum carried her forward and she hurled herself into the stone wall to brake herself.

Nothing.

There was no explosion.

Sazonov and his men were shouting triumphantly.

She leaned over the side to look down, uncaring for once of the awful abyss below.

Oh, dear God, the map case's strap had caught on a boulder just below the lip, where it swung violently. When it smashed against the rock or somebody below picked it up . . .

She raced for her life back up the path, praying the sharp corner and solid wall of granite would protect her.

"You fool, Meredith! Grab my hand and I'll pull you up!"

She leaped upward and Brian's iron fingers closed around her wrist. Her feet scrabbled for a hold and he yanked her up, her toes barely fast enough to aid him before he hauled her over the edge. He half-carried, half-flung her off the unstable overhang onto solid ground. She grabbed Morro and pulled him close just before Brian slammed down on top of her.

Brilliant yellow light flashed past the corner of her eyes, startling against the gray crags and black storm clouds.

KERBOOM! The mountain rumbled behind them.

BOOM! BOOM! The ground shook underneath them like giants hammering out a new forge. Dust surged into the air, tainted with the stench of rotten eggs and hiding the few remaining glimpses of the sun.

And the plans were gone, burned beyond even the chance of ashes. Eisengau's workers would never use them to gain their rights. They'd have to find their own road, no matter how long that took.

Meredith buried her face in the crook of her arm, hot tears burning her eyes.

Brian lifted her onto her feet the instant the dust cloud died down. "I'm sorry about the plans but thank you for saving my life. You saved many men's lives."

"I'll try to think of it as a pleasure." She leaned up to kiss him, ignoring her abominably tight throat and undoubtedly tear-streaked face. "How far back is Sazonov? Or are we lucky enough to have him disappear?"

"He and his men are alive, with the path cut before them. But they have climbing gear . . ."

"So he'll manage a way around the gap." She sighed and beat the dust out of her skirt. If—when!—they made it out of here, she'd beg Brian to indulge her in some of the nonsense her mother adored, like a long indulgent soak in a scented tub, layers of frilly, silken petticoats, or even a lacy tea gown, simply to wear something other than sweat-soaked tweeds. "We'd best be off then."

"I love you."

She glanced up at him, startled. The adoration in his eyes made her heart race. She traced his jaw and he kissed her palm.

"Do you know how many women would be having hysterics at this moment?"

"Silly fools." She sniffed. "But maybe it's something I can learn to do later, say, after we reach Switzerland."

"How far is it?"

"After the crest."

Brian followed her gaze and whistled softly. "Then we definitely need to move out."

Especially if they wanted to arrive before the coming storm or Sazonov did.

Brian glanced back at his darling, who was trudging steadily along the rocky trail. By all the saints, he didn't know how she'd kept up so long but she had, without a whimper. Perhaps it was the legendary Scots stubbornness.

Regardless, he needed to take her to safety soon. She was the only one who could re-create the cannon's plans—and that made her key to defeating Sazonov's plans to conquer Alaska.

In the shade, ice slicked the narrow path, reminding him how close they were to the crest. It filled the crevices between the boulders and glared from between fissures. But in the sun, it poured itself into waterfalls, diving out of the mountain.

"Miss Duncan?" Sazonov called through his omnipresent bullhorn.

Meredith made a very rude gesture.

Brian smothered a laugh. His darling must indeed be exhausted if she was displaying any vocabulary learned in the foundry, not the drawing room.

"Go ahead," she whispered. "I'll stay here and distract him while you two scout."

"Are you sure?"

"Of course. I can have a drink from that waterfall, while I wait."

He frowned. The jagged chunks of rock surrounding the fountaining stream seemed more artistic than stable.

"Miss Duncan, let's discuss children's education."

"Go, go!" She mimed shooing Brian away.

Still, he'd only be gone for a few minutes and Sazonov was a noticeable distance behind, despite all his noise. He dropped a kiss on her cheek.

The black dog gazed into her eyes seriously.

"Keep Brian safe for me, Morro," she ordered in Gaelic. She kissed his forehead and he licked her nose, making her giggle.

The dog followed Brian calmly enough, although not eagerly. He wouldn't have wanted to leave her either.

"What children, Herr Sazonov?" Meredith called.

Judging by her relaxed tone, he'd wager she had her back to the rock wall, away from the gorge. She'd probably also drawn her feet up to keep her heels from slipping on the trail's slippery edge. Jesus, Mary, and Joseph, how she loathed looking at any sort of drop.

The path beyond was particularly steep and narrow, doubling back on itself like the devil's idea of a ladder to hell. A pile of boulders channeled water from the mountain. But beyond them . . .

He sprang onto the rocks, straining his eyes for a glimpse of the green meadows rolling *down* the mountainside beyond.

The chunks shifted under him and he adjusted easily. Dammit, he'd grown up around mines and talus piles, where waste rock was thrown away. This stack was a small hurdle compared to those.

Surely those were Swiss meadows. And maybe, just maybe, there were men riding toward him, leading other horses.

Gravel skittered underneath and a boulder grumbled. The rocks rolled, and rolled again, bringing one tumbling down upon another.

Brian leaped for solid ground before he thought, warned by old instinct.

"Meredith, duck!"

WOOF! WOOF! Morro raced for the path downward. Brian dove for his collar, barely grabbing it before the faithful dog disappeared.

More rocks moved, tumbling forward. A bigger rock hurtled into motion, loosening a boulder, and suddenly the entire pile raced toward the edge.

Brian's stomach plummeted into his boots. How could he have been so arrogant as to stand on that unsteady rock pile? Sweet singing Jesus, if anything happened to his lady . . .

Dust ripped into the sky, blocking out any sight of her.

He rolled himself over onto her violently squirming friend. It was the only gift he could still give her, while the mountain stormed around him and his heart shredded itself.

It seemed forever before he could lift his head.

"Did you finally kill her, Donovan?" Sazonov asked conversationally.

Pity the bastard was still alive. Still, it did allow time to provide a suitably painful death.

Brian didn't bother to answer him. Instead, he released Morro and crawled forward to the edge, praying harder than he could remember. If she was alive, he'd donate a stained glass window to a convent or endow a college chair. And kiss her a dozen times every morning.

Her dusty, scratched face looked up at him from below. She unfolded one arm from around her knees and waggled her fingers at him. She was definitely the most beautiful woman in the world.

"Hello," she croaked. Her universe had shrunk to a narrow section of rocky ledge, barely ten feet long and no more than a yard wide at any point.

"Thank God you're alive." He blew her a kiss, causing a smile to break like sunshine across her face. "Can you stand up?"

"I think so." She suited action to words, rising tentatively to her feet.

His heart surged into a more normal rhythm.

"I'm glad you are still with us, Miss Duncan," Sazonov remarked. "Have you considered taking up residence in St. Petersburg?"

Meredith closed her eyes and sighed, looking exhausted for the first time.

Damn Russian bastard.

She composed herself and started trying to soothe Morro, pragmatic as ever.

He couldn't leave her to Sazonov's few mercies. What hadn't the Russians done in their dungeons to those who disagreed with them? Beatings, starvation, torture . . .

He growled, baring his teeth.

But how could he quickly rescue his darling? The landslide had carried away the trail he'd ascended by, leaving him lying on a rocky ledge nearly three storeys above her. Dust still bubbled into the air from the rubble pile below, making it even more unstable than when he'd set it rolling, even if he could reach it.

The great shift had also knocked a boulder onto the trail beyond Meredith. She couldn't go around it. But a professional climber, with time and proper gear, definitely could.

And Brian absolutely lacked ropes. Mayer and Brecht hadn't provided them and he hadn't taken any from the horse farm.

Morro was howling in frustration and he would have liked

to do the same. Instead he let out a vicious string of teamster's curses and sprang back onto his feet. He spun around, looking for any other option. Perhaps if he could persuade the Swiss border guards to leave their posts . . .

The riders were now galloping toward him, looking oddly familiar. The big man leading the way, the two more slender men, and the very slight one were sights he'd seen all his life.

By all the saints, his family had come to save them.

"Meredith, dearest, my family is coming." He leaned back over the ledge to speak as quietly as possible to her.

She frowned slightly before composing her face.

"Love, you don't need to stretch the truth to improve my morale. I know your family wouldn't expect us to take this route."

"No, it's true, they're on the way."

"So is Sazonov," she pointed out, clearly too exhausted to guard her tongue.

Shit. Dammit, he knew she didn't trust his father.

How could he quickly convince her?

"My mother will be here, plus my two brothers," Brian added, hoping that more family members to dilute the patriarch's influence would help her relax.

She hesitated a moment before her damn logical mind kicked in again. "But you can't reach me from up there."

"We'll manage. I swear to you on my grandparents' graves, we'll rescue you in time."

A single tear glittered on her eyelashes and he would have torn his heart out to spare her the agony.

"Morro! Morro, hush!" she ordered in Gaelic.

The dog immediately stopped his erratic barking and watched her closely.

"Keep Brian's mother safe, Morro! Do you hear me?" She emphasized the order's importance by using only Gaelic.

The dog whined unhappily, his ears flat against his head.

"Keep Brian's mother safe," she repeated.

He barked once, his ears still lying back.

"I swear I'll be back, Meredith." Brian put all the conviction he could into the simple words.

"I believe you, love." She smiled at him.

Meredith closed her eyes and listened to Brian's footsteps die out across the rock. She believed he would return; she simply wasn't sure he'd survive.

At least ordering Morro to guard Brian's mother should keep him away from harm. She couldn't believe any autocrat would let his wife go into battle.

"How are you this afternoon, Miss Duncan?" Sazonov asked.

"Quite well. And you?" She might as well amuse herself by talking to him. It might keep him from thinking up new plots against Brian.

"Excellent. Far better than the poor serfs in Russia."

Huh? Her brows snapped together and she stared at the unmoving rock between them, as if it could announce her enemy's intentions. She'd be greatly surprised to learn Sazonov had ever had a thought which didn't focus on himself or his country's glory.

"Russian serfs?" she queried, too startled to think of a more probing question.

"Yes, our poor peasants. So hungry, so uneducated, so lacking in medical care. Tied to the land and at the mercy of their masters . . ." He clucked his tongue.

Her eyes widened. He actually sounded as if he cared.

"Why do you mention them?"

"Doesn't every wise man want everyone else to be happy?"

"No," she retorted bluntly. If he honestly believed she thought he was wise, he needed to find a new line of argument.

He chuckled. His voice's echoes changed subtly, sounding as if he was coming a little closer.

Brian, please hurry . . .

"You might find Russia's serfs more worthy of your concern than Eisengau's workers, Miss Duncan. After all, Eisengau's people are already well-fed and housed, a situation that's not true in Russia."

"But I can't do anything for Russian serfs," she retorted. She hoped Liesel's seduction had been more delightful than these veiled hints.

"You could if you agreed to work for us willingly."

"What?!"

"You can recreate the Eisengau 155mm cannons and all of Zorndorf's other designs."

This display of logic allowed her to close her mouth. She could redraw all the designs for the cannons since she'd gone to work for Zorndorf. But if she did that, she'd be a prisoner of the Russians for the rest of her life. She'd never see Brian or her brothers again, unless the Russians let them visit her in St. Petersburg—an event which would come with a very high price.

"Do that for us and you can name your price. You would make Russia the mightiest military power in Asia and Europe. Do you think the Tsar wouldn't let you remake a few laws, especially when the liberal half of his cabinet already clamors for him to do so?"

Meredith's knees gave out and she sank down against the stone. Sazonov had come up with the one bribe that could tempt her.

Chapter Seventeen

The trail opened onto a gravel slope only a dozen yards past the rocky ledge where Brian had last seen Meredith. He raced down it, waving frantically at the riders galloping across the grassy meadow beyond. "Father!"

"Brian!" His sire sawed on the reins, swinging himself down almost before his horse could completely stop. He enveloped his son in a hug so enormous it swept Brian off his feet.

Brian only laughed and pounded the senior Donovan on the back. An instant later, he hugged and kissed his mother on both cheeks then laughed with the two twins.

"Where are we going now, son?" asked William Donovan, a tear gleaming on his cheeks.

Brian blinked; he'd expected to have to convince his family he wasn't going back to Switzerland with them. He considered their equipage a little more closely.

They had two spare horses with them, not one, and every saddle was ornamented with a rifle.

"Your mother convinced me—us!—there was somebody in Eisengau you were interested in," the founder of Donovan & Sons commented.

"Since you and the dog are the only ones who came out, I suspect we need to find her." Mother finished another of

Father's sentences. Morro had sat down and was eyeing her wistfully.

"Yes, we do." Brian swallowed hard, breaking through the tightness in his throat. Surely Meredith would come to love his family as much as he did. "And I need to introduce Mother to her new friend."

"Of course, there'd be benefits for you, too," Sazonov added. "Fashionable yet comfortable clothing, an elegant mansion in St. Petersburg, and a beautiful dacha to relax in, since we know how you love the open air."

She closed her eyes. Could she honorably put her own happiness ahead of so many others?

But did she believe Sazonov would keep his promises?

If she went with Brian, she'd have to trust he'd keep her from being trapped in a network of laws designed to enforce masculine authority.

She buried her face against her knees, her cairngorm brooch pressing into her chest under her suit jacket.

Somebody was tapping on that huge boulder, building a path for Sazonov around it.

Brian lay a few feet back from the ledge, his beloved Mauser rifle finally slung over his back. Marlowe and his father, draped in coils of rope, flanked him. All three of them were studying the scene below, while his mother and an unhappily resigned Spenser waited with the horses and Morro.

"Nice predicament," Father commented just above a whisper. "That's quite a bribe the Russian's offering."

And the only one she'd listen to, dammit. She was being swayed, too, judging by her silence. Brian clenched his fists. "We have to get her out of there."

"We'll have to lift her over the ledge," decided the very experienced freighter.

"We didn't bring a bosun's chair or any other polite contraption to hold a proper lady," Marlowe pointed out.

"One of us can go down and tie her in," Father countered.

"Is there time?" Sazonov had been successfully driving his men damn hard and fast.

The two elder Donovans looked at the party's youngest member.

"They're closer than you said." Marlowe craned his neck to get a better view. His experiments with mountain climbing and slightly larger size were why he'd come forward, instead of Spenser. "I give them maybe five minutes to finish setting ropes around that rock."

"Then there's no time to send somebody down there. We'll have to ask her to do it."

Butterflies turned into vultures and started rioting in Brian's stomach. "I'll talk her through it."

"Sweetheart?" The beloved whisper sifted down.

"Brian!" She jumped up and stretched her hands up to him along the stone wall. "My dearest love, thank God you came back."

"My family's here, too," he offered reassuringly. "My father, William Donovan, and my brother Marlowe."

"Miss Duncan." Two men, remarkably similar to Brian but very different in age to each other, poked their heads over the ledge.

She nodded, bemused. His father was going to be actively engaged in rescuing her? At least she could keep her back to the gorge while this occurred.

"Miss Duncan?" Sazonov again. She ignored him and the incessant hammering.

"We're going to drop a rope down to you with a loop tied in it."

"Why a loop?" She frowned, considering scenarios.

The men glanced at each other guiltily.

A cold chill ran down her spine.

"After you grab the rope, pull your arms through it so it rests around your chest under your armpits."

She did not like the sound of this.

"Then lower your hands and grab your belt. My father and Marlowe will lift you very quickly up here."

"But the rope will be cutting into me. Isn't there anyplace else you can put it? My legs, so I can sit down?"

"We didn't bring the equipment for a lady, miss," Brian's father apologized.

"Think about how your drawers are made, Meredith. Do you want us wrapping rope around you there?" Brian hissed.

She cringed, remembering all the bare, delicate skin under her skirt. Hardly.

But if she was lifted out on a rope, wouldn't she swing like a pendulum? Over the gorge and its incredible fall of over three thousand feet?

How high had the Scottish cliff been, that she'd been trapped on when she was eight?

"But are you sure the rope is strong enough for my weight, given these breezes?" She hesitated. Or should she be blunt and call them winds? At any event, every hair on her skin was standing up, even the ones under her sleeves and on the nape of her neck.

"I'm very glad you've decided to return to my party, Mr. Donovan," Sazonov purred.

Meredith spun to stare downhill, her outer foot slipping on the trail's verge. The Russian was far too close, judging by the echoes.

Brian's father began to rapidly tie a series of knots in the stout rope.

She looked away and pressed her fist to her mouth. A father and a rope and a crumbling cliff . . .

Something clicked—and Brian's gaze turned hard and wary.

Shots rang out from the chimney behind the boulder. Sazonov must have hidden riflemen in there, where they couldn't reach her but they could block the approaches.

Dust burst around her rescuers' heads. They stiffened but didn't retreat.

Brian promptly rolled over and brought his rifle up. He began to fire rapidly at the hidden enemy.

Brian's father came up onto his knees, exposing himself to the bullets.

No, no, no! She couldn't let this be for naught.

The heavy coil bounced heavily off the rock and landed in front of her.

Meredith gulped, her father's heavy brooch rolling over her throat. She might be able to help the serfs or she could definitely build a life with Brian. But that life would be something her father would recognize, filled with good conversation and literature and laughter. Maybe that was why she didn't trust it.

Perhaps that was why she should.

She picked up the rope and dropped it over her head before she could have second thoughts. She yanked it taut, wincing when the rope cut into her breasts through her clothes. Then she gripped the heavy leather belt holding her skirt and closed her eyes.

An instant later, her feet were ripped off the ground and her stomach rushed for her throat. Fireworks were launched more slowly.

She swung, spinning like a whirligig, back and forth in great parallel arcs. Morro was barking encouragement from somewhere.

She gritted her teeth and squeezed her eyes more tightly shut, determined not to look at the gorge.

Marriage would be easier than this.

Another hard yank and she surged upward again. Her shoulder banged hard against unyielding rock. She spun again more wildly, bouncing out again into the wild winds over the abyss.

She started to release her belt so she could defend herself against the cliff. The rope slipped, burning into her armpit.

No! She knotted her fingers into the leather and the tweed underneath. Safety depended on gripping her belt—and how well the *modiste* had stitched the skirt's loops.

BAM! Her hat blew off her head and the winds began to pick apart her hair.

Somebody was shooting at her while she was hanging there, helpless as a target at a shooting club.

BAM! Fire burned into her left arm.

Spenser slid into place beside Brian, his Winchester in his hands.

No time to argue now about Mother needing help with the horses or find out if the kid had learned to shoot well enough for this. Right now, he just needed covering fire. "Two snipers in the chimney."

"I see 'em. You take the Russian." Spenser's rifle settled easily into his shoulder. He squeezed off his first shot, splitting chips off the rock next to one sniper.

Brian rolled away, satisfied, and focused on Meredith.

Father and Marlowe pulled again, yanking her up another few feet. Sazonov had clambered over the boulder and had a clear shot at her. But he'd already missed two easy shots, so he might not be able to see too well from behind that bandage swathing his scalp. Perhaps Morro had hurt him more than they knew.

Thin thread to pin his hopes on with Meredith's life dangling in the balance.

He shoved another magazine into his rifle and took careful aim.

BAM!

Sazonov ignored him. Instead he fired again at Meredith, protected by the great boulder.

Dammit, he couldn't reach far enough forward to fire down at the bastard. He'd have to make it onto that spur to get a good shot. Who cared about what that position did to his chances for coming back, as long as it helped Meredith's?

Time stretched, slowing his pulse. The shots spitting up dust around him seemed to be very far apart.

Brian lunged onto the rock knob, gritting his teeth at how

it swayed under him. He dragged his Mauser forward and slowly brought it up to his shoulder. The rock rippled but finally steadied. He dug his toes into the ledge behind him, grateful he'd had his rifle shortened to something useful for a horseman. Sweet singing Jesus, he didn't want to be carrying any extra weight right now.

The icy winds sawed at him, trying to suck his body forward into oblivion.

Sazonov looked up at him, a killer's lust bright on his face. He deliberately worked the bolt, sending another round into the chamber, and took careful aim.

BAM! BAM! They fired simultaneously.

Chips exploded out of the spur below Brian.

Sazonov fell forward onto the boulder, a small crimson hole in his forehead. His heavy Mosin-Nagant rifle slipped sideways off his shoulder, overbalancing his corpse. It slid off the rock like an enormous, broken doll, onto the ledge, and rolled into the gorge. Heavy thuds marked its disappearance, barely audible over the whistling winds and gurgling waters.

Two bodies were slumped in the chimney, silent testimony to Spenser's expertise with a rifle.

Two strong hands seized Brian's ankles and yanked him to safety.

He gave Spenser a quick nod of thanks then rolled to help bring his darling over the ledge onto safety. Blood streaked her face and dripped onto her jacket.

He brushed it away, his hand shaking. "Meredith, darling, how badly are you hurt?"

Her beautiful gray eyes blinked open. With a glad cry, she fell forward against his shoulder and buried her face against him.

However pleasant that felt, he needed to check her face. "Sweetheart," he crooned. "Please let us take care of you."

"Your jacket is bloodstained now." Her voice was muffled.

"Do you think I care?" His father handed him a wet handkerchief and he gave it to her.

"No." She sat up and he began to gently wash her face. Morro butted his way onto her lap. She tried to pet him, flinching when she used her left arm.

The world spun around Brian. Jesus, Mary, and Joseph, she was bleeding there, too. He gritted his teeth and tried to speak normally. "Please let my mother look at your arm, Meredith."

"It hurts," she whispered and held out her blood-soaked arm.

Sazonov had died far too quickly.

He begged his mother for help with his eyes and Father fetched Mother's omnipresent first aid kit from her horse, his expression very thoughtful. Marlowe and Spenser, their rifles at the ready, edged forward to spy on Sazonov's remaining companions.

Meredith buried her face against Brian's shoulder while her sleeve was cut away. He clumsily stroked her hair and made soothing sounds while Mother tended to her. He could not, would not believe anything could happen to her now, not with his family to protect her and when they were so close to Switzerland. Not when they had the rest of their lives before them.

He ruffled Morro's fur, silently reassuring them both.

"It's a nasty graze but nothing too alarming," Mother pronounced, firmly tying off the bandage. "But you need a good meal and some rest, to say nothing of a bath."

"The other men are racing back down the mountain," Marlowe reported. "We're free to head back to Switzerland."

Brian traced Meredith's mouth with a fingertip and she kissed it.

"Will I be scarred?" she whispered.

"I don't give a damn." She wouldn't, judging by Mother's signal, but he didn't care either way.

"That wasn't my question," she snapped, recovering more of her spirits.

"It's the only important answer."

"Oh." She thought some more. She still hadn't looked directly at Father but that would come in time. She caught Brian's hand. "Will you marry me?"

Joy burst through his veins.

"Yes, of course. How about today?"

She began to giggle, a sound he'd never expected to hear from her. "Whenever you'd like, if you plan the wedding."

He'd plotted the answer to this on that interminable train ride, dreaming it would be an elopement.

"Scotland then. It's your home and we can arrange everything very quickly there."

Saint Andrew's Metropolitan Cathedral, Glasgow, Scotland, three weeks later

Meredith bounced a little, marking time to the organ music. Professor Aubrey patted her hand reassuringly and she forced herself to calm down, assuming the expected outward semblance of a decorous maiden.

The Donovans had somehow managed to persuade the chair of her father's old department at Oxford to give her away. He truly was the closest person she had to a father figure for this occasion, especially since he'd been one of her father's fellow professors. He'd already shared some delightful stories with her.

He'd been especially delighted to learn her husband was also a Roman Catholic, thus sharing her and her father's faith.

Morro was waiting on the church porch, neatly groomed for once. He'd even tolerated a white satin bow for the occasion.

The organ eased to a stop, gathered itself, and launched into Handel's *La Rejouissance*'s beautiful opening chords. A smiling, black-clad priest opened the heavy, carved doors to the sanctuary and Meredith's future with Brian.

She started forward, trying to match Professor Aubrey's conservative pace.

Rippling stone columns rose around her, leading to the arches vaulting over the ceiling high above. Great panels of stained glass poured light over the altar and those waiting for her.

Brian stood there, with his two younger brothers at his side, and the bishop behind them. His expression was solemn enough for a service in a church that had fought for life in order to serve the workers nearby. Their descendants watched from the pews around her, their clean, well-darned clothes and wide eyes making them look so very similar to her friends in Eisengau.

Brian's lips curved into a slow smile at the sight of her.

She wanted to run to him and leap into his arms for joy. Soon they'd be united forever. She grinned at him but he couldn't read her expression at this distance through the heavy lace veil. It matched her very fashionable, very frilly, satin and lace wedding dress, which Viola Donovan had somehow conjured out of Paris. The sleeves were fuller than usual at the top, to accommodate her bandage, although her arm barely hurt any more.

She'd chosen it for him, to emphasize her commitment to him and all that a traditional marriage meant, rather than living together outside wedlock.

His eyes traveled over her, lingering on her tiny waist and swaying hips, the hundreds of pleats frothing along her white satin train's edges. A month ago, she'd have thrown it at anyone who dared suggest she yield to the male establishment.

His smile broadened into a joyous grin and their eyes met through her veil, shooting her into a joyous leap. Only Professor Aubrey's quick grab for her wrist stopped her from racing toward the altar like a hoyden.

A gurgle of laughter ran through the assemblage. Brian's parents were in the front pew, while Mrs. Aubrey was her matron of honor. The American ambassador and his wife were also here, together with Gareth Blackwood and some of her father's old colleagues. There were just enough of them to add a little extra color among all the gray stones and flowers bedecking the high altar and pews, plus the parishioners' black clothing.

She didn't want to think about the strangers, or how closely Blackwood and the American Ambassador scrutinized her. It was time to start her future with Brian, not worry about the past.

The Latin words wove magic around her, tying her to Brian and him to her. She could keep these vows, of fidelity and honor for all time. She loved him with all her heart, no matter what else happened. When he slid the heavy gold ring onto her finger, she rejoiced that he accepted one from her.

Their first kiss as a married couple was very gentle, a sacred pledge for the years to come.

Finally the nuptial mass, including the prayer for Neil Donovan's safety, was over and it was time to leave for their wedding breakfast. Meredith shook out her skirts, preparing to take back her bouquet.

"Mrs. Donovan." It was a conqueror's triumphant growl.

She whirled to look up at him, her long train flinging itself around her feet.

He caught her against him, heedless of her crisply pressed dress. "*My* Mrs. Donovan."

His mouth came down on hers and she met him more than halfway, aching to give him everything in her heart.

Meredith glanced around the bedroom one more time, checking to make sure everyone was in place. It was ridiculous for her pulse to be rattling through her veins like a trolley car engine in need of repair. It was even sillier to be shaking so hard she could barely fluff up the pillows.

After all, she and Brian had shared a bed before—and very successfully, too!—although not since they'd left Eisengau. They'd decided to wait until after the wedding, so her arm could heal, and to respect his mother's feelings. She didn't think much could shock that lady, who seemed to laughingly tolerate their frequent disappearances to hug and caress each other.

Mr. Donovan was another matter, with his quiet formality toward her and his open warmth toward his sons. She had no idea what to think of him yet. He seemed to be treating her with the same courtesy she'd offer an unhappy, new puppy, although that was an absurd thought.

At least Morro was safely curled up outside the door in his new basket, as he'd done at Schloss Belvedere.

She smoothed out the sheet once again and contemplated the coverlet, brilliantly white in the lamplight. Dearest Brian had brought her to this very fancy hotel, deep in the Scottish Highlands, promising her comfort and complete privacy for anything she wanted. They could open the curtains and enjoy the view of the loch down below or dive under the blankets like a long-time married couple or . . .

He caressed her shoulders from behind. "Hmm, lace. I love it."

She turned to face him. "Do you?" She spread her hands, displaying her pleated, embroidered, beribboned, white lace peignoir. "Or is it too overblown, considering we already, ah, know each other?"

"It's beautiful, as you are, and enhances your charms." He caught her hands and drew them up to his chest. His gold chain rippled over his collar bone, carrying his crucifix and medals. Other than that, only black silk trousers clung to his form. Her fascinated eyes could find the tempting hollow at the side of his hips, the taut sweep of his ass, the heavy muscles of his flanks. All only barely hidden behind a shimmering veil of rippling black—but much less interesting than the smooth, ivory satin of his bare flesh.

Her knuckles brushed his chest and swept through his hair, caressing him. His skin was warm and soft, luring her more than the greatest books. Her fingers flexed, seeking out the broad span of his heavy muscles.

Her peignoir's folds whispered against each other, echoing

her slightest movements. Her stiff collar rose and fell over her breasts, marking her desperate quest for breath.

He kissed her palms and sought out each finger to suckle. Her breath caught and surged, sparking with lust to match his rhythm.

Her eyelids slid down, allowing her gaze to seek out his fascinating nipples, nestled like small copper coins amid his dark fur. Her knees weakened when he folded back her sleeve and raked his teeth over her wrist. Her pulse skittered frantically, racing into a world where veins carried molten desperation and breathing only added fuel to the flames.

She ran her other hand down his waist to his hip. "I should be cherishing you, not the other way around," she gasped. Hunger ached and burned, pulsing into liquid fire between her legs.

"I won't last five minutes if you do," he countered, his voice all dark, masculine certainty and laughter.

He kissed her thudding pulse and she swayed dizzily.

"Meredith?" He caught her in his arms.

"I'm dizzy with anticipation, love." She managed to open her eyes and met his brilliant gaze directly, letting him read her honesty. "I feel like a package about to be unwrapped. As if I'm about to be reborn."

"By all the saints, I don't deserve you, Meredith. But I swear I'll love you all my life."

"As I you." He rolled his hips against her and her head fell back. She managed to tease him. "And remember to love me with your body as well."

He choked with laughter. "Always."

She glided her palms up his chest, sensing him through as much of her skin as possible. Oh yes, very hot, slightly sweaty, the curves, the strength. Her man.

She moaned softly, her eyes sliding shut. Heat sparked and flared through her, pulsing between her breasts and her core.

He unfastened her collar, lingering over the fragile ribbons and tiny buttons.

She spanned her fingers over his shoulders, greedily exploring how his muscles met his bones. If she rubbed herself against him, perhaps fire would leap from her skin to his and she could explode.

"Meredith?"

"Hmm?" She stroked his biceps, jumping her fingertips lightly over to his ribcage. Her hips circled, echoing the movement, aching to approach him closer.

"Meredith darling . . ."

She looked up reluctantly, his blood pounding under her hands. His hips rocked, pushing closer to hers.

"What are you wearing under this?" His voice was a harsh whisper.

"Nothing."

"Nothing???"

"Except slippers." Her fingers slipped down the back of his pajama trousers and cupped his beautiful ass. "That's why there are so many pleats."

"I take my hat off to good women; they're more devious than I ever suspected," Brian muttered. His cock brushed against her belly like a customized invitation to frolic, every time she squeezed his rump.

He kissed her cheek and teased her lips. She sighed and opened to him, forgetting any excuse to delay. Cream heated faster, scenting the room, dripping over her folds. She rubbed herself against him, her aching nipples inciting them both as much as her fingers did.

He kissed her, plunging his tongue deep into her mouth, mating them. His fingers pulled and twisted, desperately seeking and undoing every miniscule button. Finally he yanked the frothy lace down her shoulders where it pooled on the floor.

He lifted her in his arms, stripped the sheets down, and laid her on the bed. She rolled to greet him, desperate to touch him, and found him peeling those silk trousers over his rampant cock. Oh, very definitely yes.

He reached for the packet of condoms he always placed in the nightstand drawer.

Not tonight he wouldn't. She crooned approval and leaned forward to kiss his gleaming, crimson cockhead.

"Meredith!"

She swirled her tongue over the tip, fascinated by the hot, salty taste.

"By all the saints, Meredith, I'll never fit a condom on if you do that." He beat his fists against his thighs.

She tilted her head back to look at him and cupped his balls very gently. His eyes crossed in sheer pleasure.

"Or we can simply enjoy ourselves, if you'd prefer." She shifted to finger herself but his hand caught her wrist.

"Mrs. Donovan, you're becoming greedy."

Why did that tone of voice make her core clench so fiercely? She moaned, her head tossing restlessly on the sheet. "Mr. Donovan, you're driving your wife insane."

"You could drive a saint mad, Meredith!" He leaned over her, cupping her small breasts in his big hands. He brushed his cheeks over them, inciting her with the slight roughness of his beard stubble.

She arched and pulled him closer. More, please, anything . . .

He rolled onto her, running his hands down her sides, fondling her boldly between her legs. She opened herself willingly, drunk on the whirling delight of bare skin to bare skin, curve to curve, muscle to muscle. Her hot wet folds rippling over his cock's fiery bar.

Brian. Always Brian. No matter what else happened, she'd stay with Brian.

He twisted again, his blue eyes brilliant above her, and brought her under him. She arched to meet him, wrapping her legs around him. He thrust and thrust again, driving himself home, until she was finally, gloriously, full of her husband.

Yes, oh yes.

He moved faster, harder, driving both of their bodies recklessly into exhilaration. His face locked into a rictus of pure joy, his hands clenched her like the key to all his tomorrows. Her blood pounded through her, burning down to her bones and rocketing between her breasts and her core. She fought to keep his cock within her, moaned her hunger, raked his back in blood lust.

He shouted and arched, driving deep within her. His hands locked tighter around her. He tumbled into his climax, pumping her full of his seed.

Hot, wet explosion . . . It was too much, too different, too perfect. Too Brian.

Meredith spun into orgasm, howling her pleasure like a perfectly tuned she-wolf, a creature of instinct, not intellect. Her muscles locked around him, gulping every last drop of his essence. Fireworks raced up her spine and out through her head, shattering her mind and world.

Something scratched on the door afterward.

"What the devil?" Brian lifted his head.

"Morro." Meredith closed her eyes. "We should probably rejoice he waited this long to demand entry."

Grumbling all the way, her husband climbed out of bed, stalked across the room, and admitted the small, black rogue.

Morro bounded over to a rectangular cushion under the table, scratched it once, turned around several times, and flopped down. He tilted his head at his humans and yawned.

"We've just been told it's time to go to sleep." Meredith held the covers open for Brian. He said something very rude about who really ruled the roost and rejoined her. She snuggled against him.

"Why did you stop me from wearing a condom?" Brian spoke very softly.

She yawned. "Why would you want to? We're married."

"Do you want children?"

"A husband and wife can enjoy each other any way they want, without worrying about the consequence."

"You didn't answer my question."

His very tense voice brought her fully awake. She fumbled for words to explain something deadly serious to both of them.

"Children have never been an ambition of mine, whether to adopt or bear some nameless man's babe."

Brian flinched.

"But I do want yours because you're very special. You want to have children and I'd like to live in a household with your children."

"Only mine?"

"Nobody else's. Never anybody else's." She shook her head vehemently.

"My darling, my life." He showered kisses on her and she happily wrapped her arms around his neck.

The White House, Washington, D.C., October 1901

Meredith looked out of the carriage, considering the armed soldiers gathered under the great white portico. Ceremonial troops, no doubt, but undoubtedly dangerous since the last president had been violently killed only a few weeks before.

She extended her hand to her husband and allowed him to assist her down, careful to keep her head high and her smile gracious. She wasn't about to look anxious about being abruptly summoned to the White House so early in the new administration.

She'd worn a new black, Parisian day dress for the occasion, since appointments like this called for all possible armor and ammunition. A Worth gown offered advantages few men knew how to counter, starting with the blatant reminder of wealth and privilege. She shook it out carefully, fluffing her soft skirts back into order.

Brian was immaculate, of course, in his top hat and cut-away morning jacket, the very formal black attire required for any man calling on the president.

Pounding hoofbeats and rattling wheels announced a cab suddenly pulling into the long, curving driveway. Immediately after it stopped just behind their carriage, the door flung open and William Donovan sprang down.

Thank God. She closed her eyes briefly. How had they arrived so quickly from Seattle? Who cared about that now?

She'd reached a state of armed truce with William, undoubtedly aided by her home near Stanford University which gave her a little breathing room from the family castle. What mattered now was that William would make sure his son was safe, no matter what happened to her.

"Father, Mother, how good of you to make it in time." Brian hastened forward to greet them with warm hugs. Viola gave her a quick kiss on the cheek, careful not to disturb their equally impressive gowns, while William shook hands with her in their usual greeting.

"Mr. and Mrs. Donovan?" A black-clad bureaucrat approached.

"I am William Donovan and this is my son, Brian. The ladies are our wives."

Meredith inclined her head, dozens of feathers whispering across her hat, and rested her hands on her parasol. Viola did the same beside her, each lady flanked by her husband.

"Oh yes, of course, both pairs of Donovans. We weren't expecting all of you." He blinked, studying William Donovan as if he expected the man to suddenly sprout horns. "Please come this way. The President is expecting you."

Meredith accepted Brian's arm and entered, following her in-laws. Surely her unsettled stomach was due to her increasing need for a new corset.

The rooms were smaller than she'd have expected for a house of this importance, although the ceilings were very high. Each room was decorated in a single color, following the fashion of decades earlier, with worn furniture and immense chandeliers. Men brushed past them, following the tracks beaten into the carpets, their hard eyes assessing them quickly. This was a potentate's workplace, far more so than Eisengau Citadel's crystal and gold showroom.

Their escort knocked politely on a door. "Mr. and Mrs. William Donovan, with Mr. and Mrs. Brian Donovan," he announced, holding it open for them.

"Donovan! How very good of you to come!" Teddy Roosevelt bounded up from behind a paper-strewn desk. "Mrs. Donovan!"

He rushed at her in-laws, displaying all of his notorious exuberance, and clapped William on the back. "How many years has it been?"

"Since you were riding alone and starving in Dakota?" William retorted dryly.

"Wasn't I the greenhorn! Bully for me, you happened along when you did." Roosevelt laughed, in no way disconcerted. "Mrs. Donovan, you are a lucky woman to have men like yours, who treat even dudes honestly."

"You'd have done very well on your own, Roosevelt," William demurred.

"But you took the time to teach me about supplies and freighting. Not many teamsters would have done that." He shook hands with Brian, pumping his arm as if priming a well. "Good to see you, too, young Donovan! Just two old campaigners, aren't we?"

His eyes weren't quite as innocent behind his spectacles when they considered Brian.

Whatever she chose, whatever she did, would reflect on her beloved. If they threatened him, she'd have to agree.

"Yes, colonel," Brian agreed. "May I introduce my wife, Meredith?"

"Mr. President." She curtsied, most properly of course.

He shook hands with her, studying her like a scientific specimen. She looked straight back at him, wrapping herself in ladylike behavior. Survival in this room would probably not depend on socialist tactics.

"My condolences, sir, on President McKinley's untimely

death." As the senior member of the family, William offered the necessary platitude.

Roosevelt's expression turned cold, his mobile mouth freezing into a hard line. "It was a very grievous loss to the entire nation, something we must all work to overcome."

"Of course, sir," Brian agreed.

"So what did you do with the plans for the cannon?" Roosevelt shot back at him.

Meredith turned very, very cold, far colder than the cramped room would account for.

"Everything is in my report to the War Department," Brian said steadily. "The four prototypes suffered a grievous accident and were demolished. The plans were destroyed during our departure from Eisengau, to keep them out of the Russians' hands. Alaska remains safe."

"Secretary of State Hay reports our London ambassador and Whitehall believe Mrs. Donovan can recreate those plans." Roosevelt leaned forward, his hand on a chair back, as belligerent as a battery of cannons.

"No."

"Are you saying they're wrong? That she can't redraw them?" The words shot out of his mouth like bullets.

Brian and Meredith looked at each other.

Young Grand Duke Nicholas was doing very well in Eisengau. He'd even adapted quite smoothly to the last election when the workers' party won a majority. But none of Zorndorf's assistants could rebuild the Eisengau 155 from the remaining jumble of parts.

San Francisco society already knew she could recreate any drawing she'd seen. Lying wouldn't solve this.

"No, I'm telling you . . ." Brian began.

"I won't do it." Meredith slipped her hand into Brian's and he squeezed her fingers. Her warrior was fighting for her this time, rather than blindly obeying his country. Warmth began to creep over her skin.

"Mrs. Donovan!" Roosevelt stared at her, his high-pitched voice rising even farther in astonishment. "Don't you understand how important those cannon are?"

"I've seen them in action many times, unlike you, Mr. President. I am quite sure the world doesn't need such firepower yet." Would Russia try to steal them and seize Alaska? Or would a war break out somewhere else, fueled by feelings of invulnerability? She wouldn't help that happen.

Could a president throw her into prison for refusing? What nastiness could he hurl at her and Brian, or their family?

"Donovan, will you talk some sense into them?" Roosevelt spun to face the patriarch. "You know how dangerous matters are growing overseas. We must, must have these guns." He pounded his fist on the table.

"Why? I understand the great advantage is their range."

What? She'd expected him to make the best possible deal with the War Department for her help. He could make a fortune from her knowledge.

"What need do we have for that here in America, when we have the Atlantic and Pacific to protect us? Will Canada invade us or Mexico?" Traces of Ireland swirled through William's melodious voice.

Viola stood shoulder to shoulder beside him, ghostly generations of Southern aristocracy armed for battle against impetuous New York politicians arrayed at her back.

Meredith's jaw dropped open.

"Matters could change in a moment." The former Rough Riders' colonel frowned and thrust out his jaw.

"If they do, you know where to find us. Until then, *my daughter-in-law* will be very busy in San Francisco," William said implacably.

That wasn't much of a bargain. Instead, he was claiming her as part of the family, drawing her into the dynasty.

"If you have any further questions for her, I suggest you direct them to my attorneys."

No deal whatsoever. She was free to be Brian's wife and her own woman, thanks to William Donovan. Meredith blinked rapidly, pushing back tears.

"Donovan . . ." Roosevelt's orator's voice turned coaxing.

William raised an eyebrow. "Would you let anyone turn your Alice's life upside-down?" he asked softly.

Roosevelt rubbed his chin but finally shook his head. "I'll remind Whitehall that Mrs. Donovan is an American citizen now and, as such, not to be meddled with. By golly, if we can't put those plans into immediate production, nobody else will."

"Thank you." William inclined his head.

Meredith rested her cheek against her husband's arm, enchanted by her father-in-law. He would have gained far more politically and monetarily if he'd handed her over. Yet he'd kept her within the family.

Now they could visit her brothers, while they were at school in Austria. Smuggled letters were all well and good but seeing them in person would be far more pleasant.

She squeezed Brian's hand and he grinned down at her, smug as a cat lapping milk. He'd promised her this would happen and she hadn't dared believe him.

After they returned to the hotel, she'd gift him with news of his child growing under her heart.

Author's Note

Cannons have been called "King of Battle" for a very long time. Some of the cannons invented at the start of the twentieth century were so revolutionary, they became super-weapons, the equivalent of today's intercontinental ballistic missiles.

The Canon de 75 modéle 1897, or "French 75," is one of the world's legendary artillery pieces. Harry Truman commanded a battery of them during World War One and it remained the principal armament of the French, Polish, American, Estonian, Greek, Lithuanian, Portugese, and Romanian armies until the 1940s. Unlike almost any other weapon ever made, it was commemorated by a champagne cocktail, which was very popular during the 1920s and 1930s.

The Eisengau 155 is based on Schneider & Company's Canon de 155mm Longue Mle 1917 Grand Puissance, Filloux (GPF) (or "155mm cannon of great power, designed by Filloux"), which was a radical design. It served the French Army for a long time and was turned against the Allies as coastal fortifications during World War II. It's also the direct ancestor of America's beloved "Long Tom" cannon, which served throughout World War II and Korea. The Long Tom is fondly remembered for helping beat back the Nazis at the Battle of the Bulge on December 23, 1944 with a spectacular "time-on-target serenade."

Esquimalt Harbor in British Columbia was originally built as a Royal Navy outpost, to defend against attacks by Russia. Today it contains a spectacular naval dockyard.

The Grand Duchy of Eisengau is a fictional creation, although based on several Germanic states existing in 1900.

My deepest thanks go to JS, retired artillery instructor from U.S. Army Field Artillery School at Ft. Sill, and TS (U.S.M.C.-Ret.) for help in describing artillery. A big hug goes to Fred for explaining turn-of-the-century engineering drawings and master control systems.

Further thanks go to the Stdschnauzer loop at Yahoo, who generously shared their infinite love, knowledge, and stories about the fabulous Standard Schnauzer breed. As ever, I owe a huge debt to Yahoo!Groups' Weapons Loop and Willy, who proved a preacher's son can answer the oddest questions. Any errors are entirely my own doing.

I look forward to hearing from my readers about this or any other subjects. Please visit my website at *www.DianeWhiteside.com*.

If you liked this story, pick up
INSTANT ATTRACTION
by Jill Shalvis. . . .

"Why are you in my bed?" he asked warily, as if maybe he'd put her there but couldn't quite remember.

He had a black duffel bag slung over a shoulder. Light brown hair stuck out from the edges of his knit ski cap to curl around his neck. Sharp green eyes were leveled on hers, steady and calm but irritated as he opened his denim jacket.

If he was an ax murderer, he was quite possibly the most attractive one she'd ever seen, which didn't do a thing for her frustration level. She'd been finally sleeping.

Sleeping!

He could have no idea what a welcome miracle that had been, dammit.

"Earth to Goldilocks." He waved a gloved hand until she dragged her gaze back up to his face. "Yeah, hi. My bed. Want to tell me why you're in it?"

"But I've been sleeping here for a week." Granted, she'd had a hard time of it lately, but she definitely would have noticed *him* in bed with her. Just thinking about it now had her glasses fogging up.

"Who told you to sleep here?"

"My boss, Stone Wilder. Well, technically, Annie. She's the chef here and—" She broke off when he reached toward her, clutching the comforter to her chin as if the down feathers could protect her, really wishing for that handy-dandy bat.

But instead of killing her, he hit the switch to the lamp on the nightstand and more fully illuminated the room as he dropped his duffel bag.

While Katie tried to slow her heart rate, he pulled off his jacket and gloves, and tossed them territorially to the chest at the foot of the bed.

His clothes seemed normal enough. Beneath the jacket he wore a fleece-lined sweater opened over a long-sleeved brown Henley, half untucked over faded Levi's. The jeans were loose and low on his hips, baggy over unlaced Sorels, the entire ensemble revealing that he was in prime condition.

"My name is Katie Kramer," she told him, hoping he'd return the favor. "Wilder Adventures's new office temp." She paused, but he didn't even attempt to fill the awkward silence. "So that leaves you . . ."

"What happened to Riley?"

"Who?"

"The current office manager."

"I think she's on maternity leave."

"That must be news to his wife."

She met his cool gaze. "Okay, obviously I'm new. I don't know all the details since I've only been here a week."

"Here, being my cabin, of course."

"Stone told me that the person who used to live here had left."

"Ah." His eyes were the deepest, most solid green she'd ever seen as they regarded her. "I did leave. I also just came back."

She winced, clutching the covers a little tighter to her chest. "So this cabin . . . does it belong to an ax murderer?"

That tugged a rusty-sounding laugh from him. "Haven't sunk that low. Yet." Pulling off his cap, he shoved his fingers through his hair. With those sleepy-lidded eyes, disheveled hair, and at least two days' growth on his jaw, he looked big and bad and edgy—and quite disturbingly sexy with it. "I need sleep," he said, and dropped his long, tough self to the chair by the bed, as if so weary he could no longer stand. He set first one and then the other booted foot on the mattress, grimacing as if he were hurting, though she didn't see any reason for that on his body as he settled back, lightly linking his hands together low on his flat abs. Then he let out a long, shuddering sigh.

She stared at more than six feet of raw power and testosterone in disbelief. "You still haven't said who you are."

"Too Exhausted To Go Away."

She did some more staring at him. Staring and glaring, but he didn't appear to care. "Hello?" she said after a full moment of stunned silence. "You can't just—"

"Can. And am." And with that, he closed his eyes. "Night, Goldilocks."

Try BARE NERVE,
by Katherine Garbera,
available now from Brava. . . .

Jack Savage was the kind of man Anna secretly wanted for her own. The kind of man who lived outside of the law and set his own standards.

He was everything she wasn't. Everything her life had always pointed her away from. He lived and breathed in that gray area between right and wrong. It wasn't necessarily the area between criminals and law-abiding citizens . . . it was an area she liked to think of as justice.

She knew justice didn't always come with a badge or in a courtroom. And she saw in Jack's eyes that he knew this, too.

His life had shaped him into the kind of man who'd be more than happy to get justice for himself and his client however it had to be achieved. And if that meant working outside of the normal boundaries of the law, so be it.

"Why are you staring at me like that?" he asked. His voice was deep and rough, just another thing about him that showed her he wasn't civilized.

"I don't know," she said, and then stood up and walked away before she did something really stupid like kiss him. Because giving in to a bad boy like Jack Savage was something she'd never really been tempted to do before.

But Jack Savage was temptation incarnate for her. He made her wish she was a different kind of woman so she could spend all her time with him.

Anna knew she needed to keep her mind on the mission. On making sure Demetri Andreev was captured and put out of business for good. But she couldn't help watching Jack, and he wouldn't leave her thoughts alone.

No matter how many times she tried to convince herself she didn't care what he did, she kept finding her attention drawn back to him.

She wanted him. *Oh, my God,* she thought. She was in lust for the first time in her life, and a part of her was very much afraid she was going to act on the impulse.

And don't miss Donna Kauffman's latest,
LET ME IN,
coming next month!

"I always found you to be an attractive woman, Tate."

Alarm filled her. But it didn't come close to matching the rush of . . . what? Anticipation? Surely she didn't want him to acknowledge, much less act on, the other kind of tension that was swirling around them.

"But, even in the most extreme situations, I never once considered doing what I can't seem to stop thinking about doing now."

She was the one hallucinating now, that was it. He was still in the bathroom and she'd come into the kitchen to get soup, and had somehow fallen down a rabbit hole or something, because surely he was not standing right in front of her saying what she thought he was saying. It was wild enough that she was having any thoughts in his general direction, but at least she had the excuse of being retired and no longer the sharp professional.

He was still team leader, actively on the job. And the only person who'd been even more the consummate professional during their years working together than she'd been. All work, no wink. That was Derek Cole. Not ever. With her, or anyone else. At least not that anyone had ever known. CJ had made it her favorite topic of conversation on more than one occasion. So, if he ever had . . . flung, he'd been remarkably discreet about it, which was saying something around people whose job it was to know every damn thing. It was another aspect of his character that she'd admired. So, what the hell was this?

When she finally found her voice, it was damnably shaky. "You're injured, and recently injected with God knows what, so—"

"It's not the drugs talking, Tate."

"Well, it doesn't sound like you talking, either. At least not the you I worked for. We've got enough to deal with, without—"

"Oh, I know. Believe me. I came down the hall just now to see if I could sit in here and eat some soup. No ulterior motives. No skulking intended. Then I heard you commenting on my—"

"Must you repeat it?"

His lips quirked a little then. "See?"

"See what?"

"How is it I missed this?" he asked, sounding sincerely perplexed.

"Missed what?"

"You."

He was looking at her like he'd just discovered something amazing, and couldn't quite believe it.

"I'm the same me I've—"

"No. You're not. I always admired your capable, no-nonsense work ethic. You and CJ were the best agents I ever had. Which, considering the talent I had assembled, is a high, but deserved, compliment. I've said before that I found you attractive. I did. And do. But I've always viewed that through the filter of being your team leader, looking at that as simply another attribute you possessed, to be executed professionally where and when best deployed."

"Just because I don't work for you now—"

"It's not just that. You're . . . more you now. Still everything you were, but there's so much more. I'm seeing the rest of you, probably the you you've always been, but who I never had the pleasure of meeting. You're dry, sharp, outspoken, and surprisingly sarcastic."

"You're right, the professional filter is off, but maybe I'm not who I was before, either. I'm leading a very different life now. I'll pull it back together, focus, find my professional balance once again, but only because I have to. And, believe me, no one is more motivated to get through this and make it go away as quickly as possible. To make you go away," she added truthfully. "To get back to the life I earned, the life I deserve. The life I *need*, Derek." If there was a quiet pleading in her tone, she wasn't going to apologize for it. Things were complicated enough without this sudden revelation from him. Especially considering she'd been thinking very similar things about him.

Which, if he hadn't known before, he did now, given her comment about his lack of clothing. Now he knew she was noticing him, too.

Which meant one of them had to get their act together, and get it together real quick. He moved closer and leaned his weight against the counter, along with the walking stick, so he could lift his free hand.

"Derek—" She broke off when he lightly brushed his fingertips across her cheek. His touch was gentler than she'd expected. She should be smacking his hand away, not wanting to lean in to the unanticipated warmth she found there. She didn't need nurturing, or caretaking, but that's not what the look in his eyes was telegraphing, What she saw there was bold, unwavering, unapologetic want.

And what he wanted was her.